JOHN UPDIKE

The Music School

SHORT STORIES

A Fawcett Crest Book

Fawcett Publications, Inc., Greenwich, Conn.
Member of American Book Publishers Council, Inc.

THIS BOOK CONTAINS THE COMPLETE TEXT OF THE ORIGINAL HARDCOVER EDITION.

A Fawcett Crest Book reprinted by arrangement with Alfred A. Knopf, Inc.

Library of Congress Catalog Card Number: 66-19404

All twenty of these stories first appeared in *The New Yorker*. They were written in the order they have here.

The lines from "To the One of Fictive Music" are quoted from THE COLLECTED POEMS OF WALLACE STEVENS by permission of his publisher, Alfred A. Knopf, Inc.

PRINTING HISTORY
Alfred A. Knopf edition published September 19, 1966
First printing, July 1966
Second printing, January 1967

First Fawcett Crest Printing, November 1967

Published by Fawcett World Library
67 West 44th Street, New York, N. Y. 10036
Printed in the United States of America

Contents

Now, of the music summoned by the birth
That separates us from the wind and sea,
Yet leaves us in them, until earth becomes,
By being so much of the things we are,
Gross effigy and simulacrum, none
Gives motion to perfection more serene
Than yours, out of our imperfections wrought,
Most rare, or ever of more kindred air
In the laborious weaving that you wear.

—WALLACE STEVENS,
"To the One of Fictive Music"

In Football Season

DO YOU REMEMBER a fragrance girls acquire in autumn? As you walk beside them after school, they tighten their arms about their books and bend their heads forward to give a more flattering attention to your words and in the little intimate area thus formed, carved into the clear air by an implicit crescent, there is a complex fragrance woven of tobacco, powder, lipstick, rinsed hair, and that perhaps imaginary and certainly elusive scent that wool, whether in the lapels of a jacket or the nap of a sweater, seems to yield when the cloudless fall sky like the blue bell of a vacuum lifts toward itself the glad exhalations of all things. This fragrance, so faint and flirtatious on those afternoon walks through the dry leaves, would be banked a thousandfold and lie heavy as the perfume of a flower shop on the dark slope of the stadium when, Friday nights, we played football in the city.

"We"—we the school. A suburban school, we rented for some of our home games the stadium of a college in the city of Alton three miles away. My father, a teacher, was active in the Olinger High athletic department, and I, waiting for him beside half-open doors of varnished wood and frosted glass, overheard arguments and felt the wind of the worries that accompanied this bold and at that time unprecedented decision. Later, many of the other county high schools followed our lead; for the decision was vindicated. The stadium each Friday night when we played was filled. Not only students and parents came but spectators unconnected with either school, and the money left over when the stadium rent was paid supported our entire athletic program. I remember the smell of the grass crushed by footsteps behind the end zones. The smell was more vivid than that of a meadow, and in the blue electric glare the green vibrated as if excited, like a child, by being allowed up late. I remember my father taking tickets at the far corner of the wall, wedged into a tiny wooden booth that made him seem somewhat magical, like a troll. And of course I remember the way we, the students, with all of our jealousies and antipathies and deformities, would be—beauty and boob, sexpot and grind—crushed together like flowers pressed to yield to the black sky a concentrated homage, an incense, of cosmetics, cigarette smoke, warmed wool, hot dogs, and the tang, both animal and metallic, of clean hair. In a hoarse olfactory shout, these odors ascended. A dense haze gathered along the ceiling of brightness at the upper limit of the arc lights, whose glare blotted out the stars and made the sky seem romantically void and intimately near, like the death that now and then stooped and plucked one of us out of a crumpled automobile. If we went to the back row and stood on the bench there, we could look over the stone lip of the stadium down into the houses of the city, and feel the cold November air like the black presence of the ocean beyond the rail of a ship; and when we left after the game and from the hushed residential streets of this part of the city saw behind us a great vessel steaming with light, the arches of the colonnades blazing like portholes, the stadium seemed a great ship sinking and we the survivors of a celebrated disaster.

To keep our courage up, we sang songs, usually the same song, the one whose primal verse runs,

> Oh, you can't get to Heaven
> *(Oh, you can't get to Heaven)*
> In a rocking chair.
> *(In a rocking chair)*
> 'Cause the Lord don't want
> *('Cause the Lord don't want)*
> No lazy people there!
> *(No lazy people there!)*

And then repeated, double time. It was a song for eternity; when we ran out of verses, I would make them up:

> Oh, you can't get to Heaven
> *(Oh, you can't get to Heaven)*
> In Smokey's Ford
> *(In Smokey's Ford)*

'Cause the cylinders
   ('Cause the cylinders)
Have to be rebored.
   (Have to be rebored.)

Down through the nice residential section, on through the
not-so-nice and the shopping district, past dark churches
where stained-glass windows, facing inward, warned us with
left-handed blessings, down Buchanan Street to the Running
Horse Bridge, across the bridge, and two miles out the pike
we walked. My invention would become reckless:

Oh, you can't get to Heaven
   (Oh, you can't get to Heaven)
In a motel bed
   (In a motel bed)
'Cause the sky is blue
   ('Cause the sky is blue)
And the sheets are red
   (And the sheets are red.)

Few of us had a license to drive and fewer still had visited a motel. We were at that innocent age, on the border-
line of sixteen, when damnation seems a delicious promise.
There was Mary Louise Hornberger, who was tall and held
herself with such upright and defiant poise that she was
Mother in both our class plays, and Alma Bidding, with her
hook nose and her smug smile caricatured in cerise lipstick,
and Joanne Hardt, whose father was a typesetter, and Mari-
lyn Wenrich, who had a gray front tooth and in study hall
liked to have the small of her back scratched, and Nanette
Seifert, with her button nose and black wet eyes and peach-
down cheeks framed in the fur frilling the blue hood of her
parka. And there were boys, Henny Gring, Leo Horst,
Hawley Peters, Jack Lillijedahl, myself. Sometimes these,
sometimes less or more. Once there was Billy Trupp on
crutches. Billy played football and, though only a sopho-
more, had made the varsity that year, until he broke his
ankle. He was dull and dogged and liked Alma, and she
with her painted smile led him on lovingly. We offered for
his sake to take the trolley, but he had already refused a car
ride back to Olinger, and obstinately walked with us, loping
his heavy body along on the crutches, his lifted foot a boul-
der of plaster. His heroism infected us all; we taunted the

cold stars with song, one mile, two miles, three miles. How slowly we went! With what a luxurious sense of waste did we abuse this stretch of time! For as children we had lived in a tight world of ticking clocks and punctual bells, where every minute was an admonition to thrift and where tardiness, to a child running late down a street with his panicked stomach burning, seemed the most mysterious and awful of sins. Now, turning the corner into adulthood, we found time to be instead a black immensity endlessly supplied, like the wind.

We would arrive in Olinger after the drugstores, which had kept open for the first waves of people returning from the game, were shut. Except for the street lights, the town was dark like a town in a fable. We scattered, each escorting a girl to her door; and there, perhaps, for a moment, you bowed your face into that silent crescent of fragrance, and tasted it, and let it bite into you indelibly. The other day, in a town far from Olinger, I passed on the sidewalk two girls utterly unknown to me and half my age, and sensed, very faintly, that flavor from far-off carried in their bent arms like a bouquet. And I seemed, continuing to walk, to sink into a chasm deeper than the one inverted above us on those Friday nights during football season.

For after seeing the girl home, I would stride through the hushed streets, where the rustling leaves seemed torn scraps scattered in the wake of the game, and go to Mr. Lloyd Stephens' house. There, looking in the little square window of his front storm door, I could see down a dark hall into the lit kitchen where Mr. Stephens and my father and Mr. Jesse Honneger were counting money around a worn porcelain table. Stephens, a local contractor, was the school-board treasurer, and Honneger, who taught social science, the chairman of the high-school athletic department. They were still counting; the silver stacks slipped and glinted among their fingers and the gold of beer stood in cylinders beside their hairy wrists. Their sleeves were rolled up and smoke like a fourth presence, wings spread, hung over their heads. They were still counting, so it was all right, I was not late. We lived ten miles away, and I could not go home until my father was ready. Some nights it took until midnight. I would knock and pull open the storm door and push open the real door and it would be warm in the contractor's hall. I would accept a glass of ginger ale and sit in the kitchen with the men until they were done. It was late, very late, but I was not blamed; it was permitted. Silently counting and expertly tamping the coins into little cylindrical wrappers of colored paper, the men ordered and consecrated this realm of night into which my days had never extended before. The hour or more behind me, which I had spent so wastefully, in walking when a trolley would have been swifter, and so wickedly, in blasphemy and lust, was past and forgiven me; it had been necessary; it was permitted.

Now I peek into windows and open doors and do not find that air of permission. It has fled the world. Girls walk by me carrying their invisible bouquets from fields still steeped in grace, and I look up in the manner of one who follows with his eyes the passage of a hearse, and remembers what pierces him.

The Indian

THE TOWN, in New England, of Tarbox, restrained from embracing the sea by a margin of tawny salt marshes, locates its downtown four miles inland up the Musquenomenee River, which ceases to be tidal at the waterfall of the old hosiery mill, now given over to the manufacture of plastic toys. It was to the mouth of this river, in May of 1634, that the small party of seventeen men, led by the younger son of the governor of the Massachusetts Bay Colony—Jeremiah Tarbox being only his second in command—came in three rough skiffs with the purpose of establishing amid such an unpossessed abundance of salt hay a pastoral plantation. This, with God's forbearance, they did. They furled their sails and slowly rowed, each boat being equipped with four oarlocks, in search of firm land, through marshes that must appear, now that their grass is no longer harvested by men driving horses shod in great wooden discs, much the same today as they did then—though undoubtedly the natuarl abundance of ducks, cranes, otter, and deer has been somewhat diminished. Tarbox himself, in his invaluable diary, notes that the squealing of the livestock in the third skiff attracted a great cloud of "protestating sea-fowl." The first houses (not one of which still stands, the oldest in town dating, in at least its central timbers and fireplace, from 1642) were strung along the base of the rise of firm land called Near Hill, which, with its companion Far Hill, a mile away, in effect bounds the densely populated section of the present township. In winter the population of Tarbox numbers something less than seven thousand; in summer the figure may be closer to nine thousand. The width of the river mouth and its sheltered advantage within Tarbox Bay seemed to promise the makings of a port to rival Boston; but in spite of repeated dredging operations the river has

14

proved incorrigibly silty, and its shallow winding channels, rendered especially fickle where the fresh water of the river most powerfully clashes with the restless saline influx of the tide, frustrate all but pleasure craft. These Chris-Craft and Kit-Kats, skimming seaward through the exhilarating avenues of wild hay, in the early morning may pass, as the fluttering rust-colored horizon abruptly yields to the steely blue monotone of the open water, a few dour clammers in hip boots patiently harrowing the tidewater floor. The intent posture of their silhouettes distinguishes them from the few bathers who have drifted down from the dying campfires by whose side they have dozed and sung and drunk away a night on the beach—one of the finest and least spoiled, it should be said, on the North Atlantic coast. Picturesque as Millet's gleaners, their torsos doubled like playing cards in the rosy mirror of the dawn-stilled sea, these sparse representatives of the clamming industry, founded in the eighteen-eighties by an immigration of Greeks and continually harassed by the industrial pollution upriver, exploit the sole vein of profit left in the name of old Musquenomenee. This shadowy chief broke the bread of peace with the son of the Governor, and within a year both were dead. The body of the one was returned to Boston to lie in the King's Chapel graveyard; the body of the other is supposedly buried, presumably upright, somewhere in the woods on the side of Far Hill where even now no houses have intruded, though the tract is rumored to have been sold to a divider. Until the postwar arrival of Boston commuters, still much of a minority, Tarbox lived (discounting the summer people, who came and went in the marshes each year like the migrations of mallards) as a town apart. A kind of curse has kept its peace. The hand-made-lace industry, which reached its peak just before the American Revolution, was destroyed by the industrial revolution; the textile mills, never numerous, were finally emptied by the industrialization of the South. They have been succeeded by a scattering of small enterprises, electronic in the main, which have staved off decisive depression.

Viewed from the spur of Near Hill where the fifth edifice, now called Congregationalist, of the religious society incorporated in 1635 on this identical spot thrusts its spire into the sky, and into a hundred colored postcards purchasable at all four local drugstores—viewed from this eminence, the business district makes a neat and prosperous impression.

This is especially true at Christmastime, when colored lights are strung from pole to pole, and at the height of summer, when girls in shorts and bathing suits decorate the pavements. A one-hour parking limit is enforced during business hours, but the traffic is congested only during the evening homeward exodus. A stoplight has never been thought quite necessary. A new Woolworth's with a noble façade of corrugated laminated Fiberglas has been erected on the site of a burned-out tenement. If the building which it vacated across the street went begging nearly a year for a tenant, and if some other properties along the street nervously change hands and wares now and then, nevertheless there is not that staring stretch of blank shopwindows which desolates the larger mill towns to the north and west. Two hardware stores confront each other without apparent rancor; three banks vie in promoting solvency; several luncheonettes withstand waves of factory workers and high-school students; and a small proud army of *petit-bourgeois* knights—realtors and lawyers and jewellers—parades up and down in clothes that would not look quaint on Madison Avenue. The explosive thrust of superhighways through the land has sprinkled on the town a cosmopolitan garnish; one resourceful divorcée has made a good thing of selling unabashedly smart women's clothes and Scandinavian kitchen accessories, and, next door, a foolish young matron nostalgic for Vassar has opened a combination paperback bookstore and art gallery, so that now the Tarbox town derelict, in sneaking with his cherry-red face and tot of rye from the liquor store to his home above the shoe-repair nook, must walk a garish gantlet of abstract paintings by a minister's wife from Gloucester. Indeed, the whole street is laid open to an accusatory chorus of brightly packaged titles by Freud, Camus, and those others through whose masterworks our civilization moves toward its dark climax. Strange to say, so virulent is the spread of modern culture, some of these same titles can be had, seventy-five cents cheaper, in the homely old magazine-and-newspaper store in the middle of the block. Here, sitting stoically on the spines of the radiator behind the large left-hand window, the Indian can often be seen.

He sits in this window for hours at a time, politely waving to any passerby who happens to glance his way. It is hard always to avoid his eye, his form is so unexpected, perched on the radiator above cards of pipes and pyramids of Prince Albert tins and fanned copies of *True* and *Male* and *Sport*. He looks, behind glass, somewhat shadowy and thin, but outdoors he is solid enough. During other hours he takes up a station by Leonard's Pharmaceutical on the corner. There is a splintered telephone pole here that he leans against when he wearies of leaning against the brick wall. Occasionally he even sits upon the fire hydrant as if upon a campstool, arms folded, legs crossed, gazing across at the renovations on the face of Poirier's Liquor Mart. In cold or wet weather he may sit inside the drugstore, expertly prolonging a coffee at the counter, running his tobacco-dyed fingertip around and around the rim of the cup as he watches the steam fade. There are other spots—untenanted doorways, the benches halfway up the hill, idle chairs in the barbershops—where he loiters, and indeed there cannot be a square foot of the downtown pavement where he has not at some time or other paused; but these two spots, the window of the news store and the wall of the drugstore, are his essential habitat.

It is difficult to discover anything about him. He wears a plaid lumberjack shirt with a gray turtleneck sweater underneath, and chino pants olive rather than khaki in color, and remarkably white tennis sneakers. He smokes and drinks coffee, so he must have some income, but he does not, apparently, work. Inquiry reveals that now and then he is employed—during the last Christmas rush he was seen carrying baskets of Hong Kong shirts and Italian crèche elements through the aisles of the five-and-ten—but he soon is fired or quits, and the word "lazy," given somehow more than its usual force of disapproval, sticks in the mind, as if this is the clue. Disconcertingly, he knows your name. Even though you are a young mutual-fund analyst newly bought into a neo-saltbox on the beach road and downtown on a Saturday morning to rent a wallpaper steamer, he smiles if he catches your eye, lifts his hand lightly, and says, "Good morning, Mr. ——," supplying your name. Yet his own name is impossible to learn. The simplest fact about a person, identity's very seed, is in his case utterly hidden. It can be determined, by matching consistencies of hearsay, that he lives in that tall, speckle-shingled, disreputable hotel overlooking the atrophied railroad tracks, just down from the Amvets, where shuffling Polish widowers and one-night-in-town salesmen hang out, and in whose bar, evidently, money can be wagered and women may be approached. But his name, whether it is given to you as Tugwell or Frisbee or Wigglesworth, even if it were always the same name would be in its almost parodic Yankeeness incredible. "But he's an Indian!"

The face of your informant—say, the chunky Irish dictator of the School Building Needs Committee, a dentist—undergoes a faint rapt transformation. His voice assumes its habitual whisper of extravagant discretion. "Don't go around saying that. He doesn't like it. He prides himself on being a typical run-down Yankee."

But he *is* an Indian. This is, alone, certain. Who but a savage would have such an immense capacity for repose? His cheekbones, his never-faded skin, the delicate little jut of his scowl, the drooping triangularity of his eye sockets, the way his vertically lined face takes the light, the lusterless black of his hair are all so profoundly Indian that the imagination, surprised by his silhouette as he sits on the hydrant gazing across at the changing face of the liquor store, effortlessly plants a feather at the back of his head. His air of waiting, of gazing; the softness of his motions; the odd sense of proprietorship and ease that envelops him; the good humor that makes his vigil gently dreadful—all these are totally foreign to the shambling shy-eyes and moist lower lip of the failed Yankee. His age and status are too peculiar. He is surely older than forty and younger than sixty—but *is* this sure? And, though he greets everyone by name with a light wave of his hand, the conversation never passes beyond a greeting, and even in the news store, when the political contention and convivial obscenity literally drive housewives away from the door, he does not seem to participate. He witnesses, and now and then offers in a gravelly voice a debated piece of town history, but he does not participate.

It is caring that makes mysteries. As you grow indifferent, they lift. You live longer in the town, season follows season, the half-naked urban people arrive on the beach, multiply, and like leaves fall away again, and you have ceased to identify with them. The marshes turn green and withdraw through gold into brown, and their indolent, untouched, enduring existence penetrates your fibre. You find you must drive down toward the beach once a week or it is like a week without love. The ice cakes pile up along the banks of the tidal inlets like the rubble of ruined temples.

You begin to meet, without seeking them out, the vestigial people: the unmarried daughters of vanished mill owners, the retired high-school teachers, the senile deacons in their unheated seventeenth-century houses with attics full of old church records in spidery brown ink. You enter, by way of an elderly baby-sitter, a world where at least they speak of him as "the Indian." An appalling snicker materializes in the darkness on the front seat beside you as you drive dear Mrs. Knowlton home to her shuttered house on a back road. "If you knew what they say, Mister, if you knew what they say." And at last, as when in a woods you break through miles of underbrush into a clearing, you stand up surprised, taking a deep breath of the obvious, agreeing with the trees that of course this is the case. Anybody who is anybody knew all along. The mystery lifts, with some impatience, here, in Miss Horne's low-ceilinged front parlor, which smells of warm fireplace ashes and of peppermint balls kept ready in red-tinted knobbed glass goblets for whatever open-mouthed children might dare to come visit such a very old lady, all bent double like a little gripping rose clump, Miss Horne, a fable in her lifetime. Her father had been the sixth minister before the present one (whom she does *not* care for) at the First Church, and *his* father the next but one before him. There had been a Horne among those first seventeen men. Well—where was she?—yes, the Indian. The Indian had been loitering—waiting, if you prefer—in the center of town when she was a tiny girl in gingham. And he is no older now than he was then.

Giving Blood

THE MAPLES had been married now nine years, which is almost too long. "Goddammit, goddammit," Richard said to Joan, as they drove into Boston to give blood, "I drive this road five days a week and now I'm driving it again. It's like a nightmare. I'm exhausted. I'm emotionally, mentally, physically exhausted, and she isn't even an aunt of mine. She isn't even an aunt of *yours*."

"She's a sort of cousin," Joan said.

"Well hell, every goddam body in New England is some sort of cousin of yours; must I spend the rest of my life trying to save them *all*?"

"Hush," Joan said. "She might die. I'm ashamed of you. Really ashamed."

It cut. His voice for the moment took on an apologetic pallor. "Well I'd be my usual goddam saintly self if I'd had any sort of sleep last night. Five days a week I bump out of bed and stagger out the door past the milkman and on the one day of the week when I don't even have to truck the blasphemous little brats to Sunday school you make an appointment to have me drained dry thirty miles away."

"Well it wasn't *me*," Joan said, "who had to stay till two o'clock doing the Twist with Marlene Brossman."

"We weren't doing the Twist. We were gliding around very chastely to 'Hits of the Forties.' And don't think I was so oblivious I didn't see you snoogling behind the piano with Harry Saxon."

"We weren't behind the piano, we were on the bench. And he was just talking to me because he felt sorry for me. Everybody there felt sorry for me; you could have at *least* let somebody else dance *once* with Marlene, if only for show."

20

"Show, show," Richard said. "That's your mentality exactly."

"Why, the poor Matthews or whatever they are looked absolutely horrified."

"Matthiessons," he said. "And that's another thing. Why are idiots like that being invited these days? If there's anything I hate, it's women who keep putting one hand on their pearls and taking a deep breath. I thought she had something stuck in her throat."

"They're a perfectly pleasant, decent young couple. The thing you resent about their coming is that their being there shows us what we've become."

"If you're so attracted," he said, "to little fat men like Harry Saxon, why didn't you marry one?"

"My," Joan said calmly, and gazed out the window away from him, at the scudding gasoline stations. "You honestly *are* hateful. It's not just a pose."

"Pose, show, my Lord, who are you performing for? If it isn't Harry Saxon, it's Freddie Vetter—all these dwarves. Every time I looked over at you last night it was like some pale Queen of the Dew surrounded by a ring of mushrooms."

"You're too absurd," she said. Her hand, distinctly thirtyish, dry and green-veined and rasped by detergents, stubbed out her cigarette in the dashboard ashtray. "You're not subtle. You think you can match me up with another man so you can swirl off with Marlene with a free conscience."

Her reading his strategy so correctly made his face burn; he felt again the tingle of Mrs. Brossman's hair as he pressed his cheek against hers and in this damp privacy inhaled the perfume behind her ear. "You're right," he said. "But I want to get you a man your own size; I'm very loyal that way."

"Let's not talk," she said.

His hope, of turning the truth into a joke, was rebuked. Any implication of permission was blocked. "It's that *smugness*," he explained, speaking levelly, as if about a phenomenon of which they were both disinterested students. "It's your smugness that is really intolerable. Your stupidity I don't mind. Your sexlessness I've learned to live with. But that wonderfully smug, New England—I suppose we needed it to get the country founded, but in the Age of Anxiety it really does gall."

He had been looking over at her, and unexpectedly she turned and looked at him, with a startled but uncannily crystalline expression, as if her face had been in an instant rendered in tinted porcelain, even to the eyelashes.

"I asked you not to talk," she said. "Now you've said things that I'll always remember."

Plunged fathoms deep into the wrong, his face suffocated with warmth, he concentrated on the highway and sullenly steered. Though they were moving at sixty in the sparse Saturday traffic, he had travelled this road so often its distances were all translated into time, so that they seemed to him to be moving as slowly as a minute hand from one digit to the next. It would have been strategic and dignified of him to keep the silence; but he could not resist believing that just one more pinch of syllables would restore the fine balance which with each wordless mile slipped increasingly awry. He asked, "How did Bean seem to you?" Bean was their baby. They had left her last night, to go to the party, with a fever of 102.

Joan wrestled with her vow to say nothing, but guilt proved stronger than spite. She said, "Cooler. Her nose is a river."

"Sweetie," Richard blurted, "will they hurt me?" The curious fact was that he had never given blood before. Asthmatic and underweight, he had been 4-F, and at college and now at the office he had, less through his own determination than through the diffidence of the solicitors, evaded pledging blood. It was one of those tests of courage so trivial that no one had ever thought to make him face up to it.

Spring comes carefully to Boston. Speckled crusts of ice lingered around the parking meters, and the air, grayly stalemated between seasons, tinted the buildings along Longwood Avenue with a drab and homogeneous majesty. As they walked up the drive to the hospital entrance, Richard nervously wondered aloud if they would see the King of Arabia.

"He's in a separate wing," Joan said. "With four wives."

"Only four? What an ascetic." And he made bold to tap his wife's shoulder. It was not clear if, under the thickness of her winter coat, she felt it.

At the desk, they were directed down a long corridor floored with cigar-colored linoleum. Up and down, right and left it went, in the secretive, disjointed way peculiar to hospitals that have been built annex by annex. Richard seemed to himself Hansel orphaned with Gretel; birds ate the bread crumbs behind them, and at last they timidly knocked on the witch's door, which said BLOOD DONATION CENTER. A young man in white opened the door a crack. Over his shoulder Richard glimpsed—horrors!—a pair of dismembered female legs stripped of their shoes and laid parallel on a bed. Glints of needles and bottles pricked his eyes. Without widening the crack, the young man passed out to them two long forms. In sitting side by side on the waiting bench, remembering their middle initials and childhood diseases, Mr. and Mrs. Maple were newly defined to themselves. He fought down that urge to giggle and clown and lie that threatened him whenever he was asked—like a lawyer appointed by the court to plead a hopeless case—to present, as it were, his statistics to eternity. It seemed to mitigate his case slightly that a few of these statistics (present address, date of marrige) were shared by the hurt soul scratching beside him, with his own pen. He looked over her shoulder. "I never knew you had whooping cough."

"My mother says. I don't remember it."

A pan crashed to a distant floor. An elevator chuckled remotely. A woman, a middle-aged woman top-heavy with rouge and fur, stepped out of the blood door and wobbled a moment on legs that looked familiar. They had been restored to their shoes. The heels of these shoes clicked firmly as, having raked the Maples with a defiant blue glance, she turned and disappeared around a bend in the corridor. The young man appeared in the doorway holding a pair of surgical tongs. His noticeably recent haircut made him seem an apprentice barber. He clicked his tongs and smiled. "Shall I do you together?"

"Sure." It put Richard on his mettle that this callow fellow, to whom apparently they were to entrust their liquid essence, was so clearly younger than they. But when Richard stood, his indignation melted and his legs felt diluted under him. And the extraction of the blood sample from his middle finger seemed the nastiest and most needlessly prolonged physical involvement with another human being he had ever experienced. There is a touch that good dentists, mechanics, and barbers have, and this intern did not have it; he fumbled and in compensation was too rough. Again and again, an atrociously clumsy vampire, he tugged and twisted the purpling finger in vain. The tiny glass capillary tube remained transparent.

"He doesn't like to bleed, does he?" the intern asked Joan. As relaxed as a nurse, she sat in a chair next to a table of scintillating equipment.

"I don't think his blood moves much," she said, "until after midnight."

This stab at a joke made Richard in his extremity of fright laugh loudly, and the laugh at last seemed to jar the panicked coagulant. Red seeped upward in the thirsty little tube, as in a sudden thermometer.

The intern grunted in relief. As he smeared the samples on the analysis box, he explained idly, "What we ought to have down here is a pan of warm water. You just came in out of the cold. If you put your hand in hot water for a minute, the blood just pops out."

"A pretty thought," Richard said.

But the intern had already written him off as a clowner and continued calmly to Joan, "All we'd need would be a baby hot plate for about six dollars, then we could make our own coffee too. This way, when we get a donor who needs the coffee afterward, we have to send up for it while we keep his head between his knees. Do you think you'll be needing coffee?"

"*No*," Richard interrupted, jealous of their rapport.

The intern told Joan, "You're O."

"I know," she said.

"And he's A positive."

"Why that's very good, Dick!" she called to him.

"Am I rare?" he asked.

The boy turned and explained, "O positive and A positive are the most common types." Something in the patient tilt of his close-cropped head as its lateral sheen mixed with the lazily bright midmorning air of the room sharply reminded Richard of the days years ago when he had tended a battery of teletype machines in a room much this size. By now, ten o'clock, the yards of copy that began pouring through the machines at five and that lay in great crimped heaps on the floor when he arrived at seven would have been harvested and sorted and pasted together and turned in, and there was nothing to do but keep up with the staccato appearance of the later news and to think about simple things like coffee. It came back to him, how pleasant and secure those hours had been when, king of his own corner, he was young and newly responsible.

The intern asked, "Who wants to be first?"

"Let me," Joan said. "He's never done it before."

"Her full name is Joan of Arc," Richard explained, angered at this betrayal, so unimpeachably selfless and smug.

The intern, threatened in his element, fixed his puzzled eyes on the floor between them and said, "Take off your shoes and each get on a bed." He added, "Please," and all three laughed, one after the other, the intern last.

The beds were at right angles to one another along two walls. Joan lay down and from her husband's angle of vision was novelly foreshortened. He had never before seen her quite this way, the combed crown of her hair so poignant, her bared arm so silver and long, her stocking feet toed in so childishly and docilely. There were no pillows on the beds, and lying flat made him feel tipped head down; the illusion of floating encouraged his hope that this unreal adventure would soon dissolve in the manner of a dream. "You O.K.?"

"Are you?" Her voice came softly from the tucked under wealth of her hair. From the straightness of the parting it seemed her mother had brushed it. He watched a long needle sink into the flat of her arm and a piece of moist cotton clumsily swab the spot. He had imagined their blood would be drained into cans or bottles, but the intern, whose breathing was now the only sound within the room, brought to Joan's side what looked like a miniature plastic knapsack, all coiled and tied. His body cloaked his actions. When he stepped away, a plastic cord had been grafted, a transparent vine, to the flattened crook of Joan's extended arm, where the skin was translucent and the veins were faint blue tributaries shallowly buried. It was a tender, vulnerable place where in courting days she had liked being stroked. Now, without visible transition, the pale tendril planted here went dark red. Richard wanted to cry out.

The instant readiness of her blood to leave her body pierced him like a physical pang. Though he had not so much as blinked, its initial leap had been too quick for his eye. He had expected some visible sign of flow, but from the mere appearance of it the tiny looped hose might be pouring blood *into* her body or might be a curved line added, irrelevant as a mustache, to a finished canvas. The fixed position of his head gave what he saw a certain flatness.

And now the intern turned to him, and there was the tiny felt prick of the novocain needle, and then the coarse, half-felt intrusion of something resembling a medium weight nail. Twice the boy mistakenly probed for the vein and the third time taped the successful graft fast with adhesive tape. All the while, Richard's mind moved aloofly among the constellations of the stained cracked ceiling. What was being done to him did not bear contemplating. When the intern moved away to hum and tinkle among his instruments, Joan craned her neck to show her husband her face and, upside down in his vision, grotesquely smiled.

It was not many minutes that they lay there at right angles together, but the time passed as something beyond the walls, as something mixed with the faraway clatter of pans and the approach and retreat of footsteps and the opening and closing of unseen doors. Here, conscious of a pointed painless pulse in the inner hinge of his arm but incurious as to what it looked like, he floated and imagined how his soul would float free when all his blood was underneath the bed. His blood and Joan's merged on the floor, and together their spirits glided from crack to crack, from star to star on the ceiling. Once she cleared her throat, and the sound made an abrasion like the rasp of a pebble loosened by a cliff climber's boot.

The door opened. Richard turned his head and saw an old man, bald and sallow, enter and settle in a chair. He was one of those old men who hold within an institution an ill-defined but consecrated place. The young doctor seemed to know him, and the two talked, softly, as if not to disturb the mystical union of the couple sacrifically bedded together. They talked of persons and events that meant nothing—of Iris, of Dr. Greenstein, of Ward D, again of Iris, who had given the old man an undeserved scolding, of the shameful lack of a hot plate to make coffee on, of the rumored black bodyguards who kept watch with scimitars by the bed of the glaucomatous king. Through Richard's tranced ignorance these topics passed as clouds of impressions, iridescent, massy—Dr. Greenstein with a pointed nose and almond eyes the color of ivy, Iris eighty feet tall and hurling sterilized thunderbolts of wrath. As in some theologies the proliferant deities are said to exist as ripples upon the featureless ground of Godhead, so these inconstant images lightly overlay his continuous awareness of Joan's blood, like his own, ebbing. Linked to a common loss, they were chastely conjoined; the thesis developed upon him that the hoses attached to them somewhere out of sight met. Testing this belief, he glanced down and saw that indeed the plastic vine taped to the flattened crook of his arm was the same dark red as hers. He stared at the ceiling to disperse a sensation of faintness.

Abruptly the young intern left off his desultory conversation and moved to Joan's side. There was a chirp of clips. When he moved away, she was revealed holding her naked arm upright, pressing a piece of cotton against it with the other hand. Without pausing, the intern came to Richard's side, and the birdsong of clips repeated, nearer. "Look at that," he said to his elderly friend. "I started him two minutes later than her and he's finished at the same time."

"Was it a race?" Richard asked.

Clumsily firm, the boy fitted Richard's fingers to a pad and lifted his arm for him. "Hold it there for five minutes," he said.

"What'll happen if I don't?"

"You'll mess up your shirt." To the old man he said, "I had a woman in here the other day, she was all set to leave when all of a sudden, pow!—all over the front of this beautiful linen dress. She was going to Symphony."

"Then they try to sue the hospital for the cleaning bill," the old man muttered.

"Why was I slower than him?" Joan asked. Her upright arm wavered, as if vexed or weakened.

"The woman generally is," the boy told her. "Nine times out of ten, the man is faster. Their hearts are so much stronger."

"Is that really so?"

"Sure it's so," Richard told her. "Don't argue with medical science."

"Woman up in Ward C," the old man said, "they saved her life for her out of an auto accident and now I hear she's suing because they didn't find her dental plate."

Under such patter, the five minutes eroded. Richard's upheld arm began to ache. It seemed that he and Joan were caught together in a classroom where they would never be recognized, or in a charade that would never be guessed, the correct answer being Two Silver Birches in a Meadow.

"You can sit up now if you want," the intern told them. "But don't let go of the venipuncture."

They sat up on their beds, legs dangling heavily. Joan asked him, "Do you feel dizzy?"

"With my powerful heart? Don't be presumptuous."

"Do you think he'll need coffee?" the intern asked her. "I'll have to send up for it now."

The old man shifted forward in his chair, preparing to heave to his feet.

"I do *not* want any *coffee*"—Richard said it so loud he saw himself transposed, another Iris, into the firmament of the old man's aggrieved gossip. *Some dizzy bastard down in the blood room, I get up to get him some coffee and he damn near bit my head off.* To demonstrate simultaneously his essential good humor and his total presence of mind, Richard gestured toward the blood they had given—two square plastic sacks filled solidly fat—and declared, "Back where I come from in West Virginia sometimes you pick a tick off a dog that looks like that." The men looked at him amazed. Had he not quite said what he meant to say? Or had they never seen anybody from West Virginia before?

Joan pointed at the blood, too. "Is that us? Those little doll pillows?"

"Maybe we should take one home to Bean," Richard suggested.

The intern did not seem convinced that this was a joke. "Your blood will be credited to Mrs. Henryson's account," he stated stiffly.

Joan asked him, "Do you know anything about her? When is she—when is her operation scheduled?"

"I think for tomorrow. The only thing on the tab this after is an open heart or two; that'll take about sixteen pints."

"Oh . . ." Joan was shaken. "Sixteen . . that's a full person, isn't it?"

"More," the intern answered, with the regal handwave that bestows largess and dismisses compliments.

"Could we visit her?" Richard asked, for Joan's benefit. ("Really ashamed," she had said; it had cut.) He was confident of the refusal.

"Well, you can ask at the desk, but usually before a major one like this it's just the nearest of kin. I guess you're safe now." He meant their punctures. Richard's arm bore a small raised bruise; the intern covered it with one of those

ample, salmon, unhesitatingly adhesive bandages that only
hospitals have. That was their specialty, Richard thought—
packaging. They wrap the human mess for final delivery.
Sixteen doll's pillows, uniformly dark and snug, marching
into an open heart: the vision momentarily satisfied his hun-
ger for cosmic order.

He rolled down his sleeve and slid off the bed. It startled
him to realize, in the instant before his feet touched the
floor, that three pairs of eyes were fixed upon him, fascinated and apprehensive and eager for scandal. He stood and
towered above them. He hopped on one foot to slip into
one loafer, and then on this foot to slip into the other loafer. Then he did the little shuffle-tap, shuffle-tap step that
was all that remained to him of dancing lessons he had
taken at the age of seven, driving twelve miles each Saturday into Morgantown. He made a small bow toward his
wife, smiled at the old man, and said to the intern, "All my
life people have been expecting me to faint. I have no idea
why. I never faint."

His coat and overcoat felt a shade queer, a bit slithery
and light, but as he walked down the length of the corridor,
space seemed to adjust snugly around him. At his side, Joan
kept an inquisitive and chastened silence. They pushed
through the great glass doors. A famished sun was nibbling
through the overcast. Above and behind them, the King of
Arabia lay in a drugged dream of dunes and Mrs. Henryson
upon her sickbed received like the comatose mother of
twins their identical gifts of blood. Richard hugged his
wife's padded shoulders and as they walked along leaning
on each other whispered, "Hey, I love you. Love love *love*
you."

Romance is, simply, the strange, the untried. It was un-
usual for the Maples to be driving together at eleven in the
morning. Almost always it was dark when they shared a
car. The oval of her face was bright in the corner of his
eye. She was watching him, alert to take the wheel if he
suddenly lost consciousness. He felt tender toward her in
the eggshell light, and curious toward himself, wondering
how far beneath his brain the black pit did lie. He felt no
different; but then the quality of consciousness perhaps did
not bear introspection. Something certainly had been taken
from him; he was less himself by a pint and it was not impossible that like a trapeze artist saved by a net he was sus-

tained in the world of light and reflection by a single layer
of interwoven cells. Yet the earth, with its signals and buildings and cars and bricks, continued like a pedal note.

Boston behind them, he asked, "Where should be eat?"

"Should we eat?"

"Please, yes. Let me take you to lunch. Just like a secretary."

"I do feel sort of illicit. As if I've stolen something."

"You too? But what did we steal?"

"I don't know. The morning? Do you think Eve knows
enough to feed them?" Eve was their sitter, a little sandy girl
from down the street who would, in exactly a year, Richard
calculated, be painfully lovely. They lasted three years on the
average, sitters; you got them in the tenth grade and escorted
them into their bloom and then, with graduation, like commuters who had reached their stop, they dropped out of sight,
into nursing school or marriage. And the train went on, and
took on other passengers, and itself became older and longer.
The Maples had four children: Judith, Richard Jr., poor
oversized, angel-faced John, and Bean.

"She'll manage. What would you like? All that talk about
coffee has made me frantic for some."

"At the Pancake House beyond 128 they give you coffee
before you even ask."

"Pancakes? Now? Aren't you gay? Do you think we'll
throw up?"

"Do you feel like throwing up?"

"No, not really. I feel sort of insubstantial and gentle, but
it's probably psychosomatic. I don't really understand this
business of giving something away and still somehow having
it. What is it—the spleen?"

"I don't know. Are the splenetic man and the sanguine man
the same?"

"God. I've totally forgotten the humors. What are the
others—phlegm and choler?"

"Bile and black bile are in there somewhere."

"One thing about you, Joan. You're educated. New England women are educated."

"Sexless as we are."

"That's right; drain me dry and then put me on the
rack." But there was no wrath in his words; indeed, he had
reminded her of their earlier conversation so that, in much
this way, his words might be revived, diluted, and erased. It
seemed to work. The restaurant where they served only

pancakes was empty and quiet this early. A bashfulness possessed them both; it had become a date between two people who have little as yet in common but who are nevertheless sufficiently intimate to accept the fact without chatter. Touched by the stain her blueberry pancakes left on her teeth, he held a match to her cigarette and said, "Gee, I loved you back in the blood room."

"I wonder why."

"You were so brave."

"So were you."

"But I'm supposed to be. I'm paid to be. It's the price of having a penis."

"Shh."

"Hey, I didn't mean that about your being sexless."

The waitress refilled their coffee cups and gave them the check.

"And I promise never never to do the Twist, the cha-cha, or the schottische with Marlene Brossman."

"Don't be silly. I don't care."

This amounted to permission, but perversely irritated him. That smugness; why didn't she *fight?* Trying to regain their peace, scrambling uphill, he picked up their check and with an effort of acting, the pretense being that they were out on a date and he was a raw dumb suitor, said handsomely, "I'll pay."

But on looking into his wallet he saw only a single worn dollar there. He didn't know why this should make him so angry, except the fact somehow that it was only *one.* "Goddammit," he said. "Look at that." He waved it in her face. "I work like a bastard all week for you and those insatiable brats and at the end of it what do I have? One goddam crummy wrinkled dollar."

Her hands dropped to the pocketbook beside her on the seat, but her gaze stayed with him, her face having retreated, or advanced, into that porcelain shell of uncanny composure. "We'll both pay," Joan said.

A Madman

ENGLAND ITSELF seemed slightly insane to us. The meadows skimming past the windows of the Southampton-London train seemed green deliriously, seemed so obsessively steeped in the color that my eyes, still attuned to the exhausted verdure and September rust of American fields, doubted the ability of this landscape to perform useful work. England appeared to exist purely as a context of literature. I had studied this literature for four years, and had been sent here to continue this study. Yet my brain, excited and numbed by travel, could produce only one allusion; "a' babbled of green fields," that inconsequential Shakespearean snippet rendered memorable by a classic typographical emendation, kept running through my mind, "a' babbled, a' babbled," as the dactylic scansion of the train wheels drew us and our six mute, swaying compartment-mates northward into London. The city overwhelmed our expectations. The Kiplingesque grandeur of Waterloo Station, the Eliotic despondency of the brick row in Chelsea where we spent the night in the flat of a vague friend, the Dickensian nightmare of fog and sweating pavement and besmirched cornices that surrounded us when we awoke—all this seemed too authentic to be real, too corroborative of literature to be solid. The taxi we took to Paddington Station had a high roof and an open side, which gave it to our eyes the shocked, cockeyed expression of a character actor in an Agatha Christie melodrama. We wheeled past mansions by Galsworthy and parks by A. A. Milne; we glimpsed a cobbled eighteenth-century alley, complete with hanging tavern boards, where Dr. Johnson might have reeled and gasped the night he laughed so hard—the incident in Boswell so beautifully amplified in the essay by Beerbohm. And underneath all, underneath Heaven knew how many medieval

32

plagues, pageants, and conflagrations, old Londinium itself like a buried Titan lay smoldering in an abyss and tangle of time appalling to eyes accustomed to view the land as a surface innocent of history. We were relieved to board the train and feel it tug us westward.

The train brought us into Oxford at dusk. We had no place to go. We had made no reservations. We got into a cab and explained this to the driver. Middle-aged, his huge ears frothing with hair, he seemed unable to believe us, as if in all his years he had never before carried passengers who had not already visited their destination. He seemed further puzzled by the discovery that, though we claimed to be Americans, we had never been in Stillwater, or even in Tulsa. Fifteen years ago he had spent some months in the depths of Oklahoma learning to fly Lend-Lease planes. Now he repaid his debt by piloting us down a narrow street of brick homes whose windows—queerly, for this was suppertime—were all dark. "We'll give you a try at the Potts'," he explained briefly, braking. He went with us up to the door and twisted a heavy wrought-iron knob in its center. A remote, rattling ring sounded on the other side of the opaquely stained panes. At length a tall saturnine man answered. Our driver explained to him, "Potty, we've two homeless Yanks here. They don't know the score as yet."

Early in the evening as it was, Mr. Pott wore a muttering, fuddled air of having been roused. The BED AND BREAKFAST sign in his window seemed to commit him to no hospitality. Only after impressing us with the dark difficulty of it, with the unprecedented strain we were imposing upon the arrangements he had made with a disobliging and obtusely technical world, did he lead us upstairs and into a room. The room was large, chill, and amply stocked with whatever demigods it is that supervise sleep. I remember that the deliciously cool sheets and coarse blankets were topped by a purple puff smelling of lavender, and that in the morning, dressing, my wife and I skipped in and out of the radiant influence of the electric heater like a nymph and satyr competing at a shrine. The heater's plug was a ponderous and voltish-looking affair of three prongs; plugging it in was my first real work of acclimatization. We appeared for breakfast a bit late. Of all the other boarders, only Mr. Robinson (I have forgotten his actual name) had yet to come down. Our places were laid at the dining table, and at my place—I couldn't believe my eyes—was set, an insanity, a half of a cooked tomato on a slice of fried bread.

Mr. Robinson came down as Mr. Pott was finishing explaining to us why we must quickly find permanent lodgings. Our room would soon be needed by its regular tenant, an Indian undergraduate. Any day now he would take it into his head to show up. It was a thankless job, keeping students' rooms; they were in and out and up and talking and making music at all hours, and the landlord was supposed to enforce the midnight curfew. "The short of it is," Mr. Pott snarled, "the university wants me to be a nanny and a copper's nark." His voice changed tone. "Ah, Mr. Robinson! Good morning, Professor. We have with us two lovebirds from across the Atlantic."

Mr. Robinson ceremoniously shook our hands. Was he a professor? He was of middle size, with a scholar's delicate hunch and long thinning yellowish-white hair brushed straight back. In speech, he was all courtesy, lucid patter, and flattering attention. We turned to him with relief; after our host's dark hints and dour discontents, we seemed to be emerging into the England of light. "Welcome to Oxford," he said, and from a bright little tension in his cheeks we could see he was about to quote. " 'That home of lost causes, and forsaken beliefs, and unpopular names, and impossible loyalties.' That's Matthew Arnold; if you want to understand Oxford, read Arnold. Student of Balliol, fellow of Oriel, professor of poetry, the highest bird as ever flew with a pedant's clipped wings. Read Arnold, and read Newman. 'Whispering from her towers the last enchantments of the Middle Age'—which he did not *mean,* you know, entirely sympathetically; no, not at all. Arnold was not at all church-minded. 'The Sea of Faith was once, too, at the full, but now I only hear its melancholy, long, *withdrawing* roar, retreating to the breath of the nightwind down the vast edges drear of the naked shingles of the world.' Hah! Mr. Pott, what is this I see before me? My customary egg. You are a veritable factotum, a Johannes Factotum, of kindness. Mr. Pott of St. John's Street," he confided to us in his quick, twinkling way, "an institution no less revered by the student body than the church of St. Michael's-at-the-north-gate, which contains, you should know, and will *see,* the oldest standing structure in"—he cleared his throat, as if to signal something special coming—"Oxnaford: the old Saxon tower, dating from the ninth century at the least. At the *least,* I insist, though in doing so I incur the certain wrath of the more piddling of local archaeologists, if we can dignify them with the title upon which Schliemann and Sir Leonard Woolley have heaped so much honor." He set to his egg eagerly, smashing it open with a spoon.

My wife asked him, "Are you a professor of archaeology?"

"Dear madam," he said, "in a manner of speaking, in a manner of speaking, I have taken all knowledge for my province. Do you know Ann Arbor, in, I believe, the very wooded state of Michigan? No? Have no shame, no shame; your country is so vast, a poor Englishman's head reels. My niece, my sister's daughter, married an instructor in the university there. I learn from her letters that the temperature frequently—*frequently*—drops below zero Fahrenheit. Mr. Pott, will this charming couple be spending the term with us here?" When it was explained to him, more readily than tactfully, that our presence here was an emergency measure, the result of a merciful impulse which Mr. Pott, his implication was, already regretted, Mr. Robinson bent his face low over the table to look up at us. He had perfect upper teeth. "You must know the *way,*" he said, "the ins and outs, the little short cuts and circumlocutions, circumflexions, the *circumstances;* else you will never find a flat. You have waited long, too long; in a few days the Michaelmas term will be upon us and from Woodstock to Cowley there won't be a room to be *had.* But I, I"—he lifted one finger and closed one eye sagely—"I may be of help. *'Che tu mi segui,'* as Virgil said to Dante, *'e io sarò tua guida!'* "

We were of course grateful for a guide. The three of us walked down St. John's Street (all the shades were drawn, though this was daylight), up Beaumont past the sooty, leonine sprawl of the Ashmolean, and down Magdalen Street to Cornmarket, where indeed we did see the Saxon tower. Mr. Robinson indicated points of interest continuously. His lower jaw seemed abnormally slender, as if a normal jaw had been whittled for greater flexibility and lightness. It visibly supported only one lower tooth, and that one hardly bigger than a fleck of tobacco, and set in the gum sideways; whereas his upper teeth were strikingly even and complete. Through these mismatched gates he poured an incessant stressed stream of words, broken only when, preparatory to some heightened effort of erudition, he preeningly cleared his throat. "Now we are standing in the center of town, the

very hub and beating heart of Oxfordshire, Carfax, derived
—uh-uh-*hem*—from the Norman *carrefor*, the Latin
quadrifurcus, meaning four forks, or crossroads. Do you
know Latin? The last international language, the—uh-hem
—Esperanto of Christendom." He carried an old paper bag,
and we found ourselves in a vast roofed market, surrounded
by blood-flecked butcher's stalls and bins of raw vegetables
smelling of mud. Mr. Robinson methodically filled his bag
with potatoes. He examined each potato, and hesitated with
it, as if it would be his last; but then his anxious parch-
menty hand would dart out and seize yet another. When the
bag could hold no more, he shrugged and began to wander
away. The proprietress of the stall shouted in protest. She
was fat; her face looked scorched; and she wore a man's
boots and numerous unravelling sweaters. Without a word,
Mr. Robinson returned and rather grandly dumped all the
potatoes back into the bin. Along with the potatoes some
papers fluttered out, and these he put back in the bag. He
turned to us and smiled. "Now," he said, "it is surely time
for lunch. Oxnaford is no town to storm on an empty stomach."

"But," I said, "Mr. Robinson, what about the place we
have to find?"

He audibly exhaled, as if he had just tasted a superb
wine. "*Aaaaah*. I have not forgotten, I have not forgotten.
We must tread cautiously; you do not know, you see, the
way. The ins and outs, the *circumstances*." He led us to a
cafeteria above a furniture store on the Broad and through
the chips and custard tried to distract us with a profuse
account of Oxford in its medieval heyday—Roger Bacon,
Duns Scotus, the "Mad Parliament" of 1256, the town-
gown riots of St. Scholastica's Day in 1355. Down on the
street once more, he took to plucking our arms and making
promises. One more little trip, one harmless excursion that
would be *very* useful for us, and then down to business. He
escorted us all the way down High Street to the Magdalen
Bridge, and thus we received our first glimpse of the Cher-
well. No punts were out at this time of year, and swans generally stayed downriver. But looking back toward the center
of town, we were treated to the storybook view of Oxford,
all spires and silhouette and flaking stone, under a sky by
John Constable, *R.A.* Weak, distraught, I felt myself succumb; we surrendered the day to Mr. Robinson. Triumphantly sensing this, he led us down Rose Lane, through the

botanic gardens orange and golden with fall flowers, along Merton Field, and back through a series of crooked alleys to the business district. Here he took us into a bookstore and snatched a little newspaper, the Oxfordshire weekly, out of a rack and indicated to the man behind the counter that I would pay for it. While I rummaged the fourpence out of my pocket, Mr. Robinson pranced to the other wall and came back holding a book. It was a collection of essays by Matthew Arnold. "Don't buy this book," he told me. *"Don't buy it.* I have it in a superior edition, and will lend it to you. Do you understand? I will *lend* it to you." I thanked him and, as if all he had wanted from us was a little gratitude, he announced that he would leave us now. He tapped the paper in my hand. He winked "Your problems—and don't think, *don't* think they have not been painfully on my mind—are solved; you will find your rooms in here. Very few, *very* few people know about this paper, but all the locals, *all* the locals with *good* rooms advertise in here; they don't *trust* the regular channels. You must know the *way,* you see, the ins and outs." And he left us, as at the edge of Paradise.

It was growing dark, in that long, slow, tea-shoppe-lit style of English afternoons, and we had tea to clear our heads. Then there seemed nothing to do but return to Mr. Pott's house, on St. John's Street. Now we noticed for the first time students in the streets, whirring along on their bicycles like bats, their black gowns fluttering. Only we lacked a roost. My wife lay down on top of our purple puff and silently cried. Her legs ached from all the walking. She was —our heavy secret—three months pregnant. We were fearful that if this became known not a landlord in Oxford would have us. I went out in the dusk with my newspaper to a phone booth. In fact, there were few flats advertised in the weekly, and all but one lacked a kitchen; this one was listed as on St. Aldate's Street. I called the number and a woman answered. When she heard my voice, she asked, "Are you an American?"

"I guess, yes."

"I'm sorry. My husband doesn't like Americans."

"He doesn't? Why not?" It had been impressed upon me, with the award of my fellowship, that I was to act as an ambassador abroad.

There was a pause, then she said, "If you must know, our

daughter's gone and married an airman from your base at Brize Norton."

"Oh—well, I'm not an airman. I'm a student. And I'm already married. It would just be me and my wife, we have no children."

"Hooh, Jack!" The exclamation sounded off focus, as if she had turned her mouth from the receiver. Then she returned close to my ear, confidential, murmurous. "My husband's this minute come in. Would you like to talk to him?"

"No," I said, and hung up, trembling but pleased to have encountered a conversation I could end.

The next morning, Mr. Robinson had reached the breakfast table before us. Perhaps it had cost him some sleep, for his hair was mussed and its yellow tinge had spread to his face. His eagerness in greeting us was now tipped with a penetrating whine. The falseness of his upper teeth had become painfully clear; spittle sparked from his mouth with the effort of keeping the plate in place. " 'Noon strikes on England,' " he recited at our appearance, " 'noon on Oxford town, Beauty she was statue cold, there's blood upon her gown, proud and godly kings had built her long ago, with her towers and tombs and statues all arow, with her fair and floral air and the love that lingers there, and the streets where the great men go.' "

"I thought this morning," I told him, "I'd go to my college and see if they could help."

"Which college?" he asked. His face became abnormally alert.

"Keble."

"Ah," he cried, triumphant, "they won't help. *They won't help.* They know *nothing.* They *wish* to know nothing. *Nihil ex nihilo.*"

"It's a game they play," Mr. Pott muttered sourly, "called Hands Off."

"Really?" my wife said, her voice brimming.

"Nevertheless," I insisted, "we have to begin somewhere. That weekly you got for us had only one possibility, and the woman's husband didn't like Americans."

"Your ruddy airmen," Mr. Pott explained, "from out Norton way have given you a name. They come into town with their powder-blue suits and big shoulders, some of 'em black as shoe polish, and give the local tarts what-for."

My mention of the weekly had set off a sequence in Mr.

Robinson's mind, for now he clapped his hands to his head and said, "That book. I promised to lend you that book. Forgive, for*give* a rattlebrained old man. I will get it for you *instanter*. No protest, no protest. Youth must be served."

He went upstairs to his room, and we glanced at Mr. Pott inquisitively. He nodded. "I'd beat it now, in your shoes," he said.

We had made three blocks and felt safely lost in the crowd along Cornmarket when Mr. Robinson caught up with us. He was panting and wearing his bedroom slippers. "Wait," he whined, *"wait,* you don't *see*. You can't run blind and headlong into these situations, you don't understand the *circumstances*." He carried his paper shopping bag and produced from it a book, which he pressed upon me. It was a turn-of-the-century edition of Arnold's essays, with marbled end papers. Right there, on the jostling pavement, I opened it, and nearly slammed it shut in horror, for every page was a spider's web of annotations and underlinings, in many pencils and inks and a wild variety of handwritings. "Cf.," *"videlicet,"* "He betrays himself here," "19th cent. optmsm."—these leaped at me out of the mad swarm. The annotations were themselves annotated, as his argument with the text doubled and redoubled back on itself. 'Is this so?' a firm hand had written in one margin, and below it, in a different slant and fainter pencil, had been added. "Yes it is so," with the "is" triple-underlined; and below this a wobbly ball-point pen had added, without capitals, "but is it?" It made me dizzy to look into; I shut the book and thanked him.

Mr. Robinson looked at me cleverly sideways. "You thought I had forgotten," he said. "You thought an old man's brain didn't hold water. No shame, no shame; in your circumstances you could hardly think otherwise. But no, what I promise, I fulfill; now I will be your guide. A-hem. Everyman, I will go with thee: hah!" He gestured toward the ancient town hall and told us that during the Great Rebellion Oxford had been the Royalist headquarters.

> "The king, observing with judicious eyes,
>   The state of both his universities,
>   To Oxford sent a troop of horse, and why?"

he recited, ending with a sweep of his arm that drew eyes to us.

Just as, by being pronounced definitely insane, a criminal curiously obligates the society he has injured, so now Mr. Robinson's hold upon us was made perfect. The slither of his shuffling slippers on the pavement, the anxious snagging stress of periodic syllables, the proud little throat clearings were so many filaments that clasped us to him as, all but smothered by embarrassment and frustration, we let him lead us. Our route overlapped much of the route of the day before; but now he began to develop a new theme—that all this while he had been subjecting us to a most meticulous scrutiny and we had passed favorably, with *flying* colors, and that he was going to introduce us to some of his friends, the really *important* people, the grand panjandrums, the people who knew where there were rooms and rooms. He would write letters, perform introductions, secure our admission to secret societies. After lunch, at about the hour when on the day before he had introduced us to the paper seller, he shepherded us into the library of the Oxford Union Society and introduced us to the fastidious boy behind the desk. Mr. Robinson's voice, somehow intensified by whispering, carried to every crusty corner and sacrosanct gallery. The young librarian in his agony did not suppress an ironical smile. When his eyes turned to us, they took on a polite glaze that fell a little short of concealing contempt. But with what a deal of delighted ceremony did Mr. Robinson, who evidently really was a member, superintend the signing of our names in a huge old ledger! In return for our signatures we were given, with a sourcerer's flourishes, an application form for membership. There was this to be said for Mr. Robinson: he never left you quite empty-handed.

Returning, frantic and dazed, to our room at the Potts', we were able to place the application blank and the annotated Arnold beside our first trophy, the Oxfordshire weekly. I lay down on the bed beside my wife and read through the lead article, a militant lament on the deterioration of the Norman church at Iffley. When I had regained some purpose in my legs, I walked over to Keble and found it was much as I had been warned. The patterns of paternalism did not include those students tasteless enough to take a wife. Flats were to be had, though, the underling asserted, absurdly scratching away with a dip pen in his tiny nook with its one Gothic window overlooking a quad; his desk suggested the Tenniel illustration of all the cards flying out of the pack.

I was newly enough married not to expect that my wife, once I was totally drained of hope, would supply some. She had decided in my absence that we must stop being polite to Mr. Robinson. Indeed, this did seem the one way out of the maze. I should have thought of it myself. We dressed up and ate a heartily expensive meal at a pseudo-French restaurant that Mr. Robinson had told us never, *never* to patronize, because they were brigands. Then we went to an American movie to give us brute strength and in the morning came down to breakfast braced. Mr. Robinson was not there.

This was to be, it turned out, our last breakfast at the Potts'. Already we had become somewhat acclimatized. We no longer, for example, glanced around for Mrs. Pott; we had accepted that she existed, if she existed at all, on a plane invisible to us. The other boarders greeted us by name now. There were two new faces among them—young students' faces, full of bewilderingly pertinent and respectful questions about the United States. The States, their opinion was, had already gone the way that all countries must eventually go. To be American, we were made to feel, was to be lucky. Mr. Pott told us that Karam had written he would be needing his room by the weekend and pushed across the table a piece of paper containing several addresses. "There's a three-room basement asking four pounds ten off Banbury Road," he said, "and if you want to go to five guineas, Mrs. Shipley still has her second floor over toward St. Hilda's."

It took us a moment to realize what this meant; then our startled thanks gushed. "Mr. Robinson," I blurted in conclusion, groping for some idiom suitable to Mr. Pott and not quite coming up with it, "has been leading us all around the Maypole."

"Poor Robbie," said Mr. Pott. "Daft as a daisy." He tapped the bony side of his lean dark head.

My wife asked, "Is he always—like that?"

"Only as when he finds an innocent or two to sink his choppers in; they find him out soon enough, poor Robbie."

"Does he really have a niece in Michigan?"

"Ah yes, he's not all fancy. He was a learned man before his trouble, but the university never quite took him on."

" 'So poetry, which is in Oxford made an art,' " a familiar voice sweetly insisted behind us, " 'in London only is a
trade.' Dryden. *Not* a true Oxonian, but an excellent poet
and amateur scholar nevertheless. If you enjoy his jingling
style. Mr. Pott. Can that egg be mine?" He sat down and
smashed it neatly with his spoon and turned to us jubilantly.
Perhaps the delay in his appearance had been caused by an
effort of grooming, for he looked remarkably spruce, his
long hair brushed to a tallowish lustre, his tie knotted
tightly, his denture snug under his lips, and a plaid scarf
draped around his shoulders. "Today," he said, "I will devote myself to your cause wholeheartedly, without intermis-
sions, interruptions, or intercessions. I have spent the last
hour preparing a wonderful surprise, *mirabile dictu*, as
faithful Aeneas said to his natural mother, Aphrodite."

"I think," I said, in a voice constrained by the presence
of others around the table, "we really must do other things
today. Mr. Pott says that Karam—"

"Wait, *wait*," he cried, becoming agitated and rising in
his chair. "You do not understand. You are *innocents*—
charming yes, vastly potential, yes, but innocents, you see.
You must know the *way*, the ins, the outs—"

"No, honestly—"

"*Wait*. Come with me now. I will show you my surprise
instanter, if you insist." And he bustled up from the table,
the egg uneaten, and back up the stairs toward his room.
My wife and I followed, relieved that what must be done
could now be done unwitnessed.

Mr. Robinson was already coming out of his room as we
met him on the second-floor landing. In his haste he had
left the door open behind him. Over his shoulder I glimpsed
a chaos of tumbled books and wrinkled papers. He held in
his hands a sheet of paper on which he had made a list. "I
have spent the last hour preparing," he said, "with a care
not incomparable to that of, *ih-ih-humm*, St. Jerome tran-
scribing the Vulgate, a list; these are the people that today
we will *see*." I read the list he held to my face. The offices
and titles and names at the top meant nothing to me, but
halfway down, where the handwriting began to get big and
its slant to become inconstant, there was the word "Chan-
cellor" followed by a huge colon and the name "Lord Hali-
fax."

Something in my face made the paper begin to tremble.
Mr. Robinson took it away and held it at his side. With the

other hand he fumbled with his lapel. "You're terribly kind," I said. "You've given us a wonderful introduction to Oxford. But today, really, we must go out on our own. Absolutely."

"No, no, you don't seem to comprehend; the *circum—*"

"*Please,*" my wife said sharply.

He looked at her, then at me, and an unexpected calm entered his features. The twinkle faded, the jaw relaxed, and his face might have been that of any tired old man as he sighed, "Very well, very well. No shame."

"Thank you so much," my wife said, and made to touch, but did not quite touch, the limp hand that had curled defensively against the breast of his coat.

Knees bent, he stood apparently immobilized on the landing before the door of his room. Yet as we went down the stairs, he did one more gratuitous thing; he came to the banister, lifted his hand and pronounced, as we quickened our steps to dodge his words, "God bless. God bless."

Leaves

THE GRAPE LEAVES outside my window are curiously beautiful. "Curiously" because it comes upon me as strange, after the long darkness of self-absorption and fear and shame in which I have been living, that things are beautiful, that independent of our catastrophes they continue to maintain the "effect," which is the hallmark and specialty of Nature. Nature: this morning it seems to me very clear that Nature may be defined as that which exists without guilt. Our bodies are in Nature; our shoes, their laces, the little plastic tips of the laces—everything around us and about us is in Nature, and yet something holds us away from it, like the upward push of water which keeps us from touching the sandy bottom, ribbed and glimmering with crescental fragments of oyster shell, so clear to our eyes.

A blue jay lights on a twig outside my window. Momentarily sturdy, he stands astraddle, his dingy rump towards me, his head alertly frozen in silhouette, the predatory curve of his beak stamped on a sky almost white above the misting tawny marsh. See him? I do, and, snapping the chain of my thought, I have reached through glass and seized him and stamped him on this page. Now he is gone. And yet, there, a few lines above, he still is, "astraddle," rump "dingy," his head "alertly frozen." A curious trick, possibly useless, but mine.

The grape leaves where they are not in each other's shadows are golden. Flat leaves, they take the sun flatly, and turn the absolute light, sum of the spectrum and source of all life, into the crayon yellow with which children render it. Here and there, wilt transmutes this lent radiance into a glowing orange, and the green of the still tender leaves—for green persists long into autumn, if we look—strains from the sunlight a fine-veined chartreuse. The shadows these

44

leaves cast upon each other, though vagrant and nervous in the wind that sends friendly scavenging rattles scurrying across the roof, are yet quite various and definite, containing innumerable barbaric suggestions of scimitars, flanged spears, prongs, and menacing helmets. The net effect, however, is innocent of menace. On the contrary, its intricate simultaneous suggestion of shelter and openness, warmth and breeze, invites me outward; my eyes venture into the leaves beyond. I am surrounded by leaves. The oak's are tenacious claws of purplish rust; the elm's, scant feathers of a feminine yellow; the sumac's, a savage, toothed blush. I am upheld in a serene and burning universe of leaves. Yet something plucks me back, returns me to that inner darkness where guilt is the sun.

The events need to be sorted out. I am told I behaved wantonly, and it will take time to integrate this unanimous impression with the unqualified righteousness with which our own acts, however admittedly miscalculated, invest themselves. And once the events are sorted out—the actions given motivations, the actors assigned psychologies, the miscalculations tabulated, the abnormalities named, the whole furious and careless growth pruned by explanation and rooted in history and returned, as it were, to Nature—what then? Is not such a return spurious? Can our spirits really enter Time's haven of mortality and sink composedly among the mulching leaves? No: we stand at the intersection of two kingdoms, and there is no advance and no retreat, only a sharpening of the edge where we stand.

I remember most sharply the black of my wife's dress as she left our house to get her divorce. The dress was a soft black sheath, with a V neckline, and Helen always looked handsome in it; it flattered her pallor. This morning she looked especially handsome, her face utterly white with fatigue. Yet her body, that natural thing, ignored our catastrophe, and her shape and gestures were incongruously usual. She kissed me lightly in leaving, and we both felt the humor of this trip's being insufficiently unlike any other of her trips to Boston—to Symphony, to Bonwit's. The same search for the car keys, the same harassed instructions to the complacent baby-sitter, the same little dip and thrust of her head as she settled behind the wheel of her car. And I, satisfied at last, divorced, studied my children with the eyes of one who had left them, examined my house as one does a set of snapshots from an irrevocable time, drove through

the turning landscape as a man in asbestos cuts through a
fire, met my wife-to-be—weeping yet smiling, stunned yet
brave—and felt, unstoppably, to my horror, the inner darkness burst my skin and engulf us both and drown our love.
The natural world, where our love had existed, ceased to
exist. My heart shied back; it shies back still. I retreated. As
I drove back, the leaves of the trees along the road stated
their shapes to me. There is no more story to tell. By telephone I plucked my wife back; I clasped the black of her
dress to me, and braced for the pain.

It does not stop coming. The pain does not stop coming.
Almost every day, a new installment arrives by mail or face
or phone. Every time the telephone rings, I expect it to un-
coil some new convolution of consequence. I have come
to hide in this cottage but even here, there is a telephone,
and the scraping sounds of wind and branch and unseen animal are charged with its electric silence. At any moment, it
may explode, and the curious beauty of the leaves will be
eclipsed again.

In nervousness, I rise, and walk across the floor. A spider
like a white asterisk hangs in air in front of my face. I look
at the ceiling and cannot see where its thread is attached.
The ceiling is smooth plasterboard. The spider hesitates. It
feels a huge alien presence. Its exquisite white legs spread
warily and of its own dead weight it twirls on its invisible
thread. I catch myself in the quaint and antique pose of the
fabulist seeking to draw a lesson from a spider, and become
self-conscious. I dismiss self-consciousness and do earnestly
attend to this minute articulated star hung so pointedly before my face; and am unable to read the lesson. The spider
and I inhabit contiguous but incompatible cosmoses. Across
the gulf we feel only fear. The telephone remains silent.
The spider reconsiders its spinning. The wind continues to
stir the sunlight. In walking in and out of this cottage, I have
tracked the floor with a few dead leaves, pressed flat like
scraps of dark paper.

And what are these pages but leaves? Why do I produce
them but to thrust, by some subjective photosynthesis, my
guilt into Nature, where there is no guilt? Now the marsh,
level as a carpet, is streaked with faint green amid the
shades of brown—russet, ochre, tan, *marron*—and on the
side, where the land lifts above tide level, evergreens stab
upwards sullenly. Beyond them, there is a low blue hill; in
this coastal region, the hills are almost too modest to bear

names. But I *see* it; for the first time in months I see it. I see it as a child, fingers gripping and neck straining, glimpses the roof of a house over a cruelly high wall. Under my window, the lawn is lank and green and mixed with leaves shed from a small elm, and I remember how, the first night I came to this cottage, thinking I was leaving my life behind me, I went to bed alone and read, in the way one reads stray books in a borrowed house, a few pages of an old edition of *Leaves of Grass*. And my sleep was a loop, so that in awaking I seemed still in the book, and the light-struck sky quivering through the stripped branches of the young elm seemed another page of Whitman, and I was entirely open, and lost, like a woman in passion, and free, and in love, without a shadow in any corner of my being. It was a beautiful awakening, but by the next night I had returned to my house.

The precise barbaric shadows on the grape leaves have shifted. The angle of illumination has altered. I imagine warmth leaning against the door, and open the door to let it in; sunlight falls flat at my feet like a penitent.

The Stare

THEN THERE it was, in the corner of his eye. He turned, his heart frozen. The incredibility of her being here, now, at a table in this one restaurant on the one day when he was back in the city, did not check the anticipatory freezing of his heart, for when they had both lived in New York they had always been lucky at finding each other, time after time; and this would be one more time. Already, in the instant between recognition and turning, he had framed his first words; he would rise, with the diffidence she used to think graceful, and go to her and say, "Hey. It's you."

Her face would smile apologetically, lids lowered, and undergo one of its little shrugs. "It's me."

"I'm so glad. I'm so sorry about what happened." And everything would be understood, and the need of forgiveness once again magically put behind them, like a wall of paper flames they had passed through.

It was someone else, a not very young woman whose hair, not really the color of her hair at all, had, half seen, suggested the way her hair, centrally parted and pulled back into a glossy French roll, would cut with two dark wings into her forehead, making her brow seem low and intense and emphasizing her stare. He felt the eyes of his companions at lunch question him, and he returned his attention to them, his own eyes smarting from the effort of trying to press this unknown woman's appearance into the appearance of another. One of his companions at the table—a gentle gray banker whose affection for him, like a generous check, quietly withheld at the bottom a tiny deduction of tact, a modest minus paid as an increment on their mutual security—smiled in such a way as to balk his impulse to blurt, to confess. His other companion was an elderly female underwriter, an ex-associate, whose statistical insight was remorseless but who in personal manner was all feathers and feigned dismay. "I'm seeing ghosts," he explained to her, and she nodded, for they had, all three, with the gay withering credulity of nonbelievers, been discussing ghosts. The curtain of conversation descended again, but his palms tingled, and, as if trapped between two mirrors, he seemed to face a diminishing multiplication of her stare.

The first time they met, in an apartment with huge slab-like paintings and fragile furniture that seemed to be tiptoeing, she came to the defense of something her husband had said, and he had irritably wondered how a woman of such evident spirit and will could debase herself to the support of statements so asinine, and she must have felt, across the room, his irritation, for she gave him her stare. It was, as a look, both blunt and elusive: somewhat cold, certainly hard, yet curiously wide, and even open—its essential ingredient shied away from being named. Her eyes were the only glamorous feature of a freckled, bony, tomboyish face, remarkable chiefly for its sharp willingness to express pleasure. When she laughed, her teeth were bared like a skull's, and when she stared, her great, grave, perfectly shaped eyes insisted on their shape as rigidly as a statue's.

Later, when their acquaintance had outlived the initial irritations, he had met her in the Museum of Modern Art, amid an exhibit of old movie stills, and, going forward with the innocent cheerfulness that her presence even then aroused in him, he had been unexpectedly met by her stare. "We missed you Friday night," she said.

"You did? What happened Friday night?"

"Oh, nothing. We just gave a little party and expected you to come."

"We weren't invited."

"But you *were*. I phoned your wife."

"She never said anything to me. She must have forgotten."

"Well, I don't suppose it matters."

"But it *does*. I'm so sorry. I would have loved to have come. It's very funny that she forgot it; she really just lives for parties."

"Yes." And her stare puzzled him, since it was no longer directed at him; the hostility between the two women existed before he had fulfilled its reason.

Later still, at a party they all did attend, he had, alone with her for a moment, kissed her, and the response of her

mouth had been disconcerting; backing off, expecting to
find in her face the moist, formless warmth that had taken
his lips, he encountered her stare instead. In the months that
tingled, and, as if trapped between two mirrors, he seemed to
relax. Her body gathered softness under his; late one night,
after yet another party, his wife, lying beside him in the
pre-dawn darkness of her ignorance, had remarked, with the
cool, fair appraisal of a rival woman, how beautiful she—
she, the other—had become, and he had felt, half dreaming
in the warm bed he had betrayed, justified. Her laugh no
longer flashed out so hungrily, and her eyes, brimming with
the secret he and she had made, deepened and seemed to re-
join the girlishness that had lingered in the other features of
her face. Seeing her across a room standing swathed in the
beauty he had given her, he felt a creator's, a father's, pride.
There existed, when they came together, a presence of tenderness like a ghostly child who when they parted was taken
away and set to sleeping. Yet even in those months, in the
depths of their secret, lying together as if in an intimate dun-
geon, discussing with a gathering urgency what they would
do when their secret crumbled and they were exposed, there
would now and then glint out at him, however qualified by
tears and languor, the unmistakable accusatory hardness. It
was accusing, yet that was not its essence; his conscience
shied away from naming the pressure that had formed it and
that, it imperceptibly became apparent, he was helpless to
relieve. Each time they parted, she would leave behind, in
the last instant before the door closed, a look that haunted
him, like the flat persisting ring of struck crystal.

The last time he saw her, all the gentle months had been
stripped away and her stare, naked, had become furious.
"Don't you love me?" Two households were in turmoil and
the rich instinct that had driven him to her had been re-
duced to a thin need to hide and beg.

"Not enough." He meant it simply, as a fact, as something that already had been made plain.

But she took it as a death blow, and in a face whitened
and drawn by the shocks of recent days, from beneath dark
wings of tensely parted hair, her stare revived into a life so
coldly controlled and adamantly hostile that for weeks he
could not close his eyes without confronting it—much as a
victim of torture must continue to see the burning iron with
which he was blinded.

Now, back in New York, walking alone, soothed by food and profitable talk, he discovered himself so healed that his wound ached to be reopened. The glittering city bristled with potential prongs. The pale disc of every face, as it slipped from the edge of his vision, seemed to cup the possibility of being hers. He felt her searching for him. Where would she look? It would be her style simply to walk the streets, smiling and striding in the hope of their meeting. He had a premonition—and yes, there, waiting to cross Forty-third Street between two Puerto Rican messenger boys, it was she, with her back toward him; there was no mistaking the expectant tilt of her head, the girlish curve of her high, taut cheek, the massed roll of hair pulled so glossy he used to imagine that the hairpins gave her pain. He drew abreast, timid and prankish, to surprise her profile, and she became a wrinkled painted woman with a sagging lower lip. He glanced around incredulously, and her stare glimmered and disappeared in the wavering wall-window of a modernistic bank. Crossing the street, he looked into the bank, but there was no one, no one he knew—only some potted tropical plants that looked vaguely familiar.

He returned to work. His company had lent him for this visit the office of a man on vacation. He managed to concentrate only by imagining that each five minutes were the final segment of time he would have to himself before she arrived. When the phone on his desk rang, he expected the receptionist to announce that a distraught woman with striking eyes was asking for him. When he went into the halls, a secretary flickering out of sight battered his heart with a resemblance. He returned to his borrowed office, and was startled not to find her in it, wryly examining the yellowed children's drawings—another man's children—taped to the walls. The bored afternoon pasted shadows on these walls. Outside his window, the skyscrapers began to glow. He went down the elevator and into the cool crowded dusk thankful for her consideration; it was like her to let him finish his day's work before she declared her presence. She had always assumed, in their scattered hours together, a wife's dutiful attitude toward him. But now, now she could cease considerately hiding, and he could take her to dinner with an easy conscience. He checked his wallet to make sure he had enough money. He decided he would refuse to take her to a play, though undoubtedly she would suggest it.

She loved the stage. But they had too little time together to waste it in awareness of a third thing.

He had taken a room at what he still thought of as their hotel. To his surprise, she was not waiting for him in the lobby, which seemed filled with a party, a competition of laughter. Charles Boyer was waiting for the elevator. She would have liked that, sitting on the bench before the desk, waiting and watching, her long legs crossed and one black shoe jabbing the air with the prongs of its heel and toe. He had even prepared his explanation to the clerk; this was his wife. They had had (voice lowered, eyebrows lifted, the unavoidable blush not, after all, inappropriate) a fight, and impulsively she had followed him to New York, to make up. Irregular, but . . . women. So could his single reservation kindly be changed to a double? Thank you.

This little play was so firmly written in his head that he looked into the bar to make sure the leading actress was not somewhere in the wings. The bar was bluely lit and amply patronized by fairies. Their drawled, elaborately enunciating voices, discussing musical comedies in tones of peculiar passion, carried to him, and he remembered how she when he had expressed distaste, had solemnly explained to him that homosexuals were people, too, and how she herself often felt attracted to them, and how it always saddened her that she had nothing, you know—her stare defensively sharpened—to give them. "That old bag, she's overex*posed* herself," one of the fairies stridently declared, of a famous actress.

He took the elevator up to his room. It was similar to ones they had shared, but nothing was exactly the same, except the plumbing fixtures, and even these were differently arranged. He changed his shirt and necktie. In the mirror, behind him, a slow curve of movement, like a woman's inquisitive step, chilled his spine; it was the door drifting shut. He rushed from the suffocating vacant room into the streets, to inhale the invisible possibility of finding her. He ate at the restaurant he would have chosen for them both. The waiter seemed fussed, seating a solitary man. The woman of a couple at a nearby table adjusted an earring with a gesture that belonged to her; she had never had her ears pierced, and this naïveté of her flesh had charmed him. He abstained from coffee. Tonight he must court sleep assiduously.

He walked to tire himself. Broadway was garish with the clash of mating—sailors and sweethearts, touts and tarts.

Spring infiltrates a city through the blood of its inhabitants. The side streets were hushed like the aisles of long Pullman sleepers being drawn forward by their diminishing perspective. She would look for him on Fifth Avenue; her window-shopper's instinct would send her there. He saw her silhouette at a distance, near Rockefeller Center, and up close he spotted a certain momentary plane of her face that flew away in a flash, leaving behind the rubble of a face he did not know, had never kissed or tranquilly studied as it lay averted on a pillow. Once or twice, he even glimpsed, shadowed in a doorway, huddled on a bench tipping down toward the Promethean fountain, the ghostly child of their tenderness, asleep; but never her, her in the fragrant solidity he had valued with such strange gay lightness when it was upon him. Statistically, it began to seem wonderful that out of so many faces not one was hers. It seemed only reasonable that he could skim, like interest, her presence from a sufficient quantity of strangers—that he could refine her, like radium, out of enough pitchblende. She had never been reserved with him; this terrible tact of absence was unlike her.

The moon gratuitously added its stolen glow to the harsh illumination around the iceless skating rink. As if sensing his search, faces turned as he passed. Each successive instant shocked him by being empty of her; he knew so fully how this meeting would go. Her eyes would light on him, and her mouth would involuntarily break into the grin that greeted all her occasions, however grave and dangerous; her stare would pull her body forward, and the gathering nearness of his presence would dissolve away the hardness, the controlled coldness, the—what? What was the element that had been there from the beginning and that, in the end, despite every strenuous motion of his heart, he had intensified, like some wild vague prophecy given a tyrannical authority in its fulfillment? What was the thing he had never named, perhaps because his vanity refused to believe that it could both attach to him and exist before him?

He wondered if he were tired enough now. There was an ache in his legs that augured well. He walked back to the hotel. The air of celebration had left the lobby. No celebrity was in sight. A few well-dressed young women, of the style that bloom and wither by the thousands in the city's public places, were standing waiting for an escort or an elevator;

as he pressed, no doubt redundantly, the button, a face cut into the side of his vision at such an angle that his head snapped around and he almost said aloud, "Don't be frightened. Of course I love you."

Avec la Bébé-sitter

EVERYBODY, from their friends in Boston to the stewards on the boat, wondered why Mr. and Mrs. Kenneth Harris should suddenly uproot their family of three young children and take them to the South of France in the middle of November. They had no special affection or aptitude for the country. Janet Harris knew French as well as anyone who had taken six years of it in various respectable schools without ever speaking to a Frenchman, but Kenneth himself knew hardly any—indeed, he was not, despite a certain surface knowingness, an educated person at all. The magazine illustrations, poised somewhere between the ardently detailed earth of Norman Rockwell and the breezy blue clouds of Jon Whitcomb, with which Kenneth earned his living were the outcome of a rather monomaniacal and cloistered youth devoted to art. At his drawing board, in the little room spattered and daubed from floor to ceiling, he was a kind of master, inventive and conscientious and mysteriously alert to the oscillations of chic that galvanized the New York market; outside this room he was impulsive and innocent and unduly dependent upon improvisation. It was typical of him to disembark in Cannes with three exhausted, confused children (one still in diapers) and a harried, hurt-looking wife, without a villa, a car, or a single friendly face to greet them, at a time of year when the Mediterranean sunshine merely underlined the actual chill in the air. After a week spent in a deserted hotel whose solicitous Old World personnel, apparently all members of a single whispering family, were secretly charging him ninety dollars a day, he blundered into an Antibes villa that, if it was not even in floor space equal to their Marlborough Street brownstone, at least had enough beds and a postcard view of Fort Carré and the (on fair days) turquoise harbor

beyond. It was three more weeks, while Janet wrestled alone
with the housekeeping and slowly deciphered the problems
of shopping, before they acquired a badly needed baby-sitter. It was not only that Kenneth was incompetent; he was,
like many people whose living comes to them with some
agency of luck, a miser. The expense of this trip fairly para-
lyzed him, and, in truth, the even greater expense of the divorce to which it was the alternative was, among the decisive factors, not the least decisive.

The baby-sitter—their English-French dictionary gave no
equivalent, and *bébé-sitter*, as a joke, was funnier than
une qui s'assied avec les bébés—was named, easily enough,
Marie, and was a short healthy widow of about forty who
each noon when she arrived would call *"Bonjour, Monsieur!"* to Kenneth with a gay, hopeful ring that seemed to
promise ripe new worlds of communication between them.
She spoke patiently and distinctly, and in a few days had
received from Janet an adequate image of their expectations
and had communicated in turn such intricate pieces of information as that her husband had died suddenly of a heart
attack (*"Cœur—bom!"*—her arm quickly striking from the
horizontal into the vertical) and that the owners and summer residents of their villa were a pair of homosexuals
(hands fluttering at her shoulders—*"Pas de femmes. Jamais
de femmes!"*) who hired boys from Nice and Cannes for
"dix mille pour une nuit." "Nouveaux francs?" Kenneth
asked, and she laughed delightedly, saying, *"Oui, oui,*
though this couldn't be right; no boy was worth two thousand dollars a night. Marie was tantalizing, for he felt
within her, as in a locked chest, inaccessible wealth, and he
didn't feel that Janet, whose conversations with her had an
awkward grammatical formality, was gaining access either.
As a result, the children remained hostile and frightened.
They were accustomed, in Boston, to two types of baby-sit-
ters: teen-age girls upon whom his elder daughter, aged
seven, inflicted a succession of giggling crushes, and elderly
limping women, of whom the grandest was Mrs. Shea. She
had a bosom like a bolster and a wispy saintly voice in
which apparently, as soon as the Harrises were gone, she
would tell the children wonderful stories of disease, calam-
ity, and anatomical malfunction. Marie was neither young
nor old, and, hermetically sealed inside her language, she
must have seemed to the children as grotesque as a fish
mouthing behind glass. They clustered defiantly around their

parents, routing Janet out of her nap, pursuing Kenneth into the field where he had gone to sketch, leaving Marie alone in the kitchen, whose floor she repeatedly mopped in an embarrassed effort to make herself useful. And whenever their parents left together, the children, led by the oldest, wailed shamelessly while poor Marie tried to rally them with energetic *"ooh's"* and *"ah's."* It was a humiliating situation for everyone, and Kenneth was vexed by the belief that his wife, in an hour of undivided attention, could easily have built between the baby-sitter and the children a few word bridges that would have adequately carried all this stalled emotional traffic. But she, with the stubborn shyness that was alternately her most frustrating and most appealing trait, refused, or was unable, to do this. She was exhausted. One afternoon, after they had done a little shopping for the Christmas that in this country and climate seemed so wan a holiday, Kenneth had dropped her off at the Musée d'Antibes and drove back in their rented Renault to the villa alone.

Smoke filled the living room. The children and Marie were gathered in silence around a fire she had built in the fireplace. Her eyes looked inquisitively past him when he entered. *"Madame,"* he explained, *"est,* uh, *visitée?—la Musée."*

Comprehension dawned in her quick face. *"Ah, le Musée d'Antibes! Très joli."*

"Oui. Uh"—he thought he should explain this, so she would not expect him to leave in the car again—*"Madame est marchée."* In case this was the wrong word, he made walking motions with his fingers, and unable to locate any equivalent for "back," added, *"ici."*

Marie nodded eagerly. *"À pied."*

"I guess. Yes. *Oui."*

Then came several rapid sentences that he did not understand at all. She repeated slowly, *"Monsieur,"* pointing at him, *"travaille,"* scribbling with her hands across an imaginary sketchbook.

"Oh. *Oui. Bon Merci. Et les enfants?"*

From her flurry of words and gestures he gathered an assurance that she would take care of them. But when he did go outdoors with the pad and paintbox, all three, led by Vera, the two-year-old, irresistibly followed, deaf to Marie's shrill pleas. Flustered, embarrassed, she came onto the patio.

"C'est rien," he told her, and wanted to tell her, "Don't worry." He tried to put this into his facial expression, and she laughed, shrugged, and went back into the house. Fort Carré was taking the sun crisply on one chalk-yellow side in the cubistic way that happens only in French light, the Mediterranean wore a curious double horizon of hazed blue, and Nice in the distance was like a long heap of pale flakes shed by the starkly brilliant Alps beyond. But Vera accidentally kicked the glass of water into the open paint tray, and as he bent to pick it up the freshly wet sketch fell face down into the grass. He gathered up everything and returned to the house, the children following. Marie was in the kitchen mopping the floor. "I think we should have a French lesson," he announced firmly. To Marie he added, with an apologetic note of interrogation, *"Leçon français?"*

"Une leçon de français," she said, and they all went into the smoky living room. *"Fumée—foof!"* she exclaimed, waving her hands in front of her face and opening the side doors. Then she sat down on the bamboo sofa with orange cushions—the two homosexuals had a taste for highly colored, flimsy furniture—and crossed her hands expectantly in her lap.

"Now," Kenneth said. *"Maintenant. Comment dites-vous—?"* He held up a pencil.

"Le crayon," Marie said.

"Le crayon," Kenneth repeated proudly. How simple, really, it all was. "Nancy, say, *'Le crayon.'* "

The girl giggled and shuttled her eyes between the two adults, to make sure they were serious. "Luh crrayong," she said.

"Bon," Kenneth said. "Charlie. *'Le crayon.'* "

The boy was four, and his intelligence had a way of unpredictably sinking beneath waves of infantile willfulness. But, after a moment's hesitation, he brought out *"Le crayon"* with an expert twang.

"And Vera? *'Le crayon'?"*

The baby was just learning English, and he did not press her when she looked startled and said nothing. The lesson continued, through *le feu, le bois, la cheminée,* and *le canapé orange.* Having exhausted the objects immediately before them, Kenneth drew, and Marie identified, such basic components of the universe as *l'homme, la femme, le garçon, la jeune fille, le chien, le chat, la maison,* and *les oiseaux.* The two older children took to bringing things from other parts of the room—*un livre, une bouteille d'encre, un cendrier,* and an old *soulier* of Charlie's whose mate had mysteriously vanished out in the yard among the giant cactuses. Nancy fetched from her room three paper dolls of great men she had punched from a copy of *Réalités* left in the house. *"Ah,"* Marie said. *"Jules César, Napoléon, et Charles Baudelaire."*

Vera toddled into the kitchen and came back with a stale cupcake, which she held out hopefully, her little face radiant.

"Gâteau," Marie said.

"Coogie," Vera said.

"Gâteau."

"Coogie."

"Non, non. Gâteau."

"Coogie!"

"Gâteau!"

The baby burst into tears. Kenneth picked her up and said, "You're right, Vera. That's a cookie." To the other children he said, "O. K., kids. That's all for now. Tomorrow we'll have another lesson. Go outside and play." He set the baby down. With a frightened backward look at the baby-sitter, Vera followed her brother and sister outdoors. By way of patching things up, Kenneth felt he should stay with Marie and make conversation. Both remained sitting. He wondered how much longer it would be before Janet returned and rescued them. The unaccustomed sensation of yearning for his wife made him feel itchy and suffocated.

"Le français," Marie said, spacing her words clearly, *"est difficile pour vous."*

"Je suis très stupide," he said.

"Mais non, non, Monsieur est très doué, très"—her hand scribbled over an imaginary sketch pad—*"adroit."*

Kenneth winced modestly, unable to frame any disclaimer.

She directed at him an interrogative sentence which, though she repeated it slowly, with various indications of her hands, he could not understand. "Nyew Yurrk?" she said at last. "Weshington?"

"Oh. Where do I come from? Here. *Les Etats-Unis.*" He took up the pad again, turned a new leaf, and drew the Eastern seaboard. *"Floride,"* he said as he outlined the peninsula, and growing reckless, indicated *"Le Golfe de Mexique."* He suspected from her blank face that this was wrong. He put in a few dark dots: "Washington, New York, *et ici, une heure nord à* New York *par avion,* Bos*ton! Grande ville.*"

"*Ah,*" Marie said.

"We live," Kenneth went on, "uh, *nous vivons dans une maison comme ça.*" And he found himself drawing, in avidly remembered detail, the front of their house on Marlborough Street, the flight of brown steps with the extra-tall top step, the carpet-sized front lawn with its wrought-iron fence and its single prisoner of forsythia like a weeping princess, the coarse old struggling vine that winter never quite killed, the tall windows with their many Colonial panes; he even put the children's faces in the second-story windows. This was the window of Vera's room, these were the ones that Nancy and Charlie watched the traffic jams out of, this was the living-room window that at this time of year should show a brightly burdened Christmas tree, and up here, on the third story, were the little shuttered windows of the guest bedroom that was inhabited by a ghost with a slender neck and naked moonlit shoulders. Emotion froze his hand.

Marie, looking up from the vivid drawing with very dark eyes, asked a long question in which he seemed to hear the words "*France*" and "*pourquoi.*"

"Why did we come to France?" he asked her in English. She nodded. He said what he next said in part, no doubt, because it was the truth, but mainly, probably, because he happened to know the words. He put his hand over his heart and told the baby-sitter, "*J'aime une autre femme.*"

Marie's shapely plucked eyebrows lifted, and he wondered if he had made sense. The sentence seemed foolproof; but he did not repeat it. Locked in linguistic darkness, he had thrown open the most intimate window of his life. He felt the relief, the loss of constriction, of a man glimpsing light at the end of a tunnel.

Marie spoke very carefully. "*Et Madame? Vous ne l'aimez pas?*"

There was a phrase, Kenneth knew, something like "*Comme ci, comme ça,*" which might roughly outline the immense ambiguous mass of his guilty, impatient, fond, and forlorn feelings toward Janet. But he didn't dare it, and instead, determined to be precise, measured off about an inch and a half with his fingers and said, "*Un petit peu pas.*"

"*Ahhhh.*" And now Marie, as if the languages had been reversed, was speechless. Various American phrases, traditional to his situation—"a chance to get over it," "for the sake of the kids"—revolved in Kenneth's head without encountering any equivalent French. "*Pour les enfants,*" he said at last, gesturing toward the outdoors and abruptly following the direction of his gesture, for Vera had begun to cry in the distance. About once a day she speared herself on one of the cactuses.

Janet was walking up the driveway. As he saw her go in to the baby-sitter he felt only a slight alarm. It didn't seem possible that he could have been indiscreet in a language he didn't know. When he came indoors, Marie and his wife were talking at cheerful length about what he imagined to be the charm of Le Musée d'Antibes, and it occurred to him that the reserve that had existed between the two women had been as much the baby-sitter's as Janet's. Now, from this afternoon on, Marie became voluble and jolly, open and *intime,* with her mistress; the two held long kitchen conversations in which womanly intuition replaced whatever was lost in nuances of diction. The children, feeling the new rapprochement, ceased yowling when their parents went away together, and under Marie's care developed a somewhat independent French, in which, if pencils were called crayons crayons must be called pencils. Vera learned the word "*gâteau*" and even the sentence "*Je veux un gâteau.*" As to Kenneth, he was confident, without knowing what the women said to each other, that his strange confession was never mentioned. The *bébé-sitter* kept between herself and him a clear little distance, whether as a sign of disapproval or of respect, he could not decide; at any rate when she was in the house he was encouraged to paint by himself in the fields, and this isolation, wherein his wife's growing fluency spared him much further trouble of communication, suited his preoccupied heart. In short, they became a *ménage.*

Twin Beds in Rome

THE MAPLES had talked and thought about separation so long it seemed it would never come. For their conversations, increasingly ambivalent and ruthless as accusation, retraction, blow, and caress alternated and cancelled, had the final effect of knitting them ever tighter together in a painful, helpless, degrading intimacy. And their love-making, like a perversely healthy child whose growth defies every deficiency of nutrition, continued; when their tongues at last fell silent, their bodies collapsed together as two mute armies might gratefully mingle, released from the absurd hostilities decreed by two mad kings. Bleeding, mangled, reverently laid in its tomb a dozen times, their marriage could not die. Burning to leave one another, they left, out of marital habit, together. They took a trip to Rome.

They arrived at night. The plane was late, the airport grand. They had left hastily, without plans; and yet, as if forewarned of their arrival, nimble Italians, speaking perfect English, parted them deftly from their baggage, reserved a hotel room for them by telephone from the airport, and ushered them into a bus. The bus, surprisingly, plunged into a dark rural landscape. A few windows hung lanternlike in the distance; a river abruptly bared its silver breast beneath them; the silhouettes of olive trees and Italian pines flicked past like shadowy illustrations in an old Latin primer. "I could ride this bus forever," Joan said aloud, and Richard was pained, remembering from the days when they had been content together, how she had once confessed to feeling a sexual stir when the young man at the gas station, wiping the windshield with a vigorous, circular motion, had made the body of the car, containing her, rock slightly. Of all the things she had ever told him, this remained in his mind the most revealing, the deepest glimpse she had ever permitted into the secret woman he could never reach and had at last wearied of trying to reach.

Yet it pleased him to have her happy. This was his weakness. He wished her to be happy, and the certainty that, away from her, he could not know if she were happy or not formed the final, unexpected door barring his way when all others had been opened. So he dried the very tears he had whipped from her eyes, withdrew each protestation of hopelessness at the very point when she seemed willing to give up hope, and their agony continued. "Nothing lasts forever," he said now.

"You can't let me relax a minute, can you?"

"I'm sorry. Do relax."

She stared through the window awhile, then turned and told him, "It doesn't feel as if we're going to Rome at all."

"Where are we going?" He honestly wanted to know, honestly hoped she could tell him.

"Back to the way things were?"

"No. I don't want to go back to that. I feel we've come very far and have only a little way more to go."

She looked out at the quiet landscape a long while before he realized she was crying. He found the impulse to comfort her, inwardly shouted it down as cowardly and cruel, but his hand, as if robbed of restraint by a force as powerful as lust, crept onto her arm. She rested her head on his shoulder. The shawled woman across the aisle took them for honeymooners and politely glanced away.

The bus slipped from the country. Factories and residential rows narrowed the highway. A sudden monument, a massive white pyramid stricken with light and inscribed with Latin, loomed beside them. Soon they were pressing their faces together to the window to follow the Colosseum itself as, shaped like a shattered wedding cake, it slowly pivoted and silently floated from the harbor of their vision. At the terminal, another lively chain of hands and voices rejoined them to their baggage, settled them in a taxi, and carried them to the hotel. As Richard dropped six hundred-lira pieces into the driver's hand, they seemed the smoothest, roundest, most tactfully weighted coins he had ever given away. The hotel desk was one flight up. The clerk was young and playful. He pronounced their name several times, and wondered why they had not gone to Naples. The halls of the hotel, which had been described to them at the airport as second-class, were nevertheless of rose marble.

The marble floor carried into their room. This, and the amplitude of the bathroom, and the imperial purple of the curtains blinded Richard to a serious imperfection until the clerk, his heels clicking in satisfaction with the perhaps miscalculated tip he had received, was far down the hall.

"Twin beds," he said. They had always had a double bed.

Joan asked, "Do you want to call him back?"

"How important is it to you?"

"I don't think it matters. Can you sleep alone?"

"I guess. But—" It was delicate. He felt they had been insulted. Until they finally parted, it seemed impertinent for anything, even a slice of space, to come between them. If this trip were to be kill or cure (and this was, for the tenth time, their slogan), then the attempt at a cure should have a certain technical purity, even though—or, rather, all the more because—in his heart he had already doomed it to fail. And also there was the material question of whether he could sleep without a warm proximate body to give his sleep shape.

"But what?" Joan prompted.

"But it seems sort of sad."

"Richard, don't be sad. You've been sad enough. You're supposed to relax. This isn't a honeymoon or anything, it's just a little rest we're trying to give each other. You can come visit me in my bed if you can't sleep."

"You're such a nice woman," he said. "I can't understand why I'm so miserable with you."

He had said this, or something like it, so often before that she, sickened by simultaneous doses of honey and gall, ignored the entire remark, and unpacked with a deliberate serenity. On her suggestion, they walked into the city, though it was ten o'clock. Their hotel was on a shopping street that at this hour was lined with lowered steel shutters. At the far end, an illuminated fountain played. His feet, which had never given him trouble, began to hurt. In the soft, damp air of the Roman winter, his shoes seemed to have developed hot inward convexities that gnashed his flesh at every stride. He could not imagine why this should be, unless he was sensitive to marble. For the sake of his feet, they found an American bar, entered, and ordered coffee. Off in a corner, a drunken male American voice droned through the grooves of an unintelligible but distinctly female circuit of complaints; the voice, indeed, seemed not so much a man's as a woman's deepened by being played at a slower speed on the phonograph. Hoping to cure the growing dizzy emptiness within him, Richard ordered a "hamburger" that proved to be more tomato sauce than meat. Outside, on the street, he bought a paper cone of hot chestnuts from a sidewalk vender. This man, whose thumbs and fingertips were charred black, agitated his hand until three hundred lire were placed in it. In a way, Richard welcomed being cheated; it gave him a place in the Roman economy. The Maples returned to the hotel, and side by side on their twin beds fell easily into a solid sleep.

That is, Richard assumed, in the cavernous accounting rooms of his subconscious, that Joan also slept well. But when they awoke in the morning, she told him, "You were terribly funny last night. I couldn't go to sleep, and every time I reached over to give you a little pat, to make you think you were in a double bed, you'd say 'Go away' and shake me off."

He laughed in delight. "Did I really? In my sleep?"

"It must have been. Once you shouted 'Leave me alone!' so loud I thought you must be awake, but when I tried to talk to you, you were snoring."

"Isn't that funny? I hope I didn't hurt your feelings."

"No. It was refreshing not to have you contradict yourself."

He brushed his teeth and ate a few of the cold chestnuts left over from the night before. The Maples breakfasted on hard rolls and bitter coffee in the hotel and walked again into Rome. His shoes resumed their inexplicable torture. With its strange, almost mocking attentiveness to their unseen needs, the city thrust a shoe store under their eyes; they entered, and Richard bought, from a gracefully reptilian young salesman, a pair of black alligator loafers. They were too tight, being smartly shaped, but they were dead—they did not pinch with the vital, outraged vehemence of the others. Then the Maples, she carrying the Hachette guidebook and he his American shoes in a box, walked down the Via Nazionale to the Victor Emmanuel Monument, a titanic flight of stairs leading nowhere. "What was so great about him?" Richard asked. "Did he unify Italy? Or was that Cavour?"

"Is he the funny little king in *A Farewell to Arms?*"

"I don't know. But nobody could be *that* great."

"You can see now why the Italians don't have an inferiority complex. Everything is so huge."

They stood looking at the Palazzo Venezia until they imagined Mussolini frowning from a window, climbed the many steps to the Piazza del Campidoglio, and came to the equestrian statue of Marcus Aurelius on the pedestal by Michelangelo. Joan remarked how like a Marino Marini it was, and it was; her intuition had leaped eighteen centuries. She was so intelligent. Perhaps this was what made leaving her, as a gesture, so exquisite in conception and so difficult in execution. They circled the square. The portals and doors all around them seemed closed forever, like the doors in a drawing. They entered, because it was open, the side door of the church of Santa Maria in Aracoeli. They discovered themselves to be walking on sleeping people, life-size tomb-reliefs worn nearly featureless by footsteps. The fingers of the hands folded on the stone breasts had been smoothed to finger-shaped shadows. One face, sheltered from wear behind a pillar, seemed a vivid soul trying to rise from the all but erased body. Only the Maples examined these reliefs, cut into a floor that once must have been a glittering lake of mosaic; the other tourists clustered around the chapel preserving, in slippers and vestments, behind glass, the child-sized greenish remains of a pope. They left by the same side door and descended steps and paid admission to the ruins of the Roman Forum. The Renaissance had used it as a quarry; broken columns lay everywhere, loaded with perspective, like a de Chirico. Joan was charmed by the way birds and weeds lived in the crevices of this exploded civic dream. A delicate rain began to fall. At the end of one path, they peeked in glass doors, and a small uniformed man with a broom limped forward and admitted them, as if to a speakeasy, to the abandoned church of Santa Maria Antiqua. The pale vaulted air felt innocent of worship; the seventh-century frescoes seemed recently, nervously executed. As they left, Richard read the question in the broom man's smile and pressed a tactful coin into his hand. The gentle rain continued. Joan took Richard's arm, as if for shelter. His stomach began to hurt—a light, chafing ache at first, scarcely enough to distract him from the pain in his feet. They walked along the Via Sacra, through roofless pagan temples carpeted in grass. The ache in his stomach intensified. Uniformed guards, old men standing this way and that in the rain like hungry gulls, beckoned them toward further ruins, further churches, but the pain now had blinded Richard to everything but the extremity of his distance from anything that might give him support. He refused admittance to the Basilica of Constantine, and asked instead for the *uscita*. He did not feel capable of retracing his steps. The guard, seeing a source of tips escaping, dourly pointed toward a small gate in a nearby wire fence. The Maples lifted the latch, stepped through, and stood on the paved rise overlooking the Colosseum. Richard walked a little distance and leaned on a low wall.

"Is it so bad?" Joan asked.

"Oddly bad," he said. "I'm sorry. It's funny."

"Do you want to throw up?"

"No. It's not like that." His sentences came jerkily. "It's just a . . . sort of gripe."

"High or low?"

"In the middle."

"What could have caused it? The chestnuts?"

"No. It's just, I think, being here, so far from anywhere, with you, and not knowing . . . why."

"Shall we go back to the hotel?"

"Yes. I think if I could lie down."

"Shall we get a taxi?"

"They'll cheat me."

"That doesn't matter."

"I don't know . . . our address."

"We know sort of. It's near that big fountain. I'll look up the Italian for 'fountain.' "

"Rome is . . . full of . . . fountains."

"Richard. You aren't doing this just for my benefit?"

He had to laugh, she was so intelligent. "Not consciously. It has something to do . . . with having to hand out tips . . . all the time It's really an ache. It's incredible."

"Can you walk?"

"Sure. Hold my arm."

"Shall I carry your shoebox?"

"No. Don't worry, sweetie. It's just a nervous ache. I used to get them . . . when I was little. But I was . . . braver then."

They descended steps to a thoroughfare thick with speeding traffic. The taxis they hailed carried heads in the rear and did not stop. They crossed the Via dei Fori Imperiali and tried to work their way back, against the sideways tug of interweaving streets, to the territory containing the fountain, the American Bar, the shoe store, and the hotel. They passed through a market of bright food. Garlands of sausages hung from striped canopies. Heaps of lettuce lay in the street. He walked stiffly, as if the pain he carried were precious and fragile; holding one arm across his abdomen seemed to ease it slightly. The rain and Joan, having been in some way the pressures that had caused it, now became the pressures that enabled him to bear it. Joan kept him walking. The rain masked him, made his figure less distinct to passersby, and therefore less distinct to himself, and so dimmed his pain. The blocks seemed cruelly uphill and downhill. They climbed a long slope of narrow pavement beside the Banca d'Italia. The rain lifted. The pain, having expanded into every corner of the chamber beneath his ribs, had armed itself with a knife and now began to slash the walls in hope of escape. They reached the Via Nazionale, blocks below the hotel. The shops were unshuttered, the distant fountain was dry. He felt as if he were leaning backward, and his mind seemed a kind of twig, a twig that had deviated from the trunk and chosen to be this branch instead of that one, and chosen again and again, becoming finer with each choice, until finally there was nothing left for it but to vanish into air. In the hotel room he lay down on his twin bed, settled his overcoat over him, curled up, and fell asleep.

When he awoke an hour later, everything was different. The pain was gone. Joan was lying in her bed reading the Hachette guide. He saw her, as he rolled over, as if freshly, in the kind of cool library light in which he had first seen her; only he knew, calmly, that since then she had come to share his room. "It's gone," he told her.

"You're kidding. I was all set to call up a doctor and have you taken to a hospital."

"No, it wasn't anything like that. I knew it wasn't. It was nervous."

"You were dead white."

"It was too many different things focusing on the same spot. I think the Forum must have depressed me. The past here is so heavy. Also my shoes hurting bothered me."

"Darley, it's Rome. You're supposed to be happy."

"I am now. Come on. You must be starving. Let's get some lunch."

"Really? You feel up to it?"

"Quite. It's gone." And, except for a comfortable reminiscent soreness that the first swallow of Milanese salami healed, it was. The Maples embarked again upon Rome, and, in this city of steps, of sliding, unfolding perspectives, of many-windowed surfaces of sepia and rose ochre, of buildings so vast one seemed to be outdoors in them, the couple parted. Not physically—they rarely left each other's sight. But they had at last been parted. Both knew it. They became with each other, as in the days of courtship, courteous, gay, and quiet. Their marriage let go like an overgrown vine whose half-hidden stem had been slashed in the dawn by an ancient gardener. They walked arm in arm through seemingly solid blocks of buildings that parted, under examination, into widely separated slices of style and time. At one point she turned to him and said, "Darley, I know what was wrong with us. I'm classic, and you're baroque." They shopped, and saw, and slept, and ate. Sitting across from her in the last of the restaurants that like oases of linen and wine had sustained these level elegiac days, Richard saw that Joan was happy. Her face, released from the tension of hope, had grown smooth; her gestures had taken on the flirting irony of the young; she had become ecstatically attentive to everything about her; and her voice, as she bent forward to whisper a remark about a woman and a handsome man at another table, was rapid, as if the very air of her breathing had turned thin and free. She was happy, and, jealous of her happiness, he again grew reluctant to leave her.

Four Sides
of One Story

Tristan

MY LOVE:

Forgive me, I seem to be on a boat. The shock of leaving you numbed me rather nicely to the usual humiliations of boarding—why is it that in a pier shed everyone, no matter how well-born and self-confident, looks like a Central European immigrant, and is treated accordingly?—and even though we are now two days out to sea, and I can repose, technically, in your utter inaccessibility, I still am unable to focus on my fellow-passengers, though for a split second of, as it were, absent-minded sanity, I did prophetically perceive, through a chink in my obsession, that the waiter, having sized me up as one of the helpless solitaries of the world, would give me arrogant service and expect in exchange, at journey's end, an apologetically huge tip. No matter. The next instant, I unfolded the napkin, and your sigh, shaped exactly like a dove, the blue tint of its throat visibly clouding for a moment the flame of the candle on the table, escaped; and I was plunged back into the moist murmurs, the eclipsed whispers, the vows instantly hissingly retracted, the exchanged sweats, of our love.

The boat shakes. The vibration is incessant and ubiquitous; it has sniffed me out even here, in the writing room, a dark nook staffed by a dour young Turinese steward and stocked, to qualify as a library, with tattered copies of Paris *Match* and, behind glass, seventeen gorgeously bound and impeccably unread volumes of D'Annunzio, in of course Italian. So that the tremor in my handwriting is a purely motor affair, and the occasional splotches you may consider droplets of venturesome spray. As a matter of fact, there is a goodly roll, though we have headed into sunny latitudes.

When they try to fill the swimming pool, the water thrashes and pitches so hysterically that I peek over the edge expecting to see a captured mermaid. In the bar, the bottles tinkle like some immensely dainty Swiss gadget, and the Daiquiris come to you aquiver, little circlets of agitation spinning back and forth between the center and the rim. The first day, having forgotten, in my landlocked days with you, the feel of an ocean voyage, I was standing in the cabin-class lobby, waiting to try to buy my way toward a higher deck and if possible a porthole, when, without any visible change in the disposition of furniture, lighting fixtures, potted palms, or polylingual bulletin board, the floor like a great flat magnet suddenly rendered my blood heavy—extraordinarily heavy. There were people around me, and their facial expressions did not alter by one millimeter. It was quite comic, for as the ship rolled back the other way my blood absolutely *swung* upward in my veins—do you remember how your arm feels in the first instant after a bruise?—and it seemed imminent that I, and, if I, all these dead-panned others too, would lift like helium balloons and be bumpingly pasted to the ceiling, from which the ship's staff would have to rescue us, irritably, with broom handles. The vision passed. The ship rolled again. My blood went heavy again. It seemed that you were near.

Iseult. I must write your name. Iseult. I am bleeding to death. Certainly I feel bloodless, or, more precisely, diluted, diluted by half, since everything around me—the white ropes, the ingenious little magnetic catches that keep the doors from swinging, the charmingly tessellated triangular shower stall in my cabin, the luxurious and pampered textures on every side—I seem to see, or touch, or smile over, with you, which means, since you are not here, that I only half-see, only half-exist. I keep thinking what a pity all this luxury is wasted on me, Tristan the Austere, the Perpetually Grieving, the Orphaned, the Homeless. The very pen I am writing this with is an old-fashioned dip, or nib, pen, whose flexibility irresistibly invites flourishes that sit up wet and bluely gleaming for minutes before finally deigning to dry. The holder is some sort of polished Asiatic wood. Teak? Ebony? You would know. It was enchanting for me, how you knew the names of surfaces, how you had the innocence to stroke a pelt and not flinch from the panicked little quick-eyed death beneath; for me, who have always been on the verge of becoming a vegetarian, which Mark, I know, would say was a form of death-wish (I can't describe to you how stupid that man seems to me; unfairly enough, even what tiny truth there is in him seems backed by this immense capital—these armies, this downright kingdom—of stupidity, so that even when he says something intelligent it affects me like Gospel quoted in support of social injustice. This parenthesis has gotten out of all control. If it seems ugly to you, blame it on jealousy. I am not sure, however, if I hate your husband because he—if only legally—possesses you, or if, more subtly, because he senses my own fear of just such legal possession, which gives him, for all his grossness, his grotesque patronization and prattling, a curious moral hold over me which I cannot, writhe as I will, break. End parenthesis).

An especially, almost maliciously, prolonged roll of the boat just slid the ink bottle, unspilled, the width of my cubbyhole and gave me the choice of fixing my eyes on the horizon or beginning to be seasick.

Where was I?

For me it was wonderful to become a partner in your response to textures. Your shallowness, as my wife calls it—and like everything she says, there is something in it which, at the least, gives dismissal pause—broke a new dimension into my hitherto inadequately superficial world. Now, adrift in this luxurious island universe, where music plays like a constant headache, I see everything half through your eyes, conduct circular conversations with you in my head, and rest my hand on the wiped mahogany of the bar as if the tremor beneath the surface is you, a mermaid rising. What are our conversations about? I make, my mind tediously sifting the rubble of the emotional landslide, small discoveries about us that I hasten to convey to you, who are never quite as impressed by them as I thought you would be. Yesterday, for example, at about 3:30 p.m., when the sallow sun suddenly ceased to justify sitting in a deck chair, I discovered, in the act of folding the blanket, that I had never, in my heart, taken your sufferings as seriously as my own. That you were unhappy, I knew. I could diagram the mechanics of the bind you were in, could trace the vivacious contours and taste the bright flat colors of your plight—indeed I could picture your torment so clearly that I felt I was feeling it with you. But no, there was a final kind of credence I denied your pain, that cheated it of dimension and weight, and for this I belatedly apologized. In my head you accepted the apology with a laugh, and then wished to go on and discuss the practical aspects of our elopement. Two hours later, pinning a quivering Daiquiri to the bar with my fingers, I rather jerkily formulated this comforting thought: however else I failed you, I never pretended to feel other than love for you, I never in any way offered to restrict, or control, the love you felt for me. Whatever sacrifices you offered to make, whatever agony you volunteered to undergo for me, I permitted. In the limitless extent of my willingness to accept your love, I was the perfect lover. Another man, seeing you flail and lacerate yourself so mercilessly, might have out of timid squeamishness (calling it pity) pretended to turn his back, and saved your skin at the price of your dignity. But I, whether merely hypnotized or actually suicidal, steadfastly kept my face turned toward the blaze between us, though my eyes watered, my nose peeled, and my eyebrows disappeared in twin whiffs of smoke. It took all the peculiar strength of my egotism not to flinch and flaw the purity of your generous fury. No? For several hours I discussed this with you, or rather vented exhaustive rewordings upon your silent phantom, whose comprehension effortlessly widened, like ringing water, to include every elaboration.

Then, at last weary, brushing my teeth while the shower curtains moved back and forth beside me like two sluggish, rustling pendulums, I received, as if it were a revelation absolutely gravitational in importance, the syllogism that (major premise) however much we have suffered because of each other, it is quite out of the question for me to blame you for my pain, though strictly speaking you were the cause; and, since (minor premise) you and I as lovers were mirrors and always felt the same, therefore (conclusion) this must also be the case with you. Ergo, my mind is at peace. That is, it is a paradoxical ethical situation to be repeatedly wounded by someone *because he or she is beloved*. Those small incidentals within my adoration, those crumbs of Mark's influence that I could never digest, those cinders from past flames unswept from your corners, the flecks of mediocrity, glimpses of callousness, even moments of physical repulsiveness—it was never these that hurt me. It was your *perfection* that destroyed me, demented my logical workings, unmanned my healthy honor, bled me white. But I bear no grudge. And thus know that you bear none; and this knowledge, in the midst of my restless misery, gives me ease. As if what I wish to possess forever is not your presence but your good opinion.

I was rather disturbed to learn, from Brangien, just before I left, that you are seeing a psychiatrist. I cannot believe there is anything abnormal or curable about our predicament. We are in love. The only way out of it is marriage, or some sufficiently pungent piece of overexposure equivalent to marriage. I am prepared to devote my life to avoiding this death. As you were brave in creating our love, so I must be brave in preserving it. My body aches for the fatal surfeit of you. It creaks under the denial like a strained ship. A hundred times a day I consider casting myself loose from this implacable liner and giving myself to the waves on the implausible chance that I might again drift to you as once I drifted, pustular, harping, and all but lifeless, into Whitehaven. But I who slew the Morholt slay this Hydra of yearning again and again. My ship plows on, bleeding a straight wake of aquamarine, heading Heaven knows where, but away, away from the realms of compromise and muddle wherein our love, like a composted flower, would be returned to the stupid earth. Yes, had we met as innocents, we could have indulged our love and let it run its natural course of passion, consummation, satiety, contentment, boredom, betrayal. But, being guilty, we can seize instead a purity that will pass without interruption through death itself. Do you remember how, by the river, staking your life on a technicality, you seized the white-hot iron, took nine steps, and showed all Cornwall your cold clean palms? It is from you that I take my example. Do you remember in the Isak Dinesen book I gave you the story in which God is described as He who says No? By saying No to our love we become, you and I, gods. I feel this is blasphemy and yet I write it.

The distance between us increases. Bells ring. The Turinese steward is locking up the bookcase. I miss you. I am true to you. Let us live, forever apart, as a shame to the world where everything is lost save what we ourselves deny.

T.

Iseult of the White Hands

DEAR KAHERDIN:

Sorry not to have written before. This way of life we've all been living doesn't conduce to much spare time. I haven't read a book or magazine in weeks. Now the brats are asleep (I think), the dishes are chugging away in the washer, and here I sit with my fifth glass of Noilly Prat for the day. You were the only one he ever confided in, so I tell you. He's left me again. On the other hand, he's also left her. What do you make of it? She is taking it, from appearances, fairly well. She was at a castle do Saturday night and seemed much the same, only thinner. Mark kept a heavy eye on her all evening. At least she has *him;* all I seem to have is a house, a brother, a bank account, and a ghost. The night before he sailed, he explained to me, with great tenderness, etc., that he married me as a kind of pun. That the thing that drew him to me was my having her name. It was all—seven years, three children—a kind of Freudian slip, and he was really charmingly boyish as he begged to be excused. He even made me laugh about it.

If I had any dignity I'd be dead or insane. I don't know if I love him or what love is or even if I want to find out. I tried to tell him that if he loved her and couldn't help it he should leave me and go to her, and not torment us both indefinitely. I've never much liked her, which oddly enough offends him, but I really do sympathize with what he must have put her through. But he seems to think there's something so beautiful about hanging between us that he won't let go with either hand. He's rapidly going from the sublime to the ridiculous. Mark, who in his bullying way wants to be sensible and fair, had his lawyer on the move, and I was almost looking forward to six weeks on a ranch somewhere. But no. After spending the whole summer climbing fences, faking appointments, etc., anything that looks like real action terrifies him and he gets on a boat. And through it all, making life a hell for everybody concerned, including the children, he wears this saintly pained look and insists he's trying to do the right thing. What was really annihilating wasn't his abuse of me, but his kindness.

I've mentally fiddled with your invitation to come back to Carhaix, but there seems no point. The children are in school, I have friends here, life goes on. I've explained his absence as a business trip, which everybody accepts and nobody believes. The local men are both a comfort and a menace—I guess it's their being a menace that makes them a comfort. My virtue is reasonably safe. It all comes back to me, this business of managing suitors, keeping each at the proper distance, not too close and not too far, trying to remember exactly what has been said to each. Mark's eye, for that matter, was heavy on *me* for a few moments at the party. It's essentially disgusting. But nothing else is keeping my ego afloat.

I could never get out of him what she had that I didn't. If you know, as a man, don't tell me, please. But I can't see that it was our looks, or brains, or even in bed. The better I was in bed, the worse it made him. He took it as a reproach, and used to tell me I was beautiful as if it were some cruel joke I had played on him. The harder I tried, the more I became a kind of distasteful parody. But of what? She is really too shallow and silly even for me to hate. Maybe that's it. I feel I'm dropped, *bump*, as one drops any solid object, but she, she is sought in her abandonment. His heart rebounds from shapeless surfaces—the sky, the forest roof, the sea—and gives him back a terror which is her form. The worst of it is, I sympathize. I'm even jealous of his misery. At least it's a kind of pointed misery. His version is that they drank from the same cup. It has nothing to do with our merits but she loves him and I don't. I just think I do. But if I don't love him, I've never loved anything. Do you think this is so? You've known me since I was born, and I'm frightened of your answer. I'm frightened. At night I take one of the children into bed with me and hold him/her for hours. My eyelids won't close, it scalds when I shut them. I never knew what jealousy was. It's an endlessly hungry thing. It really just consumes and churns and I can't focus on anything. I remember how I used to read a newspaper and care and it seems like another person. In the day I can manage, and on the nights when I go out, but in the evenings when I'm alone, there is an hour, right now, when everything is so hollow there is no limit to how low I and my Noilly Prat can go. I didn't mean to put this into a letter. I wanted to be cheerful, and brave, and funny about it. You have your own life. My love to your family. The physical health here is oddly good. Please, *please* don't say anything to Mother and Daddy. They wouldn't understand and their worrying would just confuse me. I'm really all right, except right now. My fundamental impression I think is of the incredible wastefulness of being alive.

Love,
Iseult

Iseult the Fair
(Unsent)

TRISTAN:
 Tristan
 Tristan Tristan
 flowers—books—
 Your letter confused and dismayed me—I showed it to Mark—he is thinking of suing you again—pathetic—his attempts to make himself matter. Between words I listen for his knock on the door—if he knew what I was writing he would kick me out—and he's right.
 my king brought low
 forgive?????
 an easy word for you
 I wanted to grow fat in your arms and sleep—you ravished me with absences—enlarged our love at our expense —tore me every time we parted—I have lost 12 pounds and live on pills—I dismay myself.
 Your wife looks well.
 Trist
 Mr.
 Mrs.
 the flowers are dead and the books hidden and heavy winter here—his knock on the door—
 Kill You. I must kill you in my heart—shut you out—don't knock even if I listen. Return to your wife—try—honestly try with her. She hates me but I love her for the sorrow I have brought her—no—I hate her because she would not admit what everybody could see—she had given you up. I had earned you.

the pen in my hand
the whiteness of the paper
a draft on my ankles the stone floor—the sounds of the castle—your step?

Beware of Mark—he is strong—pathetic—my king brought low—he protects me. I am teaching myself to love him.

I would have loved the boat.

Love is too painful.

If the narcissi you planted come up next spring I will dig them out.

What a funny thing to write—I can't tell if this is a letter to you or not—I dismay myself—Mark thinks I should be committed—he is more mature than you and I

do you remember the flowers and the books you gave me?

For my sake end it—your knock never comes—the winter here is heavy—children sledding—the mountains are sharp through the window—I have a scratchy throat—Mark says psychosomatic—I hear you laugh.

Tr

Please return—nothing matters

King Mark

MY DEAR DENOALEN:

Your advice has been followed with exemplary success. Confronted with the actuality of marriage, the young man bolted even sooner than we had anticipated. The Queen is accordingly disillusioned and satisfactorily tractable.

Therefore I think that the several legal proceedings against them both may be for the time being halted at this time. By no means, however, do I wish to waive all possibility of further legal action. I am in possession of an interminable, impudent, and incriminating letter written by the confessed lover subsequent to his defection. If you desire, I will forward it to you for photostatic reproduction as a safeguard.

In the case that, through some event or events unforeseen, the matter were after all to come to court, I agree wholeheartedly that their plea of having accidentally partaken of a magic potion will not stand up. Yet your strong suggestion that execution should be the punishment for both does not seem to me to allow for what possible extenuating circumstances there are. It is indisputable, for example, that throughout the affair Tristan continued to manifest, in battle, perfect loyalty to me, and prowess quite in keeping with the standards he had set in the days prior to his supposed enchantment. Also, their twin protestations of affection for me, despite their brazen and neurotic pursuance of physical union, did not ring entirely falsely. It was, after all, Tristan's feat (i.e., slaying the dragon of Whitehaven) that brought her to Tintagel; and, while of course this is in no sense a legally defensible claim, I can appreciate that, in immature and excitable minds, it might serve as a shadow of a claim. It will do us both good, as fair-minded Englishmen, to remember that we are dealing here with a woman of Irish blood and a man whose upbringing was entirely Continental. In addition, there is the Queen herself as a political property to consider. Alive, she adorns my court. The populace is fond of her. Further, the long peace between Ireland and Cornwall which our marriage has assured should not be rashly jeopardized.

Weighing all these factors, then, and not excluding the private dispositions of my heart, I have settled on a course of action more moderate than that which you now advise. Tristan's banishment we may assume to be permanent. Return will result in recapture, trial, and death. The Queen will remain by my side. Her long sojourn in the Wood of Morois has without doubt heightened her appreciation of the material advantages she enjoys in my palace. My power and compassion have been manifested to her, and she is essentially too rational to resist their imperative appeal. As long as her present distracted state obtains, I am compelling her to submit to psychoanalysis. If her distraction persists without improvement, I will have her committed. I am confident this will not be necessary. On the remote chance that the "magic potion" is more than a fable, I have instructed my alchemists to develop an antidote. I am fully in control of matters at last.

All the best,
(*Dictated but not signed*)
MARK: REX

The Morning

HE LIVED ALONE, in a room only she had ever made habitable. Each morning he awoke to the same walls and was always slightly surprised at the sameness of the cracks and nail holes and replastered patches, as if this pattern were a set of thoughts to which a night's solid meditation had not added the merest nick of a new idea. He awoke to the same ticking clock on the mock mantel, the same shivering half-height refrigerator, the same nagging sour smell that, behind the baseboard and around the sink, had come to live with him. He would dress, and boil an egg, and crack it on a piece of toast, and heat last evening's coffee, and rinse the plate and cup, and take up a book and sit and wait. The chair would grow suffocating. The sense of the words would skid and circle senselessly under the print. He would rise, and walk around the room, pausing at every place where they had lain together, staring, as if terrified, at the bed that still bore two pillows. She was a nurse, and worked afternoons and evenings, and used to come to him in the mornings. He was a student, but of what, he had forgotten. As if to remember, he would look out the window.

Of the city outside, he could see several brick walls, and a small flat roof of pebbles her bare feet had consecrated in the summer past, and a rusty construct of metal, almost organically complex, that was a chimney or a vent or the mouth of a chute and that may or may not have been in use. In the broad gaps between brick walls he could see a skyline that had a gold dome in it, and delicate smokestacks which the morning sun whittled like church balusters, and parallel plumes of smoke quickly indistinguishable from natural clouds, and a kind of subdued twinkle that testified to the world of activity the city, like the surface of a sea, concealed. At moments his dull attention caught, like a slack sail idly filling, a breath, from this multifaceted horizon, of the hope that set in motion and sustained so many industrial efforts, so much commercial traffic, such ingenious cross-fertilization of profit, such energetic devotion to the metamorphosis of minerals, the transport of goods, the interplay of calculations, the efficiency of machines. The skyline then spread itself before his eyes like one of those laborious Asiatic pictorial conceits that compose an elephant out of naked maidens, or depict a tree of gods whose faintest twig doubles as a smile and whose smallest bud is also a fingernail. A sense of human constructiveness would seize him and try to lift him again into the airy realm of fresh ideas, eddying notes, scholarly ambition, and purpose. The forgotten object of his studies would present itself to him like a long-scorned wife who has taken a lover and again grown beautiful. He would panic with jealousy. But the pang, like a flitting glimmer from something reflective in the horizon, would pass; his eyes would shorten their focus and he would leadenly observe how the rectangular windowpanes were being rounded by the infringement of successive layers of paint carelessly applied to the mullions. A kind of demon of disconnection would abruptly occupy his body, and he felt his heart as an angrily pulsing intruder, his hands as hanging presences weighted with blood sent from a great distance. He realized within himself the intricate scaffolding of mechanical connection and chemical coöperation that upheld his life, and felt its complexity as a terrible tenuousness. He would go to the sofa and lift one of the cushions. There, in a dingy sanctum of upholstery, lay a few long hairs, almost invisible on the black cloth. He would study them as if to re-create the head from which they had strayed, and the face that had masked this head with a soul, and the body that had given this soul extension. By picking up one hair and holding it to the light he could detect a faint ghost of the golden color that often had spilled, a vivid gift, across his bare shoulders. He would replace the hair, and restore the cushion, as spinsters press a flower into a Bible.

The room was, if anything, bigger than it needed to be. When he sat and tried to read, the unused space seemed to watch him with eyes of knobs and nail holes and knotted configurations in the carpet. The space cried for another person to occupy it. Two had just fitted in this room; their voices had flattened the walls, pressed the furniture back into its servile state of being wood and cloth, submerged the shuddering of the refrigerator and the ticking of the clock. When he opened the door to her (she always looked a little startled and wary, but why?—who could she expect it to be but him?), his heart would fill his chest so tightly he had to hold her against him, like a compress, for minutes while the threat of its bursting subsided.

From the first, their embrace had seemed predetermined. His hands always went to the same places on her back, one at the nape of her neck, the other at the base of her spine. Always he rested his face on the same side of her head, so that for all he knew now she might have worn a different perfume behind the other ear. The perfume he inhaled was powdery, a hushed fragrance less of flowers than of spice, strangely far away in the galactic mansion of her hair, and tinged, perhaps only in his imagination, with an ethereal sweetness left from the hospital corridors. She was clean, beautifully clean, and he had associated this also with her work in the hospital, work which, it seemed to him, in its daily experience of bodies enabled her to accept, so totally, so frontally, his own.

Usually she would be wearing a street dress when she came, blue or green or brown, and when she left, at noon, she would be wearing a nurse's white uniform. Between these two costumes there was a third, when she was clothed in herself; so that the morning, which in the days before she first came had been so single in its purpose and so monotonous in its execution, became instead a triptych, whose two side panels, when her footsteps had receded down the stairs and the outer door of the building had closed behind her, folded in memory over the central panel, whose beauty could not be remembered but had to be, each time, revealed. In time, the very hours took their tint from the pattern of her visits, the hour after nine being blue or green or brown, the hour after that tan and blond and pink and pale, and the final hour, the most hurried, often a few quick minutes, sheer white, like the flash that engulfs the screen when the film has run out and clatters loosely in the projector. Perhaps because these minutes were closest to him, across the long gap that separated him from her last visit, he saw them most distinctly—the square folds of her starched blouse, the sudden bun she composed with the hairpins they could find, the flat white shoes and plain cotton stockings that, in innocently shaping her calves and starkly emphasizing her female solidity, revived the erotic fire her natural body, in its pliant naturalness, had damped.

He loved her in her uniform, and on the occasions when he had ventured into the hospital for a glimpse of her he felt in the corridors of identically uniformed women as if he were raiding a harem, or a cloister of the lascivious nuns who throng French pornography. There was, in her rising from beside him to don white, something blasphemous and yet holy, a reassumption of virginity emblematic of the (to a man) mysterious inviolability of a woman. It was like nothing else in his experience. A book, once read, can only be reread; a machine, used, imperceptibly wears out. But she, she came to him always beautifully clean, and unexperienced, and slightly startled, like a morning, and left, at noon, immaculate.

Dressed otherwise, she was in comparison disappointing. Often she left her heels and silk stockings and street dress behind in his room, as a pledge to return. Their presence was not as satisfying as it should have been; there was an unease surrounding them, a vague request to be explained and justified. And when, in the night, she returned, and passed from the uniform into them, it was a descent. Dressed as other women, she became one of them, a woman who sat in restaurants, and ate the food, and drank sometimes too much, and nervously crossed and recrossed the legs self-consciously lengthened by high spike heels, and talked a little awry. He impossibly expected of her conversation the same total frontal fit her body gave him. The woman separated from him by a restaurant table was a needless addition to the woman who was perfect; she wished to add needlessly to the love that needed nothing but endless continuance. It was this woman who hinted of marriage, and it was this woman who, in the dim restaurant light, misread his word "unable" to mean "unwilling," and took offense.

These evenings with her, which ended sharply and chastely at midnight, when the curfew fell in the supervised apartment where she lived, were less than entirely real and blended with the cramped dreams that dissolved under the triumphal advent of morning. Morning brought him onto another plane altogether, as when one looks up from a crowded printed page to a pale door upon which a knock has just sounded. Awake, he would gratefully drink the radiance that renewed every detail of his room, and rise, and shed his dreams, and make enough fresh coffee for them both, and begin to listen. The outer door downstairs would softly open; there was an alto squeak only she produced from the hinges. Her first steps on the flight of stairs would be inaudible. Her stealth seemed the breathy lightness of expectation. Her feet would press the top treads firmly, evenly, like piano pedals; an abrasive slither would cross the linoleum hall; and her knock, three blurred beats with an inquisitive pause between the second and third, would sound.

He listened now. The downstairs door opened. In the little skip of silence following the squeak of the hinges, his heart found space to erect a towering certainty, which toppled as the first brutal, masculine steps assaulted the stairs. Still, perhaps she was wearing boots, perhaps in the empty months her manner of mounting had changed, perhaps she was angry, or rigid with determination, or heavy with fright. He noiselessly went to his door, his hand lifted to turn the knob. The footsteps slithered on the linoleum and passed by. He felt relieved. He had lived so long with the vain expectation of her coming that it, the expectation, had become a kind of companion he was afraid of losing. He stared at the wall, dumbstruck by its stupidity. He turned sick of himself, physically sick, so that his arms ached and his stomach fell and the nagging sour smell behind the baseboard seemed the odor of his own rotting body. He returned to the chair and tried to study.

The outer door opened again, delicately this time. His heartbeats timed the silence. He saw her, dressed in blue or green or brown, ascending the diagonal corridor toward him, her lips a little parted in the effort of stealth, her hand, slightly reddened and bony from antiseptic scrubbings, lightly touching the wall for balance. The silence lengthened, lengthened beyond recall, and he forced himself to admit that there was no one on the stairs, that the wind or a child had idly opened the door from outside and let it fall shut. He rose from the chair in a rage; why didn't she *know*, know how he wanted her now, not in white, but in blue or green or brown? This was the woman he wanted, the woman much like other women, the woman who talked awry in restaurants, who wanted to marry him, the woman who came to him and not the woman, in white, who left. He had accepted her leaving because of the pledge to return she left behind, the clothes that at last he recognized as her essential clothes, the everyday clothes that contained her other costumes, as skin is beneath all cloth and white is the spin of all colors. He had dreaded in marriage the loss of their mornings, their transposition into the shadowy scale of night. But she had not explained to him that the mornings were a gift, an extravagance on her part which could be curtailed. She had been neglectful not to explain this, and she was wrong now not to know that he, lagging behind her a distance of months, had followed in the steps of her love and now had reached the exact point she had reached when they had last parted, and that she had only to stop, and turn, and take one step up the stairs to meet him. Yes, she was stupid, hasty, and cruel not to know his heart, not to hear the great cry issuing from this room; and this blunt vision of her limitations failed to dull his love but instead dreadfully sharpened it, for love begins in earnest when we love what is limited.

"My nurse," he whispered aloud, at last putting forth, in conscious competition with the tiny notched sighing of the clock, the shuddering of the refrigerator, and the empty scratches of sound in the stairway and hallway, a sound of his own. This speaking, this invoking her aloud, was the only action he was capable of taking. To seek her out would be to risk the final refusal which the silence withheld. To leave the room would be to abandon the possibility of receiving her visit. Even to install a telephone would be to heap another silence upon the furious silence of the stairs and of the doors. He did nothing. He did nothing all morning but maintain, with the full strength of his scattered mind and disconnected body, an unanswered vigil.

At noon, the day's reprieve arrived. She could not come now. She would be at work. His strenuous wrestle with her absence could be suspended, and did not need to be resumed until tomorrow morning. Perhaps tomorrow he would be weaker and, therefore, less caring, stronger. He felt that these mornings were aging him; he looked in the mirror for traces of the strange painless pain that punished him, like a punctual masseur, for three hours each day. The mirror, too, was unanswering. If anything were to show, it would be in the eyes, and one's eyes, self-confronted, lose all expression. His frame slowly relaxed, and ceased to feel his heart as an intruder. Like someone dressing in clothes wildly scattered about on the night before, he could reassemble his presence and leave the room. He could enter the twinkling city, eat, keep appointments, confront people, confident that his outward appearance had not altered, that just as his body had refused to burst in its fullness before, so now it failed to collapse in its emptiness. Resuming, in part, a student's detached interestedness, he heard himself talk, give answers, even laugh. He saw, with a blurring double sense of being a fraud and defrauded both, that a passable life could be patched together out of afternoons and evenings. But his mornings had been destroyed, and the morning of his life taken from him.

At a Bar in
Charlotte Amalie

BLOWFISH with light bulbs inside their dried skins glowed above the central fortress of brown bottles. The bar was rectangular; customers sat on all four sides. A slim school-teacherish-looking girl, without much of a tan and with one front tooth slightly overlapping the other, came in, perched on a corner stool, and asked for a Daiquiri-on-the-rocks. She wore a yellow halter, turquoise shorts, and white tennis sneakers. The bartender, who was not visibly malformed, nevertheless moved like a hunchback, with a sideways bias and the scuttling nimbleness peculiar to cripples. He wore a powder-blue polo shirt, and now and then paused to take a rather avid sip from a tall glass containing perhaps orange juice; his face was glazed with sweat and he kept peering toward the outdoors, as if expecting to be relieved of duty. The green sea was turning gray under round pink clouds. A boat dully knocked against the cement wharf, and suddenly the noise had the subtle importance noises in these latitudes assume at night. A member of the steel band, a tall, long-jawed Negro, materialized in the rear of the place, on a shallow shadowy platform where the cut and dented steel drums were stacked. After unstacking and mounting them, this Negro, who wore a tattered red shirt and held a dead cigarette in the center of his lips, picked up a mallet and experimentally tapped into the air a succession, a cluster, an overlapping cascade of transparent notes that for a moment rendered everyone at the bar silent.

Then a homosexual with a big head turned to the school-teacherish girl, who had been served, and said, "See my pretty hat?" His head seemed big because his body was small, a boy's body, knobby and slack and ill-fitted to his veined man's hands and to his face. His eyes were very close togeth-

87

er, making him seem to concentrate, without rest, upon a disagreeable internal problem, and his lips—which in their curt cut somehow expressed New York City—were too quick, snapping in and out of a grin as if he were trying to occupy both sides of his situation, being both the shameless clown and the aloof, if amused, onlooker. He had been talking about his hat, half to himself, since four o'clock this afternoon, and when he held it out to the girl an eddy of sighs and twisted eyebrows passed through the faces in the yellow darkness around the bar. The hat was a cheap broadweave straw with a bird's nest of artificial grass set into the crown, a few glass eggs fixed in the nest, and several toy birds suspended on stiff wires above it, as if in flight. "I designed it myself," he explained. "For the carnival this weekend. Isn't it marvellously uninhibited?" He glance around, checking on the size of his audience.

He was well known here. If he had scraped, from the surface of indifference, a few shreds of attention, it was because of the girl. Her coming in here, at this twilight hour, alone, bearing herself with such prim determined carelessness, was odd enough to attract notice, even at a tropical bar, where everything is permitted to happen.

"It's lovely," she said, of the hat, and sipped her drink.

"Do you want to put it on? Please try it."

"I don't think so, thank you."

"I designed it myself," he said, looking around and deciding to make a speech. "That's the way I am. I just give my ideas away." He flung up his hands in a gesture of casting away, and a breeze moved in from the street as if to accept his gift. "If I were like other people, I'd make money with my ideas. Money, monnney. It's excrement, but I love it." A brief anonymous laugh rose and was borne off by the breeze. The homosexual returned to the girl with a tender voice. "You don't have to put it on," he told her. "It's not really finished. When I get back to my room, where I've been meaning to go all day, if that *fiend*"—he pointed at the bartender, who with his slightly frantic deftness was pouring a rum Collins—"would let me go. He says I owe him monnney! When I get back to my room, I'm going to add a few touches, here, and here. A few spangly things, just a few. It's for the carnival this weekend. Are you down here for the carnival?"

"No," the girl said. "I'm flying back tomorrow."

"You should stay for the carnival. It's wonderfully unin-hibited."

"I'd like to, but I must go back." Unexpectedly blushing, she lowered her voice and murmured something containing the word "excursion."

The homosexual slapped the bar. "Forgive me, forgive me, dear Lord above"—he rolled his eyes upward, to the glowing blowfish and the great roaches and tarantulas of straw which decorated the walls—"but I *must* see how my hat looks on you, you're so pretty."

He reached out and set the hat with its bright hovering birds on her head. She took another sip of her drink, doc-ilely wearing the hat. A child laughed.

The homosexual's eyes widened. This unaccustomed ex-pression was painful to look at; it was as if two incisions were being held open by clamps. The child who had laughed was looking straight at him: a bright round face fine-featured as the moon, rising just barely to the level of the bar and topped by hair so fair it was white. The little boy sat between his parents, a man and a woman oddly alike, both wearing white and having stout sun-browned arms, crinkled weather-whipped faces, and irises whose ex-tremely pale blue seemed brittle, baked by days of concen-tration on a glaring sea. Even their hair matched. The man's had not been cut in months, except across his fore-head, and was salt-bleached in great tufts and spirals, like an unraveling rope of half-dark strands. The woman's, finer and longer, was upswept into a tumultuous blond crown that had apparently sheltered the roots enough to leave them, for an inch or two, dark. They looked, this husband and wife, like two sexless chieftains of a thickset, seagoing Nordic tribe. As if for contrast, they were accompanied by a gaunt German youth with swarthy skin, protruding eyes, close-cropped hair, and protruding ears. He stood behind and between them, a shadow uniting three luminaries.

The homosexual crouched down on the bar and fiddled his fingers playfully. "Hi," he said. "Are you laughing at me?"

The child laughed again, a little less spontaneously.

His parents stopped conversing.

"What a gorgeous child," the homosexual called to them. "He's so—so *fresh*. So uninhibited. It's wonderful." He blinked; truly he did seem dazzled.

The father smiled uneasily toward the wife; the pale

creases around his eyes sank into his tan, and his face, still young, settled into what it would become—the toughened, complacent, blind face of an old Scandinavian salt, the face that, pipe in teeth, is mimicked on carved bottle stoppers.

"No, really," the homosexual insisted. "He's darling. You should take him to Hollywood. He'd be a male Shirley Temple."

The child, his tiny pointed chin lifting in mute delight, looked upward from one to the other of his parents. His mother, in a curious protective motion, slipped from her stool and placed a sandalled foot on the rung of her child's stool, her tight white skirt riding up and exposing half her thigh. It was stout yet devoid of fat, like the trunk of a smooth-skinned tree.

The father said, "You think?"

"I *think*?" the homosexual echoed eagerly, crouching further forward and touching his chin to his glass. "I *know*. He'd be a male Shirley Temple. My judgment is infallible. If I was willing to leave all you lovely people and go dig in the dung, I'd be a stinking rich talent scout living in Beverly Hills."

The father's face collapsed deeper into its elderly future. The mother seized her thigh with one hand and ruffled the child's hair with the other. The dark German boy began to talk to them, as if to draw them back into their radiant privacy. But the homosexual had been stirred. "You know," he called to the father, "just looking at you I can feel the brine in my face. You both look as if you've been on the ocean all of your life."

"Not quite," the father said, so tersely it wasn't heard.

"I beg your pardon?"

"I haven't been on the sea all my life."

"You know, I *love* sailing. I love the life of the open sea. It's so"—his lips balked, rejecting "uninhibited"—"it's so free, so pure, all that wind, and the waves, and all that jazz. You can just be yourself. No, really. I think it's wonderful. I love Nature. I used to live in Queens."

"Where do you live now?" the girl beside him asked, setting his hat on the bar between them.

The homosexual didn't turn his head, answering as if the sailing couple had asked the question. "I live here," he called. "In dear old St. Thomas. God's own beloved country. Do you need a cook on your boat?"

The child tugged at his mother's waist and pulled her

down to whisper something into her ear. She listened and
shook her head; a brilliant loop of hair came undone. The
father drank from the glass in front of him and in a fresh-
ened voice called across, "Not at the moment."

"I wish you did, I wish to heaven you did, I'm a beautiful
cook, really. I make the *best* omelets. You should see me; I
just put in the old eggs and a little bit of milk and a glass of
brandy and some of those little green things, what are they
called?—chives, I put in the chives and stir until my arm
breaks off and it comes out just *won*derful, so light and
fluffy. If I cared about money, I'd be a chef in the Wal-
dorf."

The child's whispered request seemed to recall the group
to itself. The father turned and spoke to the German boy,
who, in the instant before bowing his head to listen, threw,
the whites of his eyes glimmering, a dark glance at the
homosexual. Misunderstanding, the homosexual left his
stool and hat and drink and went around the corner of the
bar toward them. But, not acknowledging his approach,
they lifted the child and walked away toward the rear of the
place, where there was a jukebox. Here they paused, their
brilliant hair and faces bathed in boxed light.

The homosexual returned to his stool and watched them.
His head was thrown back like that of a sailor who has
suffered a pang at the sight of land. "Oh dear," he said
aloud, "I can't decide which I want to have, the man or the
woman."

The schoolteacherish girl sipped her Daiquiri, dipping
her head quickly, as if into a bitter birdbath. One stool
away from her down the bar, there sat a beefy unshaven
customer, perhaps thirty years old, drinking a beer and
wearing a T-shirt with a ballpoint pen clipped to the center
of the sweat-soaked neckline. Squinting intently into space
and accenting some inner journey with soft grunts, he
seemed a truck driver transported, direct and intact, from
the counter of an Iowa roadside diner. Next to him, across
a space of empty stools, behind an untouched planter's
punch, sat a very different man of about the same age, a
man who, from his brick-red complexion, his high knobbed
forehead, the gallant immobility of his posture, and the
striking corruption of his teeth, could only have been English.

Into the space of three stools between them there now entered a dramatic person—tall, gaunt, and sandy. He dis-

played a decrepit Barrymore profile and a gold ring in one ear. He escorted a squat powdered woman who looked as though she had put on her lipstick by eating it. She carried a dachshund under one arm. The bartender, unsmiling, awkwardly pivoting, asked, "How's the Baron?"

"Rotten," the Baron said; and as he eased onto his stool his stiff wide shoulders seemed a huge coat hanger left, out of some savage stubbornness, in his coat. The woman set the dachshund on the bar. When their drinks came, the dog lapped hers, which was a lime rickey. When he tried to lap the Baron's—a straight Scotch—the man gripped the dachshund's thirstily wagging rump, snarled "Damn alcoholic," and sent him skidding down the bar. The dog righted himself and sniffed the truck driver's beer; a placid human paw softly closed over the mouth of the glass, blocking the animal's tongue. His nails clicking and slipping on the polished bar, the dog returned to his mistress and curled up at her elbow like a pocketbook. The girl at the corner shyly peeked at the man beside her, but he had resumed staring into space. The pen fixed at his throat had the quality of a threat, or of a scar.

The blond family returned from having put a quarter into the jukebox, which played "Loco Motion," by Little Eva, "Limbo Rock," by Chubby Checker, and "Unchain My Heart," by Ray Charles. The music, like an infusion of letters from home, froze the people at the bar into silence. Beyond the overhang that sheltered the tables, night dominated. The bar lit up a section of pavement where pedestrians flitted like skittish actors from one wing of darkness into the other. The swish of traffic on the airport road had a liquid depth. The riding lights of boats by the wharf bobbed up and down, and a little hard half-moon rummaged for its reflection in the slippery sea. The Baron muttered to the painted old woman an angry and long story in which the obscene expressions were peculiarly emphasized, so that only they hung distinct in the air, the connecting threads inaudible. The Englishman at last moved his forearm and lowered the level of his planter's punch by a fraction of an inch, making a stoic face afterward, as if the sweetness had hurt his teeth. The homosexual, nettled by the attention received by the drinking dachshund, took off his hat and addressed the ceiling of the bar as if it were God. "Hey there, Great White Father," he said. "You haven't been very good to me this month. I know You love me—how could You help it, I'm so beautiful—but I haven't seen any money coming out of the sky. I mean, really, You put us down here in the manure and we need it to live, like. You know? I mean, don't get too uninhibited up there. Huh?" He listened, and the Baron, undistracted, set another blue word burning in the hushed air. "That's O.K.," the homosexual continued. "You've kept the sun shining, and I appreciate it. You just keep the sun shining, Man, and don't send me back to Queens." At prayer's end, he put the hat on his head and looked around, his curt lips pursed defiantly.

Five Negroes, uncostumed, in motley clothes and as various in size as their instruments, had assembled on the shadowy platform, kidding and giggling back and forth and teasing the air with rapid, stop-and-start gusts of tuning up. Abruptly they began to play. The ping-pong, the highest pan, announced itself with four harsh solo notes, and on the fifth stroke the slightly deeper guitar pans, the yet deeper cello pans, and the bass boom, which was two entire forty-four-gallon oil drums, all at once fell into the tune, and everything—cut and peened drums, rubber-tipped sticks, tattered shirtsleeves, bobbing heads, munching jaws, a frightened-looking little black child whipping a triangle as fast as he could—was in motion, in flight. The band became a great loose-jointed bird feathered in clashing, rippling bells. It played "My Basket," and then, with hardly a break, "Marengo Jenny," "How You Come to Get Wet?," and "Madame Dracula." Nobody danced. It was early, and the real tourists, the college students and Bethlehem Steel executives and Westchester surgeons, had not yet come down from dinner in the hills to sit at the tables. There was a small dance floor on one side of the bar. A young Negro appeared here. He wore canary-yellow trousers and a candy-striped jersey with a boat neck and three-quarter sleeves. He had a broad, hopeful face and an athletic, triangular back. From his vaguely agitated air of responsibility, he seemed to be associated with the establishment. He asked the schoolteacherish girl, who looked alone and lost, to dance; but she, with a pained smile and a nervous dip of her head into her second Daiquiri, refused. The young Negro stood stymied on the dance floor, clothed only, it seemed, in music and embarrassment, his pale palms dangling foolishly. When the band, in a final plangent burst cut short as if with a knife, stopped, he went to the leader, the long-jawed red shirt on the ping-pong, and said, "Ey mon, le peo-*ple* wan I bet 'Ye*llow* Bird.' " He phrased it, as the West Indian accent phrases all statements, like a question.

The leader took offense. He answered deliberately, unintelligibly, as if, the music still ringing in the pan of his skull, he were softly tapping out a melody with his tongue. The man on the bass boom, a coarse thick-lipped mulatto in a blue work shirt unbuttoned down to his navel, joined in the argument and gave the young man a light push that caused him to step backward off the platform. The bass-boom man growled, and the strip of hairy cocoa skin his skirt exposed puffed up like a rooster's throat. No one had danced; the band was defensive and irritable. The leader, biting the butt of his cigarette, rattled a venomous toneless tattoo on the rim of his ping-pong. Then the shadow manning the cello pans—he had a shaved head, and was the oldest of them—spoke an unheard word, and all the Negroes, including the boy with the triangular back, broke into disjointed laughter.

When the band resumed playing, they began with "Yellow Bird"—played flat, at a grudging tempo. The young Negro approached the blond mother of the little boy. She came with him into the center of the floor and lifted her fat-fair arms. They danced delicately, sleepily, the preening shuffle of the mambo, her backside switching in its tight white dress, his broad face shining as his lips silently mouthed the words: *Ye-ell-o-oh bi-ird, up in the tree so high, ye-ell-o-oh bi-ird, you sit alone like I.* Her thick waist seemed at home in the wide curve of his hand.

When the song finished, he bowed thank you and she returned to her family by the bar and, as if sighing, let down her hair. Apparently it had been held by one pin; she pulled this pin, the fluffy sun-bleached crown on the top of her head cascaded down her back in a blinding stream, and she looked, with her weather-pinched face, like a negative of a witch, or what relates to witches as angels relate to devils. The little boy, as if his heart were climbing the golden rope she had let down, whispered up to her, and she, after bowing her head to listen, glanced up at the homosexual, who was complaining to the bartender that his vodka-and-tonic had gone watery.

"You owe me," the bartender said, "a dollar-fifty, and if you let the drink sit there hour after hour, damn right it'll melt."

"I don't have a dollar-fifty," was the answer. "I have washed my hands, forever and ever, amen, of filthy lucre.

People want me to get a job but I won't; that's the way I am. It's a matter of principle with me. Why should I work all day for a pittance and starve when I can do nothing whatsoever and starve anyway?"

Now the whole blond family was staring at him fascinated. The glow of their faces caught the corner of his eye, and he turned toward them inquisitively; memory of the snub they had given him made his expression shy.

"I want one dollar and fifty cents from you," the bartender insisted, with unconvincing emphasis; his anxious sweat and obscurely warped posture seemed that of a warden trapped in his own prison, among inmates he feared. He gulped some orange from his glass and looked toward the outdoors for relief. Pale square clouds rested above the sea, filtering stars. Laughter like spray was wafted from a party on a yacht.

The homosexual called, "Really, he is the most cunning little boy I have ever seen in all my *life*. In Hollywood he could be a male Shirley Temple, honestly, and when he grows up a little he could be a male what's-her-name—oh, what *was* her name? Jane Withers. I have a beautiful memory. If I cared, I could go back to New York and get on a quiz show and make a million dollars."

The German boy spoke for the group. "He vunts—your hatt."

"Does he? Does he really? The little angel wants to wear my hat. I designed it myself for the carnival this weekend." He left his stool, scrambled around the corner, set the hat with its glade of decoration squarely on the child's spherical head, and, surprisingly, knelt on the floor. "Come on," he said, "come on, darling. Get on my shoulders. Let's go for a ride."

The father looked a question at his wife, shrugged, and lifted his son onto the stranger's shoulders. The birds on their wires bobbed unsteadily, and fear flickered not only in the child's face but in the grown face to which he clung. The homosexual, straightening up, seemed startled that the child was a real weight. Then, like a frail monster overburdened with two large heads, one on top of the other and the upper one sprouting a halo of birds, he began to jog around the rectangular bar, his shaved legs looking knobbed and bony in their shorts. The steel band broke into a pachanga. Some tourist families had come down from the hills to occupy the tables, and the athletic young Negro, whose flesh

seemed akin to rubber, successfully invited a studiously
tanned girl with orange hair, a beauty, to dance. She had
long green eyes and thin lips painted paler than her skin,
and an oval of nakedness displayed her fine shoulder-bones.
The Baron cursed and yanked his own lady onto the floor;
as they danced, the dachshund nipped worriedly at their
stumbling feet. The Baron kicked the dog away, and in
doing so turned his head, so that, to the dizzy little boy riding by, the gold ring in his ear flashed like the ring on a
merry-go-round. A stately bald man, obviously a North
American doctor, rose, and his wife, a midget whose Cop-
pertone face was wrinkled like a walnut, rose to dance with
him. The homosexual's shoulders hurt. He galloped one last
lap around the bar and lifted the child back onto the stool.
The airy loss of pressure around his neck led him to exhale
breathlessly into the bright round face framed by straw,
"You know, Mark Twain wrote a lovely book *just* about
you." He took the hat from the child's head and replaced it
on his own. The child, having misunderstood the bargain,
burst into tears, and soon his mother carried him from the
bar.

The dancing gathered strength. The floor became
crowded. From her high vantage at the corner of the bar,
the schoolteacherish girl studied with downcast eyes the
dancing feet. They seemed to be gently tamping smooth a
surface that was too hot to touch for more than an instant.
Some females, of both races, had removed their shoes; their
feet looked ugly and predatory, flickering, spread-toed, in
and out of shadows and eclipses of cloth. When the music
stopped, black hands came and laid, on the spot of floor
where her eyes were resting, two boards hairy with upright
rusty nails. A spotlight was focused on them. The band
launched into a fierce limbo. The young Negro with the
handsome rubbery back leaped, nearly naked, into the light.
His body was twitching in rhythm, he was waving two
flaming torches, and he was clad in knit swimming trunks
and orange streamers representing, she supposed, Caribbean
slave dress. His eyes shut, he thrust the torches alternately
into his mouth and spit out flame. Indifferent applause rippled through the tables.

The Baron, drunker than anyone had suspected, pushed
off from the bar and, as the young Negro lay down on a
board of nails and stroked the skin of his chest with the
sticks of fire, lay down beside him and kicked his trousered

legs high in parody. No one dared laugh, the Baron's face was so impassive and rapt. The young Negro, his back resting on the nails, held one torch at arm's length, so that the flame rested on the Baron's coat lapel and started a few sparks there; but the Baron writhed on obliviously, and the smoldering threads winked out. When the Negro stood, now clearly shaken, and with a great mock-primitive grimace leaped on one board of nails with his bare feet, the Baron leaped in his sandals on the other, and through sandy eyelashes blindly peered into the surrounding darkness of applause, his earring glinting, his shoulders still seeming to have a coat hanger in them. Two black waiters, nervous as deer, ventured into the spotlight and seized his upraised arms; as they led him out of the light, the tall figure of the white man, gasping as if he had surfaced after a shipwreck, yet expressed, in profile, an incorrigible dignity. There was murmuring at the tables as the tourists wondered if this had been part of the act.

The music pitched into an even fiercer tempo. The young Negro, handing away his torches, was given a cloth sack, which he dropped on the floor. It fell open to reveal a greenish heap of smashed bottles. He trod on the heap with both feet. He got down and rolled in it as a dog rolls ecstatically in the rotten corpse of a woodchuck. He rested his back on the pillow of shards and the heavy mulatto left the bass boom and stood on his chest. There was applause. The mulatto jumped off and walked away. The Negro got up on his knees, cupped a glittering quantity of broken glass in his palms, and scrubbed his face with it. When he stood to take the applause, the girl observed that his back, which gleamed, heaving, a foot from her eyes, indeed did bear a few small unbleeding cuts. The applause died, the music halted, and the bright lights went on before the slave, hugging his nailboards and bag of glass, had reached the haven of the door behind the platform. As he passed among them, the members of the steel band cackled.

Now there was an intermission. The bartender, his hands trembling and his eyes watering, it seemed, on the edge of tears, scuttled back and forth mixing a new wave of drinks. More tourists drifted in, and the families containing adolescents began to leave. The traffic on the airport road had diminished, and the bumping of the boats on the wharf, beneath the moon that had lost its reflection, regained importance. The people on the decks of these boats could see the windows burning in the dry hills above Charlotte Amalie, lights spread through the middle of the night sky like a constellation about to collide with our Earth but held back, perpetually poised in the just bearable distance, by that elusive refusal implicit in tropical time, which like the soft air seems to consist entirely of circles. Within the bar, the German boy wandered over and spoke to the homosexual, who looked up from under the brim of his hat with alert lips and no longer preoccupied eyes, all business. The very English-appearing man left his place behind the undiminishing planter's punch, sauntered around the bar, and commenced a conversation with the now deserted Nordic father; the Englishman's first words betrayed a drawling American accent. The Baron laid his handsome head on the bar and fell asleep. The dachshund licked his face, because it smelled of alcohol. The woman slapped the dog's nose. The beefy man abruptly pulled the pen from the neck of his T-shirt, removed the cardboard coaster from under his beer, and wrote something on it, something very brief—one word, or a number. It was as if he had at last received a message from the ghostly trucking concern that had misplaced him here. The ping-pong sounded; the music resumed. The young Negro, changed out of costume back into his yellow pants and candy-striped boat-necked shirt, returned. Flexing his back and planting his palms on his hips, he again asked the strange girl at the corner of the bar to dance. This time, with a smile that revealed her slightly overlapping front teeth, she accepted.

The Christian
Roommates

ORSON ZIEGLER came straight to Harvard from the small South Dakota town where his father was the doctor. Orson, at eighteen, was half an inch under six feet tall, with a weight of 164 and an I.Q. of 152. His eczematous cheeks and vaguely irritated squint—as if his face had been for too long transected by the sight of a level horizon—masked a definite self-confidence. As the doctor's son, he had always mattered in the town. In his high school he had been class president, valedictorian, and captain of the football and baseball teams. (The captain of the basketball team had been Lester Spotted Elk, a full-blooded Chippewa with dirty fingernails and brilliant teeth, a smoker, a drinker, a discipline problem, and the only boy Orson ever had met who was better than he at anything that mattered.) Orson was the first native of his town to go to Harvard, and would probably be the last, at least until his son was of age. His future was firm in his mind, the pre-med course here, medical school either at Harvard, Penn, or Yale, and then back to South Dakota, where he had his wife already selected and claimed and primed to wait. Two nights before he left for Harvard, he had taken her virginity. She had cried, and he had felt foolish, having, somehow, failed. It had been his virginity, too. Orson was sane, sane enough to know that he had lots to learn, and to be, within limits, willing. Harvard processes thousands of such boys and restores them to the world with little apparent damage. Presumably because he was from west of the Mississippi and a Protestant Christian (Methodist), the authorities had given him as a freshman roommate a self-converted Episcopalian from Oregon.

When Orson arrived at Harvard on the morning of Registration Day, bleary and stiff from the series of airplane rides that had begun fourteen hours before, his roommate was already installed. "H. Palamountain" was floridly inscribed in the upper of the two name slots on the door of Room 14. The bed by the window had been slept in, and the desk by the window was neatly loaded with books. Standing sleepless inside the door, inertly clinging to his two heavy suitcases, Orson was conscious of another presence in the room without being able to locate it; optically and mentally, he focused with a slight slowness.

The roommate was sitting on the floor, barefoot, before a small spinning wheel. He jumped up nimbly. Orson's first impression was of the wiry quickness that almost magically brought close to his face the thick-lipped, pop-eyed face of the other boy. He was a head shorter than Orson, and wore, above his bare feet, pegged sky-blue slacks, a lumberjack shirt whose throat was dashingly stuffed with a silk foulard, and a white cap such as Orson had seen before only in photographs of Pandit Nehru. Dropping a suitcase, Orson offered his hand. Instead of taking it, the roommate touched his palms together, bowed his head, and murmured something Orson didn't catch. Then he gracefully swept off the white cap, revealing a narrow crest of curly blond hair that stood up like a rooster's comb. "I am Henry Palamountain." His voice, clear and colorless in the way of West Coast voices, suggested a radio announcer. His handshake was metallically firm and seemed to have a pinch of malice in it. Like Orson, he wore glasses. The thick lenses emphasized the hyperthyroid bulge of his eyes and their fishy, searching expression.

"Orson Ziegler," Orson said.

"I know."

Orson felt a need to add something adequately solemn, standing as they were on the verge of a kind of marriage. "Well, Henry"—he lamely lowered the other suitcase to the floor—"I guess we'll be seeing a lot of each other."

"You may call me Hub," the roommate said. "Most people do. However, call me Henry if you insist. I don't wish to diminish your dreadful freedom. You may not wish to call me anything at all. Already I've made three hopeless enemies in the dormitory."

Every sentence in this smoothly enunciated speech bothered Orson, beginning with the first. He himself had never been given a nickname; it was the one honor his classmates had withheld from him. In his adolescence he had coined

nicknames for himself—Orrie, Ziggy—and tried to insinu-
ate them into popular usage, without success. And what was
meant by "dreadful freedom"? It sounded sarcastic. And
why might he not wish to call him anything at all? And how
had the roommate had the time to make enemies? Orson
asked irritably, "How long have you *been* here?"

"Eight days." Henry concluded every statement with a
strange little pucker of his lips, a kind of satisfied silent
click, as if to say, "And what do you think of *that*?"

Orson felt that he had been sized up as someone easy to
startle. But he slid helplessly into the straight-man role that,
like the second-best bed, had been reserved for him. "That
long?"

"Yes. I was totally alone until the day before yesterday.
You see, I hitch-hiked."

"From *Or*egon?"

"Yes. And I wished to allow time enough for any contin-
gency. In case I was robbed, I had sewed a fifty-dollar bill
inside my shirt. As it turned out, I made smooth connec-
tions all the way. I had painted a large cardboard sign saying 'Harvard.' You should try it sometime. One meets some
very interesting Harvard graduates."

"Didn't your parents worry?"

"Of course. My parents are divorced. My father was furious. He wanted me to fly. I told him to give the plane fare
to the Indian Relief Fund. He never gives a penny to charity. And, of course, I'm old. I'm twenty."

"You've been in the Army?"

Henry lifted his hands and staggered back as if from a
blow. He put the back of his hand to his brow, whimpered
"Never," shuddered, straightened up smartly, and saluted.
"In fact, the Portland draft board is after me right now."
With a preening tug of his two agile hands—which did
look, Orson realized, old: bony and veined and red-tipped,
like a woman's—he broadened his foulard. "They refuse to
recognize any conscientious objectors except Quakers and
Mennonites. My bishop agrees with them. They offered me
an out if I'd say I was willing to work in a hospital, but I
explained that this released a man for combat duty and if it
came to that I'd just as soon carry a gun. I'm an excellent
shot. I mind killing only on principle."

The Korean War had begun that summer, and Orson,
who had been nagged by a suspicion that his duty was to

enlist, bristled at such blithe pacifism. He squinted and asked, "What *have* you been doing for two years, then?"

"Working in a plywood mill. As a gluer. The actual gluing is done by machines, but they become swamped in their own glue now and then. It's a kind of excessive introspection—you've read *Hamlet*?"

"Just *Macbeth* and *The Merchant of Venice*."

"Yes. Anyway. They have to be cleaned with solvent. One wears long rubber gloves up to one's elbows. It's very soothing work. The inside of a gluer is an excellent place for revolving Greek quotations in your head. I memorized nearly the whole of the *Phaedo* that way." He gestured toward his desk, and Orson saw that many of the books were green Loeb editions of Plato and Aristotle, in Greek. Their spines were worn; they looked read and reread. For the first time, the thought of being at Harvard frightened him. Orson had been standing between his suitcases and now he moved to unpack. "Have you left me a bureau?"

"Of course. The better one." Henry jumped on the bed that had not been slept in and bounced up and down as if it were a trampoline. "And I've given you the bed with the better mattress," he said, still bouncing, "and the desk that doesn't have the glare from the window."

"Thanks," Orson said.

Henry was quick to notice his tone. "Would you rather have my bed? My desk?" He jumped from the bed and dashed to his desk and scooped a stack of books from it.

Orson had to touch him to stop him, and was startled by the tense muscularity of the arm he touched. "Don't be silly," he said. "They're exactly alike."

Henry replaced his books. "I don't want any bitterness," he said, "or immature squabbling. As the older man, it's my responsibility to yield. I'll give you the shirt off my back." And he began to peel off his lumberjack shirt, leaving the foulard dramatically knotted around his naked throat. He wore no undershirt.

Having won from Orson a facial expression that Orson himself could not see, Henry smiled and rebuttoned the shirt. "Do you mind my name being in the upper slot on the door? I'll remove it. I apologize. I did it without realizing how sensitive you would be."

Perhaps it was all a kind of humor. Orson tried to make a joke. He pointed and asked, "Do I get a spinning wheel, too?"

"Oh, *that*." Henry hopped backward on one bare foot and became rather shy. "That's an experiment. I ordered it from Calcutta. I spin for a half hour a day, after Yoga."

"You do Yoga, too?"

"Just some of the elementary positions. My ankles can't take more than five minutes of the Lotus yet."

"And you say you have a bishop."

The roommate glanced up with a glint of fresh interest. "Say. You listen, don't you? Yes. I consider myself an Anglican Christian Platonist strongly influenced by Gandhi." He touched his palms before his chest, bowed, straightened, and giggled. "My bishop hates me," he said. "The one in Oregon, who wants me to be a soldier. I've introduced myself to the bishop here and I don't think he likes me, either. For that matter, I've antagonized my adviser. I told him I had no intention of fulfilling the science requirement."

"For God's sake, why *not*?"

"You don't really want to know."

Orson felt this rebuff as a small test of strength. "Not really," he agreed.

"I consider science a demonic illusion of human *hubris*. Its phantasmal nature is proved by its constant revision. I asked him, "Why should I waste an entire fourth of my study time, time that could be spent with Plato, mastering a mass of hypotheses that will be obsolete by the time I graduate?"

"My Lord, Henry," Orson exclaimed, indignantly defending the millions of lives saved by medical science, "you can't be serious!"

"Please. Hub. I may be difficult for you, and I think it would help if you were to call me by my name. Now let's talk about you. Your father is a doctor, you received all A's in high school—I received rather mediocre grades myself—and you've come to Harvard because you believe it affords a cosmopolitan Eastern environment that will be valuable to you after spending your entire life in a small provincial town."

"Who the hell told you all this?" The recital of his application statement made Orson blush. He already felt much older than the boy who had written it.

"University Hall," Henry said. "I went over and asked to see your folder. They didn't want to let me at first but I explained that if they were going to give me a roommate, after I had specifically requested to live alone, I had a right to information about you, so I could minimize possible friction."

"And they *let* you?"

"Of course. People without convictions have no powers of resistance." His mouth made its little satisfied click, and Orson was goaded to ask, "Why did *you* come to Harvard?"

"Two reasons." He ticked them off on two fingers. "Raphael Demos and Werner Jaeger."

Orson did not know these names, but he suspected that "Friend of yours?" was a stupid question, once it was out of his mouth.

But Henry nodded, "I've introduced myself to Demos. A charming old scholar, with a beautiful young wife."

"You mean you just went to his house and pushed yourself *in*?" Orson heard his own voice grow shrill; his voice, rather high and unstable, was one of the things about himself that he liked least.

Henry blinked, and looked unexpectedly vulnerable, so slender and bravely dressed, his ugly, yellowish, flat-nailed feet naked on the floor, which was uncarpeted and painted black. "That isn't how I would describe it. I went as a pilgrim. He seemed pleased to talk to me." He spoke carefully, and his mouth abstained from clicking.

That he could hurt his roommate's feelings—that this jaunty apparition had feelings—disconcerted Orson more deeply than any of the surprises he had been deliberately offered. As quickly as he had popped up, Henry dropped to the floor, as if through a trapdoor in the plane of conversation. He resumed spinning. The method apparently called for one thread to be wound around the big toe of a foot and to be kept taut by a kind of absent-minded pedal motion. While engaged in this, he seemed hermetically sealed inside one of the gluing machines that had incubated his garbled philosophy. Unpacking, Orson was slowed and snagged by a complicated mood of discomfort. He tried to remember how his mother had arranged his bureau drawers at home—socks and underwear in one, shirts and handkerchiefs in another. Home seemed infinitely far from him, and he was dizzily conscious of a great depth of space beneath his feet, as if the blackness of the floor were the color of an abyss. The spinning wheel steadily chuckled. Orson's buzz of unease circled and settled on his roommate, who, it was clear, had thought earnestly about profound matters, matters that Orson, busy as he had been with the practical business of being a good student, had hardly considered. It was also clear that Henry had thought unintelligently. This unintelligence ("I received rather mediocre grades myself") was more of a menace than a comfort. Bent above the bureau drawers, Orson felt cramped in his mind, able neither to stand erect in wholehearted contempt nor to lie down in honest admiration. His mood was complicated by the repugnance his roommate's physical presence aroused in him. An almost morbidly clean boy, Orson was haunted by glue, and a tacky ambience resisted every motion of his unpacking.

The silence between the roommates continued until a great bell rang ponderously. The sound was near and yet far, like a heartbeat within the bosom of time, and it seemed to bring with it into the room the muffling foliation of the trees in the Yard, which to Orson's prairie-honed eyes had looked tropically tall and lush; the walls of the room vibrated with leaf shadows, and many minute presences—dust motes, traffic sounds, or angels of whom several could dance on the head of a pin—thronged the air and made it difficult to breathe. The stairways of the dormitory rumbled. Boys dressed in jackets and neckties crowded the doorway and entered the room, laughing and calling "Hub. Hey, Hub."

"Get up off the floor, dad."

"Jesus, Hub, put your shoes on."

"Pee-*yew*."

"And take off that seductive sarong around your neck."

"Consider the lilies, Hub. They toil not, neither do they spin, and yet I say unto you that Solomon in all his glory was not arrayed like one of these."

"Amen, brothers!"

"Fitch, you should be a preacher."

They were all strangers to Orson. Hub stood and smoothly performed introductions.

In a few days, Orson had sorted them out. That jostling conglomerate, so apparently secure and homogeneous, broke down, under habitual exposure, into double individuals: roommates. There were Silverstein and Koshland, Dawson and Kern, Young and Carter, Petersen and Fitch.

Silverstein and Koshland, who lived in the room overhead, were Jews from New York City. All Orson knew about non-biblical Jews was that they were a sad race, full of music, shrewdness, and woe. But Silverstein and Koshland were always clowning, always wisecracking. They played bridge and poker and chess and Go and went to the movies in Boston and drank coffee in the luncheonettes around the Square. They came from the "gifted" high schools of the Bronx and Brooklyn respectively, and treated Cambridge as if it were another borough. Most of what the freshmen year sought to teach them they seemed to know already. As winter approached, Koshland went out for basketball, and he and his teammates made the floor above bounce to the thump and rattle of scrimmages with a tennis ball and a wastebasket. One afternoon, a section of ceiling collapsed on Orson's bed.

Next door, in Room 12, Dawson and Kern wanted to be writers. Dawson was from Ohio and Kern from Pennsylvania. Dawson had a sulky, slouching bearing, a certain puppyish facial eagerness, and a terrible temper. He was a disciple of Anderson and Hemingway and himself wrote as austerely as a newspaper. He had been raised as an atheist, and no one in the dormitory incited his temper more often than Hub. Orson, feeling that he and Dawson came from opposite edges of that great psychological realm called the Midwest, liked him. He felt less at ease with Kern, who seemed Eastern and subtly vicious. A farm boy driven by an unnatural sophistication, riddled with nervous ailments ranging from conjunctivitis to hemorrhoids, Kern smoked and talked incessantly. He and Dawson maintained between them a battery of running jokes. At night Orson could hear them on the other side of the wall keeping each other awake with improvised parodies and musical comedies based on their teachers, their courses, or their fellow-freshmen. One midnight, Orson distinctly heard Dawson sing, "My name is Orson Ziegler, I come from South Dakota." There was a pause, then Kern sang back, "I tend to be a niggler, and masturbate by quota."

Across the hall, in 15, lived Young and Carter, Negroes. Carter was from Detroit and very black, very clipped in speech, very well dressed, and apt to collapse, at the jab of a rightly angled joke, into a spastic giggling fit that left his cheeks gleaming with tears; Kern was expert at breaking Carter up. Young was a lean, malt-pale colored boy from North Carolina, here on a national scholarship, out of his depth, homesick, and cold. Kern called him Br'er Possum. He slept all day and at night sat on his bed playing the mouthpiece of a trumpet to himself. At first, he had played the full horn in the afternoon, flooding the dormitory and its green envelope of trees with golden, tremulous versions of languorous tunes like "Sentimental Journey" and "The Tennessee Waltz." It had been nice. But Young's sombre sense of tact—a slavish drive toward self-effacement that the shock of Harvard had awakened in him—soon cancelled these harmless performances. He took to hiding from the sun, and at night the furtive spitting sound from across the hall seemed to Orson, as he struggled to sleep, music drowning in shame. Carter always referred to his roommate as "Jonathan," mouthing the syllables fastidiously, as if he were pronouncing the name of a remote being he had just learned about, like Rochefoucauld or Demosthenes.

Cattycorner up the hall, in unlucky 13, Petersen and Fitch kept a strange household. Both were tall, narrow-shouldered, and broad-bottomed; physiques aside, it was hard to see what they had in common, or why Harvard had put them together. Fitch, with dark staring eyes and the flat full cranium of Frankenstein's monster, was a child prodigy from Maine, choked with philosophy, wild with ideas, and pregnant with the seeds of the nervous breakdown he was to have, eventually, in April. Petersen was an amiable Swede with a transparent skin that revealed blue veins in his nose. For several summers he had worked as a reporter for the Duluth *Herald*. He had all the newsman's tricks: the side-of-the-mouth quip, the nip of whiskey, the hat on the back of the head, the habit of throwing still-burning cigarettes onto the floor. He did not seem quite to know why he was at Harvard, and in fact did not return at the end of the freshman year. But, while those two drifted toward their respective failures, they made a strangely well-suited couple. Each was strong where the other was helpless. Fitch was so uncoördinated and unorganized he could not even type; he would lie on his bed in pajamas, writhing and grimacing, and dictate a tangled humanities paper, twice the requested length and mostly about books that had not been assigned, while Petersen, typing with a hectic two-finger system, would obligingly turn this chaotic monologue into "copy." His patience verged on the maternal. When Fitch appeared for a meal wearing a coat and tie, the joke ran in the dormitory that Petersen had dressed him. In return, Fitch gave Petersen ideas out of the superabundance painfully cramming his big flat head. Petersen had absolutely no ideas; he could neither compare, contrast, nor criticize St. Augustine and Marcus Aurelius. Perhaps having seen, so

young, so many corpses and fires and policemen and prosti-
tutes had prematurely blighted his mind. At any rate,
mothering Fitch gave him something practical to do, and
Orson envied them.

He envied all the roommates, whatever the bond between
them—geography, race, ambition, physical size—for between himself and Hub Palamountain he could see no link
except forced cohabitation. Not that living with Hub was
superficially unpleasant. Hub was tidy, industrious, and os-
tentatiously considerate. He rose at seven, prayed, did Yoga,
spun, and was off to breakfast, often not to be seen again
until the end of the day. He went to sleep, generally, at elev-
en sharp. If there was noise in the room, he would insert
rubber plugs in his ears, put a black mask over his eyes, and
go to sleep anyway. During the day, he kept a rigorous
round of appointments: he audited two courses in addition
to taking four, he wrestled three times a week for his physi-
cal-training requirement, he wangled tea invitations from
Demos and Jaeger and the Bishop of Massachusetts, he attended free evening lectures and readings, he associated
himself with Phillips Brooks House and spent two afternoons a week supervising slum boys in a Roxbury redevel-
opment house. In addition, he had begun to take piano lessons in Brookline. Many days, Orson saw him only at meals
in the Union, where the dormitory neighbors, in those first
fall months when their acquaintance was crisp and young
and differing interests had not yet scattered them, tended
to regroup around a long table. In these months there was
often a debate about the subject posed under their eyes:
Hub's vegetarianism. There he would sit, his tray heaped
high with a steaming double helping of squash and lima
beans, while Fitch would try to locate the exact point at
which vegetarianism became inconsistent. "You eat eggs,"
he said.

"Yes," Hub said.

"You realize that every egg, from the chicken's point of
reference, is a newborn baby?"

"But in fact it is not unless it has been fertilized by a
rooster."

"But suppose," Fitch pursued, "as sometimes happens—
which I happen to know, from working in my uncle's hen-
house in Maine—an egg that *should* be sterile has in fact
been fertilized and contains an embryo?"

"If I see it, I naturally don't eat that particular egg," Hub said, his lips making that satisfied concluding snap.

Fitch pounced triumphantly, spilling a fork to the floor with a lurch of his hand. "But *why?* The hen feels the same pain on being parted from an egg whether sterile or fertile. The embryo is unconscious—a vegetable. As a vegetarian, you should eat it with special relish." He tipped back in his chair so hard he had to grab the table edge to keep from toppling over.

"It seems to me," Dawson said, frowning darkly—these discussions, clogging some twist of his ego, often spilled him into a vile temper—"that psychoanalysis of hens is hardly relevant."

"On the contrary," Kern said lightly, clearing his throat and narrowing his pink, infected eyes, "it seems to me that there, in the tiny, dim mind of the hen—the minimal mind, as it were—is where the tragedy of the universe achieves a pinpoint focus. Picture the emotional life of a hen. What does she know of companionship? A flock of pecking, harsh-voiced gossips. Of shelter? A few dung-bespattered slats. Of food? Some flecks of mash and grit insolently tossed on the ground. Of love? The casual assault of a polygamous cock—cock in the Biblical sense. Then, into this heartless world, there suddenly arrives, as if by magic, an egg. An egg of her own. An egg, it must seem to her, that she and God have made. How she must cherish it, its beautiful baldness, its gentle lustre, its firm yet somehow fragile, softly swaying weight."

Carter had broken up. He bent above his tray, his eyes tight shut, his dark face contorted joyfully. "Puhleese," he gasped at last. "You're making my stomach hurt."

"Ah, Carter," Kern said loftily, "if that were only the worst of it. For then, one day, while the innocent hen sits cradling this strange, faceless, oval child, its little weight swaying softly in her wings"—he glanced hopefully at Carter, but the colored boy bit his lower lip and withstood the jab—"an enormous man, smelling of beer and manure, comes and tears the egg from her grasp. And why? Because *he*"—Kern pointed, arm fully extended, across the table, so that his index finger, orange with nicotine, almost touched Hub's nose—"*he*, Saint Henry Palamountain, wants more eggs to eat. 'More eggs!' he cries voraciously, so that brutal steers and faithless pigs can continue to menace the children of American mothers!"

Dawson slammed his silver down, got up from the table, and slouched out of the dining room. Kern blushed. In the silence, Petersen put a folded slice of roast beef in his mouth and said, chewing, "Jesus, Hub, if somebody else kills the animals you might as well eat 'em. They don't give a damn any more."

"You understand nothing," Hub said simply.

"Hey, Hub," Silverstein called down from the far end of the table. "What's the word on milk? Don't calves drink milk? Maybe you're taking milk out of some calf's mouth."

Orson felt impelled to speak. *"No,"* he said, and his voice seemed to have burst, its pitch was so unsteady and excited. "As anybody except somebody from New York would know, milch cows have weaned their calves. What I wonder about, Hub, is your shoes. You wear leather shoes."

"I do." The gaiety left Hub's defense of himself. His lips became prim.

"Leather is the skin of a steer."

"But the animal has already been slaughtered."

"You sound like Petersen. Your purchase of leather goods—what about your wallet and belt, for that matter?—encourages the slaughter. You're as much of a murderer as the rest of us. More of one—because you think about it."

Hub folded his hands carefully in front of him, propping them, almost in prayer, on the table edge. His voice became like that of a radio announcer, but an announcer rapidly, softly describing the home stretch of a race. "My belt, I believe, is a form of plastic. My wallet was given to me by my mother years ago, before I became a vegetarian. Please remember that I ate meat for eighteen years and I still have an appetite for it. If there were any other concentrated source of protein, I would not eat eggs. Some vegetarians do not. On the other hand, some vegetarians eat fish and take liver extract. I would not do this. Shoes are a problem. There is a firm in Chicago that makes non-leather shoes for extreme vegetarians, but they're very expensive and not comfortable. I once ordered a pair. They killed my feet. Leather, you see, 'breathes' in a way no synthetic substitute does. My feet are tender; I have compromised. I apologize. For that matter, when I play the piano I encourage the slaughter of elephants, and in brushing my teeth, which I must do faithfully because a vegetable diet is so heavy in carbohydrates, I use a brush of pig bristles. I am covered with blood, and pray daily for forgiveness." He took up his fork and resumed eating the mound of squash.

Orson was amazed; he had been impelled to speak by a kind of sympathy, and Hub had answered as if he alone were an enemy. He tried to defend himself. "There are perfectly wearable shoes," he said, "made out of canvas, with crêpe-rubber soles."

"I'll look into them," Hub said. "They sound a little sporty to me."

Laughter swept the table and ended the subject. After lunch Orson walked to the library with the beginnings of indigestion; a backwash of emotion was upsetting his stomach. There was a growing confusion inside him he could not resolve. He resented being associated with Hub, and yet felt attacked when Hub was attacked. It seemed to him that Hub deserved credit for putting his beliefs into practice, and that people like Fitch and Kern, in mocking, merely belittled themselves. Yet Hub smiled at their criticism, took it as a game, and fought back in earnest only at Orson, forcing him into a false position. Why? Was it because in being also a Christian he alone qualified for serious rebuke? But Carter went to church, wearing a blue pin-striped suit with a monogrammed handkerchief peaked in the breast pocket, every Sunday; Petersen was a nominal Presbyterian; Orson had once seen Kern sneaking out of Mem Chapel; and even Koshland observed his holidays, by cutting classes and skipping lunch. Why, therefore, Orsen asked himself, should Hub pick on him? And why should he care? He had no real respect for Hub. Hub's handwriting was childishly large and careful and his first set of hour exams, even in the course on Plato and Aristotle, had yielded a batch of C's. Orson resented being condescended to by an intellectual inferior. The knowledge that at the table he had come off second best galled him like an unfair grade. His situation with Hub became in his head a diagram in which all his intentions curved off at right angles and his strengths inversely tapered into nothing. Behind the diagram hung the tuck of complacence in Hub's lips, the fishy impudence of his eyes, and the keenly irksome shape and tint of his hands and feet. These images—Hub disembodied—Orson carried with him into the library, back and forth to classes, and along the congested streets around the Square; now and then the glaze of an eye or the flat yellowish nail of a big toe welled up distinctly through the pages of a book and, greatly magnified, slid with Orson into the unconsciousness of sleep. Nevertheless, he surprised himself, sitting one February afternoon in Room 12 with Dawson and Kern, by blurting, "I hate him." He considered what he had said, liked the taste of it, and repeated, "I hate the bastard. I've never hated anybody before in my life." His voice cracked and his eyes warmed with abortive tears.

They had all returned from Christmas vacation to plunge into the weird limbo of reading period and the novel ordeal of midyear exams. This was a dormitory, by and large, of public-school graduates, who feel the strain of Harvard most in their freshman year. The private-school boys, launched by little Harvards like Exeter and Groton, tend to glide through this year and to run aground later on strange reefs, foundering in alcohol, or sinking in a dandified apathy. But the institution demands of each man, before it releases him, a wrenching sacrifice of ballast. At Christmas, Orson's mother thought he looked haggard, and set about fattening him up. On the other hand, he was struck by how much his father had aged and shrunk. Orson spent his first days home listening to the mindless music on the radio, hours of it, and driving through farmland on narrow straight roads already banked bright with plowed snow. The South Dakota sky had never looked so open, so clean; he had never realized before that the high dry sun that made even sub-zero days feel warm at noon was a local phenomenon. He made love to his girl again, and again she cried. He said to her he blamed himself, for ineptitude; but in his heart he blamed her. She was not helping him. Back in Cambridge, it was raining, raining in January, and the entryway of the Coop was full of gray footprints and wet bicycles and Radcliffe girls in slickers and sneakers. Hub had stayed here, alone in their room, and had celebrated Christmas with a fast.

In the monotonous, almost hallucinatory month of re-reading, outlining, and memorizing, Orson perceived how little he knew, how stupid he was, how unnatural all learning is, and how futile. Harvard rewarded him with three A's and a B. Hub pulled out two B's and two C's. Kern, Dawson, and Silverstein did well; Petersen, Koshland, and Carter got mediocre grades; Fitch flunked one subject, and Young flunked three. The pale Negro slunk in and out of the dorm as if he were diseased and marked for destruction;

he became, while still among them, a rumor. The suppressed whistling of the trumpet mouthpiece was no longer heard. Silverstein and Koshland and the basketball crowd adopted Carter and took him to movies in Boston three or four times a week.

After exams, in the heart of the Cambridge winter, there is a grateful pause. New courses are selected, and even the full-year courses, heading into their second half, sometimes put on, like a new hat, a fresh professor. The days quietly lengthen; there is a snowstorm or two; the swimming and squash teams lend the sports pages of the *Crimson* an unaccustomed note of victory. A kind of foreshadow of spring falls bluely on the snow. The elms are seen to be shaped like fountains. The discs of snow pressed by boots into the sidewalk by Albiani's seem large precious coins; the brick buildings, the arched gates, the archaic lecterns, and the barny mansions along Brattle Street dawn upon the freshman as a heritage he temporarily possesses. The thumbworn spines of his now familiar textbooks seem proof of a certain knowingness, and the strap of the green book bag tugs at his wrist like a living falcon. The letters from home dwindle in importance. The hours open up. There is more time. Experiments are made. Courtships begin. Conversations go on and on; and an almost rapacious desire for mutual discovery possesses acquaintances. It was in this atmosphere, then, that Orson made his confession.

Dawson turned his head away as if the words had menaced him personally. Kern blinked, lit a cigarette, and asked, "What don't you like about him?"

"Well"—Orson shifted his weight uncomfortably in the black but graceful, shapely but hard Harvard chair—"it's little things. Whenever he gets a notice from the Portland draft board, he tears it up without opening it and scatters it out the window."

"And you're afraid that this incriminates you as an accessory and they'll put you in jail?"

"No—I don't know. It seems exaggerated. He exaggerates everything. You should see how he prays."

"How do you know how he prays?"

"He shows me. Every morning, he gets down on his knees and *throws* himself across the bed, his face in the blanket, his arms way out." He showed them.

"God," Dawson said. "That's marvellous. It's medieval. It's more than medieval. It's Counter-Reformation."

"I mean," Orson said, grimacing in realization of how deeply he had betrayed Hub, "I pray, too, but I don't make a show of myself."

A frown clotted Dawson's expression, and passed.

"He's a saint," Kern said.

"He's *not*," Orson said. "He's not intelligent. I'm taking Chem 1 with him, and he's worse than a child with the math. And those Greek books he keeps on his desk, they look worn because he bought them second-hand."

"Saints don't have to be intelligent," Kern said. "What saints have to have is energy. Hub has it."

"Look how he wrestles," Dawson said.

"I doubt if he wrestles very *well*," Orson said. "He didn't make the freshman team. I'm sure if we heard him play the piano, it'd be awful."

"You seem to miss the point," Kern said, eyes closed, "of what Hub's all about."

"I know goddam well what he thinks he's all about," Orson said, "but it's fake. It doesn't go. All this vegetarianism and love of the starving Indian—he's really a terribly cold bastard. I think he's about the coldest person I've ever met in my life."

"I don't think Orson thinks that; do you?" Kern asked Dawson.

"No," Dawson said, and his puppyish smile cleared his cloudy face. "That's not what Orson the Parson thinks."

Kern squinted. "Is it Orson the Parson, or Orson the Person?"

"I think Hub is the nub," Dawson said.

"Or the rub," Kern added, and both burst into grinding laughter. Orson felt he was being sacrificed to the precarious peace the two roommates kept between themselves, and left, superficially insulted but secretly flattered to have been given, at last, a nickname of sorts: Orson the Parson.

Several nights later they went to hear Carl Sandburg read in New Lecture Hall—the four adjacent roommates, plus Fitch. To avoid sitting next to Hub, who aggressively led them into a row of seats, Orson delayed, and so sat the farthest away from the girl Hub sat directly behind. Orson noticed her immediately; she had a lavish mane of coppery red hair which hung down loose over the back of her seat. The color of it, and the abundance, reminded him, all at once, of horses, earth, sun, wheat, and home. From Orson's angle she was nearly in profile; her face was small, with a tilted shadowy cheekbone and a pale prominent ear. Toward the pallor of her profile he felt an orgasmic surge; she seemed suspended in the crowd and was floating, a crest of whiteness, toward him. She turned away. Hub had leaned forward and was saying something into her other ear. Fitch overheard it, and gleefully relayed it to Dawson, who whispered to Kern and Orson; *"Hub said to the girl, 'You have beautiful hair.'"*

Several times during the reading, Hub leaned forward to add something more into her ear, each time springing spurts of choked laughter from Fitch, Dawson, and Kern. Meanwhile, Sandburg, his white bangs as straight and shiny as a doll's wig of artificial fibre, incanted above the lectern and quaintly strummed a guitar. Afterward, Hub walked with the girl into the outdoors. From a distance Orson saw her white face turn and crumple into a laugh. Hub returned to his friends with the complacent nick in the corner of his mouth deepened, in the darkness, to a gash.

It was not the next day, or the next week, but within the month that Hub brought back to the room a heap of red hair. Orson found it lying like a diaphanous corpse on a newspaper spread on his bed. "Hub, what the hell is this?"

Hub was on the floor playing with his spinning wheel. "Hair."

"Human hair?"

"Of course."

"Whose?"

"A girl's."

"What happened?" The question sounded strange; Orson meant to ask, "What girl's?"

Hub answered as if he had asked that question. "It's a girl I met at the Sandburg reading; you don't know her."

"This is *her* hair?"

"Yes. I asked her for it. She said she was planning to cut it all off this spring anyway."

Orson stood stunned above the bed, gripped by an urge to bury his face and hands in the hair. "You've been *seeing* her?" This effeminate stridence in his voice: he despised it and only Hub brought it out.

"A little. My schedule doesn't allow for much social life, but my adviser has recommended that I relax now and then."

"You take her to movies?"

"Once in a while. She pays her admission, of course."

"Of *course*."

Hub took him up on his tone. "Please remember I'm here on my savings alone. I have refused all financial assistance from my father."

"Hub"—the very syllable seemed an expression of pain—"what are you going to do with her hair?"

"Spin it into a rope."

"A *rope?*"

"Yes. It'll be very difficult; her hair is terribly fine."

"And what will you do with the rope?"

"Make a knot of it."

"A *knot?*"

"I think that's the term. I'll coil it and secure it so it can't come undone and give it to her. So she'll always have her hair the way it was when she was nineteen."

"How the hell did you talk this poor girl into it?"

"I didn't talk her into it. I merely offered, and she thought it was a lovely idea. Really, Orson, I don't see why this should offend your bourgeois scruples. Women cut their hair all the time."

"She must think you're insane. She was humoring you."

"As you like. It was a perfectly rational suggestion, and my sanity has never been raised as an issue between us."

"Well, *I* think you're insane. Hub, you're a *nut*."

Orson left the room and slammed the door, and didn't return until eleven, when Hub was asleep in his eye mask. The heap of hair had been transferred to the floor beside the spinning wheel, and already some strands were entangled with the machine. In time a rope was produced, a braided cord as thick as a woman's little finger, about a foot long, weightless and waxen. The earthy, horsy fire in the hair's color had been quenched in the process. Hub carefully coiled it and with black thread and long pins secured and stiffened the spiral into a disc the size of a small saucer. This he presented to the girl one Friday night. The presentation appeared to satisfy him, for, as far as Orson knew, Hub had no further dates with her. Once in a while Orson passed her in the Yard, and without her hair she scarcely seemed female, her small pale face fringed in curt tufts, her ears looking enormous. He wanted to speak to her; some obscure force of pity, or hope of rescue, impelled him to greet this wan androgyne, but the opening word stuck in his throat. She did not look as if she pitied herself, or knew what had been done to her.

Something magical protected Hub; things deflected from him. The doubt Orson had cast upon his sanity bounced back onto himself. As spring slowly broke, he lost the ability to sleep. Figures and facts churned sluggishly in an insomnious mire. His courses became four parallel puzzles. In mathematics, the crucial transposition upon which the solution pivoted consistently eluded him, vanishing into the chinks between the numbers. The quantities in chemistry became impishly unstable; the unbalanced scales clicked down sharply and the system of interlocked elements that fanned from the lab to the far stars collapsed. In the history survey course, they had reached the Enlightenment, and Orson found himself disturbingly impressed by Voltaire's indictment of God, though the lecturer handled it calmly, as one more dead item of intellectual history, neither true nor false. And in German, which Orson had taken to satisfy his language requirement, the words piled on remorselessly, and the existence of languages other than English, the existence of so many, each so vast, intricate, and opaque, seemed to prove cosmic dementia. He felt his mind, which was always more steady than quick, grow slower and slower. His chair threatened to adhere to him, and he would leap up in panic. Sleepless, stuffed with information he could neither forget nor manipulate, he became prey to obsessive delusions; he became convinced that his girl in South Dakota had taken up with another boy and was making love to him happily, Orson having shouldered the awkwardness and blame of taking her virginity. In the very loops that Emily's ballpoint pen described in her bland letters to him he read the pleased rotundity, the inner fatness of a well-loved woman. He even knew the man. It was Spotted Elk, the black-nailed Chippewa, whose impassive nimbleness had so often mocked Orson on the basketball court, whose terrible ease and speed of reaction had seemed so unjust, and whose defense—he recalled now—Emily had often undertaken. His wife had become a whore, a squaw; the scraggly mute reservation children his father had doctored in the charity clinic became, amid the sliding transparencies of Orson's mind, his own children. In his dreams—or in those limp elisions of imagery which in the absence of sleep passed for dreams—he seemed to be rooming with Spotted Elk, and his roommate, who sometimes wore a mask, invariably had won, by under-

handed means, the affection and admiration that were right-
fully his. There was a conspiracy. Whenever Orson heard
Kern and Dawson laughing on the other side of the wall, he
knew it was about him, and about his most secret habits.
This ultimate privacy was outrageously invaded; in bed,
half-relaxed, he would suddenly see himself bodily involved
with Hub's lips, Hub's legs, with Hub's veined, vaguely
womanish hands. At first he resisted these visions, tried to
erase them; it was like trying to erase ripples on water. He
learned to submit to them, to let the attack—for it was an
attack, with teeth and sharp acrobatic movements—wash
over him, leaving him limp enough to sleep. These dives became the only route to sleep. In the morning he would
awake and see Hub sprawled flamboyantly across his bed in
prayer, or sitting hunched at his spinning wheel, or gau-
dily dressed, tiptoeing to the door and with ostentatious care
closing it softly behind him; and he would hate him—hate
his appearance, his form, his manner, his pretensions with
an avidity of detail he had never known in love. The tiny
details of his roommate's physical existence—the wrinkles
flickering beside his mouth, the slightly withered look about
his hands, the complacently polished creases of his leather
shoes—seemed a poisonous food Orson could not stop eating. His eczema worsened alarmingly.

By April, Orson was on the verge of going to the student
clinic, which had a department called Mental Health. But at
this point Fitch relieved him by having, it seemed, his nervous breakdown for him. For weeks, Fitch had been taking
several showers a day. Toward the end he stopped going to
classes and was almost constantly naked, except for a towel
tucked around his waist. He was trying to complete a humanities paper that was already a month overdue and twenty pages too long. He left the dormitory only to eat and to
take more books from the library. One night around nine,
Petersen was called to the phone on the second-floor landing. The Watertown police had picked Fitch up as he was
struggling through the underbrush on the banks of the
Charles four miles away. He claimed he was walking to the
West, where he had been told there was enough space to
contain God, and proceeded to talk with wild animation to
the police chief about the differences and affinities between
Kierkegaard and Nietzsche. Hub, ever alert for an oppor-
tunity to intrude in the guise of doing good, went to the
hall proctor—a spindly and murmurous graduate student of

astronomy engaged, under Harlow Shapley, in an endless galaxy count—and volunteered himself as an expert on the case, and even conferred with the infirmary psychologist. Hub's interpretation was that Fitch had been punished for *hubris*. The psychologist felt the problem was fundamentally Oedipal. Fitch was sent back to Maine. Hub suggested to Orson that now Petersen would need a roommate next year. "I think you and he would hit it off splendidly. You're both materialists."

"I'm *not* a materialist."

Hub lifted his dreadful hands in half-blessing. "Have it your way. I'm determined to minimize friction."

"Dammit, Hub, all the friction between us comes from *you*."

"How? What do I do? Tell me, and I'll change. I'll give you the shirt off my back." He began to unbutton, and stopped, seeing that the laugh wasn't going to come.

Orson felt weak and empty, and in spite of himself he cringed inwardly, with a helpless affection for his unreal, unreachable friend. "I don't know, Hub," he admitted. "I don't know what it is you're doing to me."

A paste of silence dried in the air between them.

Orson with an effort unstuck himself. "I think you're right, we shouldn't room together next year."

Hub seemed a bit bewildered, but nodded, saying, "I told them in the beginning that I ought to live alone." And his hurt eyes bulging behind their lenses settled into an invulnerable Byzantine stare.

One afternoon in middle May, Orson was sitting stumped at his desk, trying to study. He had taken two exams and had two to go. They stood between him and release like two towering walls of muddy paper. His position seemed extremely precarious: he was unable to retreat and able to advance only along a very thin thread, a high wire of sanity on which he balanced above an abyss of statistics and formulae, his brain a firmament of winking cells. A push would kill him. There was then a hurried pounding up the stairs, and Hub pushed into the room carrying cradled in his arm a metal object the color of a gun and the size of a cat. It had a red tongue. Hub slammed the door behind him, snapped the lock, and dumped the object on Orson's bed. It was the head of a parking meter, sheared from its post. A keen quick pain cut through Orson's groin. "For

God's sake," he cried in his contemptible high voice, "what's *that?*"

"It's a parking meter."

"I *know*, I can *see* that. Where the hell did you *get* it?"

"I won't talk to you until you stop being hysterical," Hub said, and crossed to his desk, where Orson had put his mail. He took the top letter, a special delivery from the Portland draft board, and tore it in half. This time, the pain went through Orson's chest. He put his head in his arms on the desk and whirled and groped in the black-red darkness there. His body was frightening him; his nerves listened for a third psychosomatic slash.

There was a rap on the door; from the force of the knock, it could only be the police. Hub nimbly dashed to the bed and hid the meter under Orson's pillow. Then he pranced to the door and opened it.

It was Dawson and Kern. "What's up?" Dawson asked, frowning as if the disturbance had been created to annoy him.

"It sounded like Ziegler was being tortured," Kern said.

Orson pointed at Hub and explained, "He's castrated a parking meter!"

"I did not," Hub said. "A car went out of control on Mass. Avenue and hit a parked car, which knocked a meter down. A crowd gathered. The head of the meter was lying in the gutter, so I picked it up and carried it away. I was afraid someone might be tempted to steal it."

"Nobody tried to stop you?" Kern asked.

"Of course not. They were all gathered around the driver of the car."

"Was he hurt?"

"I doubt it. I didn't look."

"You didn't *look!*" Orson cried. "You're a great Samaritan."

"I am not prey," Hub said, "to morbid curiosity."

"Where were the police?" Kern asked.

"They hadn't arrived yet."

Dawson asked, "Well why didn't you wait till a cop arrived and give the meter to him?"

"Why should I give it to an agent of the State? It's no more his than mine."

"But it *is*," Orson said.

"It was a plain act of Providence that placed it in my hands," Hub said, the corners of his lips dented securely. "I haven't decided yet which charity should receive the money it contains."

Dawson asked, "But isn't that stealing?"

"No more stealing than the State is stealing in making people pay money for space in which to park their own cars."

"Hub," Orson said, getting to his feet. "You give it back or we'll both go to jail." He saw himself ruined, the scarcely commenced career of his life destroyed.

Hub turned serenely. "I'm not afraid. Going to jail under a totalitarian regime is a mark of honor. If you had a conscience, you'd understand."

Petersen and Carter and Silverstein came into the room. Some boys from the lower floors followed them. The story was hilariously retold. The meter was produced from under the pillow and passed around and shaken to demonstrate the weight of pennies it contained. Hub always carried, as a vestige of the lumberjack country he came from, an intricate all-purpose pocket knife. He began to pry open the little money door. Orson came up behind him and got him around the neck with one arm. Hub's body stiffened. He passed the head of the meter and the open knife to Carter, and then Orson experienced sensations of being lifted, of flying, and of lying on the floor, looking up at Hub's face, which was upside down in his vision. He scrambled to his feet and went for him again, rigid with anger and yet, in his heart, happily relaxed; Hub's body was tough and quick and satisfying to grip, though, being a wrestler, he somehow deflected Orson's hands and again lifted and dropped him to the black floor. This time, Orson felt a blow as his coccyx hit the wood; yet even through the pain he perceived, gazing into the heart of this marriage, that Hub was being as gentle with him as he could be. And that he could try in earnest to kill Hub and be in no danger of succeeding was also a comfort. He renewed the attack and again enjoyed the tense defensive skill that made Hub's body a kind of warp in space through which his own body, after an ecstatic instant of contention, was converted to the supine position. He got to his feet and would have gone for Hub the fourth time, but his fellow-freshmen grabbed his arms and held him. He shook them off and without a word returned to his desk and concentrated down into his book, turning the page. The type looked extremely distinct, though it was trembling too hard to be deciphered.

The head of the parking meter stayed in the room for one night. The next day, Hub allowed himself to be persuaded (by the others; Orson had stopped speaking to him) to take it to the Cambridge police headquarters in Central Square. Dawson and Kern tied a ribbon around it, and attached a note: "Please take good care of my baby." None of them, however, had the nerve to go with Hub to the headquarters, though when he came back he said the chief was delighted to get the meter, and had thanked him, and had agreed to donate the pennies to the local orphans' home. In another week, the last exams were over. The freshmen all went home. When they returned in the fall, they were different: sophomores. Petersen and Young did not come back at all. Fitch returned, made up the lost credits, and eventually graduated *magna cum* in History and Lit. He now teaches in a Quaker prep school. Silverstein is a biochemist, Koshland a lawyer. Dawson writes conservative editorials in Cleveland, Kern is in advertising in New York. Carter, as if obliged to join Young in oblivion, disappeared between his junior and senior years. The dormitory neighbors tended to lose sight of each other, though Hub, who had had his case shifted to the Massachusetts jurisdiction, was now and then pictured in the *Crimson,* and once gave an evening lecture, "Why I Am an Episcopalian Pacifist." As the litigation progressed, the Bishop of Massachusetts rather grudgingly vouched for him, and by the time of his final hearing the Korean War was over, and the judge who heard the case ruled that Hub's convictions were sincere, as witnessed by his willingness to go to jail. Hub was rather disappointed at the verdict, since he had prepared a three-year reading list to occupy him in his cell and was intending to memorize all four Gospels in the original Greek. After graduation, he went to Union Theological Seminary, spent several years as the assistant rector of an urban parish in Baltimore, and learned to play the piano well enough to be the background music in a Charles Street cocktail lounge. He insisted on wearing his clerical collar, and as a consequence gave the bar a small celebrity. After a year of overriding people of less strong convictions, he was allowed to go to South Africa, where he worked and preached among the Bantus until the government requested that he leave the country. From there he went to Nigeria, and when last heard from—on a Christmas card, with French salutations and Negro Magi, which arrived, soiled and wrinkled, in

South Dakota in February—Hub was in Madagascar, as a "combination missionary, political agitator, and soccer coach." The description struck Orson as probably facetious, and Hub's childish and confident handwriting, with every letter formed individually, afflicted him with some of the old exasperation. Having vowed to answer the card, he mislaid it, uncharacteristically.

Orson didn't speak to Hub for two days after the parking-meter incident. By then, it seemed rather silly, and they finished out the year sitting side by side at their desks as amiably as two cramped passengers who have endured a long bus trip together. When they parted, they shook hands, and Hub would have walked Orson to the subway kiosk except that he had an appointment in the opposite direction. Orson received two A's and two B's on his final exams; for the remaining three years at Harvard, he roomed uneventfully with two other colorless pre-med students, named Wallace and Neuhauser. After graduation, he married Emily, attended the Yale School of Medicine, and interned in St. Louis. He is now the father of four children and, since the death of his own father, the only doctor in the town. His life has gone much the way he planned it, and he is much the kind of man he intended to be when he was eighteen. He delivers babies, assists the dying, attends the necessary meetings, plays golf, and does good. He is honorable and irritable. If not as much loved as his father, he is perhaps even more respected. In one particular only—a kind of scar he carries without pain and without any clear memory of the amputation—does the man he is differ from the man he assumed he would become. He never prays.

My Love Has
Dirty Fingernails

THE MAN stood up when the woman entered the room, or, to be exact, was standing behind his desk when she opened the door. She closed the door behind her. The room was square and furnished in a strange cool manner, midway between a home (the pale-detailed Japanese prints on the wall, the thick carpet whose blue seemed a peculiarly intense shade of silence, the black slab sofa with its single prism-shaped pillow of Airfoam) and an office, which it was, though no instruments or books were on view. It would have been difficult to imagine the people who could appropriately inhabit this room, were they not already here. The man and woman both were impeccably groomed. The woman wore a gray linen suit, with white shoes and a white pocketbook, her silvery blond hair done up tightly in a French roll. She never wore a hat. Today she wore no gloves. The man wore a summer suit of a gray slightly lighter than the woman's, though perhaps it was merely that he stood nearer the light of the window. In this window, like the square muzzle of a dragon pinched beneath the sash, an air conditioner purred, a little fiercely. Venetian blinds dimmed the light, which, since this side of the building faced away from the sun, was already refracted. The man had a full head of half-gray hair, rather wavy, and scrupulously brushed, a touch vainly, so that a lock overhung his forehead, as if he were a youth. The woman had guessed he was about ten years older than she. In addition to the possibility of vanity, she read into this casually overhanging forelock a suggestion of fatigue—it was afternoon; he had already listened to so much—and an itch to apologize, to excuse herself, scratched her throat and made her limbs bristle with girlish nervousness. He waited to sit down

until she had done so; and even such a small concession to
her sex opened a window in the wall of impersonality between them. She peeked through and was struck by the fact
that he seemed neither handsome nor ugly. She did not
know what to make of it, or what she was expected to
make. His face, foreshortened downward, looked heavy and
petulant. It lifted, and innocent expectation seemed to fill it.
The customary flutter of panic seized her. Both bare hands
squeezed the pocketbook. The purring of the air conditioner
threatened to drown her first words. She felt the lack in the
room of the smell of a flower; in her own home the sills
were crowded with potted plants.

"I saw him only once this week," she said at last. Out
of polite habit she waited for a reply, then remembered
that there was no politeness here, and forced herself to go on
alone. "At a party. We spoke a little; I began the conversation. It seemed so unnatural to me that we shouldn't even
speak. When I did go up to him, he seemed very pleased,
and talked to me about things like cars and children. He
asked me what I was doing these days, and I told him,
'Nothing.' He would have talked to me longer, but I walked
away. I couldn't take it. It wasn't his voice so much, it was
his smile; when we were . . . seeing each other, I used to
think that there was a smile only I could bring out in him, a
big grin whenever he saw me that lit up his whole face and
showed all his crooked teeth. There it was, when I w— —l
up to him, that same happy smile, as if in all these months
. . . nothing had changed."

She looked at the catch on her purse and decided she had
begun badly. The man's disapproval was as real to her as the
sound of the air conditioner. It flowed toward her, enveloped
her in gray coolness, and she wondered if it was wrong of
her to feel it, wrong of her to desire his approval. She tried
to lift her face as if she were not flirting. In another room
she would have known herself to be considered a beautiful
woman. Here beauty ceased to exist, and she was disarmed,
realizing how much she depended on it for protection and
concealment. She wondered if she should try to express this.
"He sees through me," she said. "It's what made him so
wonderful then, and what makes him so terrible now. He
knows me. I can't hide behind my face when he smiles, and
he seems to be forgiving me, forgiving me for not coming to
him even though . . . I can't."

The man readjusted himself in the chair with a quickness that she took for a sign of impatience. She believed she had an honest gift for saying what he did not want to hear. She tried to say something that, in its frankness and confusion, would please him. "I'm suppressing," she said. "He did say one thing that if he hadn't been my lover he wouldn't have said. He looked down at my dress and asked me, in this shy voice, 'Did you put that on just to hurt me?' It was so un*fair*, it made me a little angry. I only have so many dresses, and I can't throw out all the ones that . . . that I wore when I was seeing him."

"Describe the dress."

When he did speak, the level of his interest often seemed to her disappointingly low. "Oh," she said, "an orangey-brown one, with stripes and a round neckline. A summer dress. He used to say I looked like a farm girl in it."

"Yes." He cut her short with a flipping gesture of his hand; his occasional rudeness startled her, since she could not imagine he had learned it from any book. She found herself, lately, afraid for him; he seemed too naïve and blunt. She felt him in constant danger of doing something incorrect. Once she had a piano teacher who, in performing scales with her side by side on the bench, made a mistake. She had never forgotten it, and never learned the piano. But as always she inspected his responses conscientiously, for a clue. She had reverted, in their conversations, again and again to this rural fantasy, as if, being so plainly a fantasy, it necessarily contained an explanation of her misery. Perhaps he was, with this appearance of merely male impatience, trying to head her into acknowledgment that she was too eager to dive to the depths. His effort, insofar as it was visible, seemed rather to direct her attention to what was not obvious about the obvious. He asked, "Have you ever worn the dress here?"

How strange of him! "To see you?" She tried to remember, saw herself parking the car, Thursday after Thursday, locking the door, feeding the meter, walking down the sunny city street of bakeries and tailor shops and dentists' signs, entering the dour vestibule of his building, and with its metal wall-sheathing stamped with fleurs-de-lis, seeing the shadow of her gloved hand reach to darken his bell. . . . "No. I don't think so."

"Do you have any thoughts as to why not?"

"There's nothing profound about it. It's a casual dress. It's young. It's not the identity a woman comes to the city in. I don't come in just to see you; I buy things, I visit people, sometimes I meet Harold afterward for a drink and we have dinner and go to a movie. Do you want me to talk about how I feel in the city?" She was suddenly full of feelings about herself in the city, graceful, urgent feelings of sunlight and release that she was sure explained a great deal about her.

He insisted. "Yet you wore this quite informal dress to a dinner party last weekend?"

"It was a party of our *friends*. It's summer in the suburbs. The dress is simple. It's not *shabby*."

"When you picked it to wear to this party where you knew he would see you, did you remember his special fondness for it?"

She wondered if he wasn't overdirecting her. She was sure he shouldn't. "I don't remember," she said, realizing, with a flash of impatience, that he would make too much of this. "You think I did."

He smiled his guarded, gentle smile and shrugged. "Tell me about clothes."

"Just anything? You want me to free-associate about clothes in general?"

"What comes to your mind."

The air conditioner flooded her silence with its constant zealous syllable. Time was pouring through her and she was wasting her session. "Well, he"—it was queer, how her mind, set free, flew like a magnet to this pronoun—"was quite funny about my clothes. He thought I overdressed, and used to kid me about what an expensive wife I'd make. It wasn't true, really; I sew quite well, and make a lot of my things, while Nancy wears these quiet clothes from R. H. Stearns that are really quite expensive. I suppose you could say my clothes were a fetish with him; he'd bury his face in them after I'd taken them off, and in making love sometimes he'd bring them back, so they'd get all tangled up between us." She stared at him defiantly, rather than blush. He was immobile, smiling the lightest of listening smiles, his brushed hair silvered by the window light. "Once I remember, when we were both in the city together, I took him shopping with me, thinking he'd like it, but he didn't. The salesgirls didn't know quite who he was, a brother or a husband or what, and he acted just like a man—you know, restless and embarrassed. In a way, I liked his reacting that way, because one of my fears about him, when I was thinking of him as somebody I owned, was that he might be effeminate. Not on the surface so much as down deep. I mean, he had this passive streak. He had a way of making me come to him without actually asking." She felt she was journeying in the listening mind opposite her and had come to a narrow place; she tried to retreat. What had she begun with? Clothes. "He was quite lazy about his own clothes. Do you want to hear about *his* clothes, or just *my* clothes? Next thing, I'll be talking about the children's clothes." She permitted herself to giggle.

He didn't respond, and to punish him she went ahead with the topic that she knew annoyed him. "He was sloppy. Even dressed up, the collars of his shirts looked unbuttoned, and he wore things until they fell apart. I remember, toward the end, after we had tried to break it off and I hadn't seen him for several weeks, he came to the house to see how I was for a minute, and I ran my hand under his shirt and my fingers went through a hole in his T-shirt. It just killed me, I had to have him, and we went upstairs. I can't describe it very well, but something about the idea of this man, who had just as much money as the rest of us, with this big hole in his undershirt, it made me weak. I suppose there was something mothering about it, but it felt the opposite, as if his dressing so carelessly made him strong, strong in a way that I wasn't. I've always felt I had to pay great attention to my appearance. I suppose it's insecurity. And then in lovemaking, I'd sometimes notice—is this too terrible, shall I stop?—I'd notice that his fingernails were dirty."

"Did you like that?"

"I don't know. It was just something I'd notice."

"Did you like the idea of being caressed by dirty hands?"

"They were *his* hands."

She had sat bolt upright, and his silence, having the quality of a man's pain, hurt her. She tried to make it up to him. "You mean, did I like being—what's the word, I've suppressed it—debased? But isn't that a sort of womanly thing that everybody has, a little? Do you think I have it too much?"

The man reshifted his weight in the chair and his hands moved in the air diagrammatically; a restrained agitation possessed his presence like a soft gust passing over a silver pond. "I think there are several things working here," he said. "On the one hand you have this aggressiveness toward the man—you go up to him at parties, you drag him on shopping expeditions that make him uncomfortable, you go to bed with him, you've just suggested, on your initiative rather than his."

She sat shocked. It hadn't been like that. Had it?

The man went on, running one hand through his hair so that the youthful lock, recoiling, fell farther over his forehead. "Even now, when the affair is supposedly buried, you continue to court him by wearing a dress that had a special meaning for him."

"I've explained about the dress."

"Then there is this dimension, which we keep touching on, of his crooked teeth, of his being effeminate, feeble, in tatters; of your being in comparison healthy and masterful. In the midst of an embrace you discover a hole in his undershirt. It confirms your suspicion that he is disintegrating, that you are destroying him. So that, by way of *repair* in a sense, you take him to bed."

"But he was *fine* in bed."

"At the same time you have these notions of 'womanliness.' You feel guilty at being the dynamic party; hence your rather doctrinaire slavishness, your need to observe that his fingernails are dirty. Also in this there is something of earth, of your feelings about dirt, earth, the country versus the city, the natural versus the unnatural. The city, the artificial, represents life to you; earth is death. This man, this unbuttoned, unwashed man who comes to you in the country and is out of his element shopping with you in the city, is of the earth. By conquering him, by entangling him in your clothes, you subdue your own death; more exactly, you pass through it, and become a farm girl, an earth-girl, who has survived dying. These are some of my impressions. It is along these lines, I think, that we need more work."

She felt sorry for him. There it was, he had made his little Thursday effort, and it was very pretty and clever, and used most of the strands, but it didn't hold her; she escaped. Shyly she glanced at the air conditioner and asked, "Could that be turned lower? I can hardly hear you."

He seemed surprised, rose awkwardly, and turned it off. She giggled again. "I'm just being masterful." He returned to his chair and glanced at his watch. Street noises—a bus shifting gears, a woman in heels walking rapidly—entered the room through the new silence at the window, and diluted its unreal air. "Can't earth," she asked, "mean life as much as death?"

He shrugged, displeased with himself. "In this sort of language, opposites can mean the same thing."

"If that's what I saw in him, what did he see in me?"

"I feel you fishing for a compliment."

"I'm not, I'm *not* fishing. I don't want compliments from you, I want the truth. I need help. I'm ridiculously unhappy, and I want to know why, and I don't feel you're telling me. I feel we're at cross-purposes."

"Can you elaborate on this?"

"Do you really want me to?"

He had become totally still in his chair, rigid—she brushed away the impression—as if with fright.

"Well"—she returned her eyes to the brass catch of her purse, where there was a mute focus that gave her leverage to lift herself—"when I came to you, I'd got the idea from somewhere that by this time something would have happened between us, that I, in some sort of way, perfectly controlled and safe, would have . . . fallen in love with you." She looked up for help, and saw none. She went on, in a voice that, since the silencing of the air conditioner, seemed harsh and blatant to her. "I don't feel that's happened. What's worse—I might as well say it, it's a waste of Harold's money if I keep anything back—I feel the opposite has happened. I keep getting the feeling that you've fallen in love with *me*." Now she hurried. "So I feel tender toward you, and want to protect you, and pretend not to reject you, and it gets in the way of everything. You put me into the position where a woman can't be honest, or weak, or herself. You make me be strategic, and ashamed of what I feel toward Paul, because it bothers you. There. That's the first time today either of us has dared mention his name. You're jealous. I pity you. At least, in a minute or two—I saw you look at your watch—I can go out into the street, and go buy a cheesecake or something at the bakery, and get into the car and drive through the traffic over the bridge; at least I loved somebody who loved me, no matter how silly you make the reasons for it seem. But you—I can't picture you ever getting out of this room, or getting drunk, or making love, or needing a bath, or anything. I'm sorry." She had expected, after this outburst, that she would have to cry, but she found herself staring wide-eyed at the man, whose own eyes—it must have been the watery light from the window—looked strained.

He shifted lazily in the chair and spread his hands on the

glass top of his desk. "One of the arresting things about you," he said, "is your insistence on protecting men."

"But I wasn't *like* that with *him*. I mean, I knew I was giving him something he needed, but I did feel protected. I felt like nothing when I was with him, like the—center of a circle."

"Yes." He looked at his watch, and his nostrils dilated with the beginnings of a sigh. "Well." He stood and made worried eyebrows. A little off guard, she stood a fraction of a second later. "Next Thursday?" he asked.

"I'm sure you're right," she said, turning at the door to smile; it was a big countryish smile, regretful at the edges. The white of it matched, he noticed with an interior decorator's eye, her hair, her suit, and the white of her pocketbook and her shoes. "I *am* neurotic."

She closed the door. The sigh that he had begun while she was in the room seemed to have been suspended until she had left. He was winning, it was happening; but he was weary. Alone, in a soundless psychic motion like the hemispherical protest of a bubble, he subsided into the tranquil surface of the furniture.

Harv Is Plowing Now

OUR LIVES submit to archaeology. For a period in my life which seems longer ago than it was, I lived in a farmhouse that lacked electricity and central heating. In the living room we had a fireplace and, as I remember, a kind of chocolate-colored rectangular stove whose top was a double row of slots and whose metal feet rested on a sheet of asbestos. I have not thought of this stove for years; its image seems to thrust one corner from the bottom of a trench. It was as high as a boy and heated a rectangular space of air around it; when I was sick, my parents would huddle me, in blankets, on a blue sofa next to the stove, and I would try to align myself with its margin of warmth while my fever rose and fell, transforming at its height my blanketed knees into weird, intimate mountains at whose base a bowl of broth seemed a circular lake seen from afar. The stove was fueled with what we called coal oil. I wonder now, what must have been obvious then, if coal oil and kerosene are exactly the same thing. Yes, they must be, for I remember filling the stove and the kerosene lamps from the same can, a five-gallon can with a side spout and a central cap which had to be loosened when I poured—otherwise by some trick of air pressure the can would bob and buck in my hands like an awkwardly live thing, and the spurting liquid, transparent and pungent, would spill. What was kerosene in the lamps became coal oil in the stove: so there are essential distinctions as well as existential ones. What is bread in the oven becomes Christ in the mouth.

When spring came, our attention thawed and was free to run outdoors. From where we lived not a highway, not a tower, not even a telephone pole was visible. We lived on the side of a hill, surrounded by trees and grass and clouds. Across a shallow valley where a greening meadow lay idle, another farm faced ours from a mirroring rise of land. Though the disposition of the barns and sheds was different, the houses were virtually identical—Pennsylvania sandstone farmhouses, set square to the compass and slightly tall for their breadth, as if the attic windows were straining to see over the trees. They must have been built at about the same time in the last century, and had been similarly covered, at a later date, with sandy, warm-colored stucco now crumbling away in patches. On chill April and May mornings, thin blue smoke from the chimney of the far house would seem to answer the smoke from the chimney of ours and to translate into another dimension the hissing blaze of cherry logs I had watched my father build in our fireplace.

The neighboring farm was owned and run by a mother, Carrie, and a son, Harvey. Even in her unimaginable prime Carrie could not have been much over five feet tall. Now she was so bent by sixty years of stooping labor that in conversation her face was roguishly uptwisted. She wore tight high-top shoes that put a kind of hop into all her motions, and an old-fashioned bonnet, so that in profile she frightened me with her resemblance to the first bogy of my childhood, the faceless woman on the Dutch Cleanser can, chasing herself around and around with a stick. Harvey—called, in the country way, Harv—was fat but silent-footed; his rap would rattle our door before we knew he was on the porch. There he would stand, surrounded by beagles, an uncocked shotgun drooping from his arm, while my parents vainly tried to invite him in. He preferred to talk outdoors, and his voice was faint and far, like wind caught in a bottle; when at night he hunted coons in our woods, which merged with his, the yapping of his beagles seemed to be escorting a silent spirit that traveled through the trees as resistlessly as the moon overhead traveled through the clouds.

In the spring, Harv hitched up their mule and horizontally plowed the gradual rise of land that mirrored the one where I stood. The linked silhouettes of the man and the mule moved back and forth like a slow brush repainting the parched pallor of the winter-faded land with the wet dark color of loam. It seemed to be happening *in me;* and as I age with this century, I hold within myself this memory, this image unearthed from a pastoral epoch predating my birth, this deposit lower than which there is only the mineral void.

The English excavators of Ur, as they deepened their trench through the strata of rubbish deposited by successive epochs of the Sumerian civilization, suddenly encountered a bed of perfectly clean clay, which they at first took to be the primordial silt of the delta. But measurements were taken and the clay proved too high to be the original riverbed; digging deeper, they found that after eight feet the clay stopped, yielding to soil again pregnant with flints and potsherds. But whereas Sumerian pottery had been turned on a wheel and not painted, these fragments bore traces of color and had been entirely hand-formed. In fact, the remnants were of an entirely different civilization, called "al 'Ubaid," and the eight feet of clay were the physical record of the legendary Flood survived by Noah.

My existence seems similarly stratified. At the top there is a skin of rubbish, of minutes, hours, and days, and the events and objects that occupy these days. At the bottom there is the hidden space where Harv—who since his mother died has sold the farm and married and moved to Florida—eternally plows. Between them, as thick as the distance from the grass to the clouds and no more like clay than fire is like air, interposes the dense vacancy where like an inundation the woman came and went. Let us be quite clear. She is not there. But she *was* there: proof of this may be discerned in the curious hollowness of virtually every piece of debris examined in the course of scavenging the days. While of course great caution should attend assertions about evidence so tenuous, so disjointed, and so befouled with the mud of phlegm and fatigue, each fragment seems hollow *in the same way;* and a kind of shape, or at least a tendency of motion which if we could imagine it continuing uninterrupted would produce a shape, might be hypothesized. But we will be on firmer ground simply describing the surface layer of days.

Abundantly present are small items of wearing apparel, particularly belts and shoelaces; china plates, patterned and plain; stainless-steel eating implements; small tables with one loose leg; glasses containing, like irregular jewels hurriedly stashed at the cataclysmic end of an antique queen's reign, ice cubes; children's faces, voices, and toys; newspapers; and isolated glimpses of weather, sky, towers, and vegetation. The order of occurrence is not random; generally, in the probing of each fresh stratum, a toothbrush is the first object encountered, often followed by an automobile gearshift and a ballpoint pen, or a fountain pen which is invariably dry. Contraceptive devices and phials apparently of medicine are not uncommon. Sometimes the page of a book is found involved with a bar of soap, and confusing snowstorms of cigarette filters and golf balls must be painstakingly-worked through. Care is crucial; days, though in sum their supply of rubbish seems endless, are each an integument of ghostly thinness. At Ur, in the delicate excavations of the tomb of Queen Shub-ad, a clumsy foot might crush a hidden skull, or a pick driven an inch too deep might prematurely bring to light a bit of gold ribbon, or a diadem, or a golden beech leaf more fragile than a wafer.

So, too, the days of my life threaten, even where the crust appears to be most solid, to crumble and plunge my vision into a dreadful forsaken gold. At the touch of an old hope, the wallpaper parts and reveals the lack of a wall. A lilac bush, and the woman's hair engulfs me. Guitar music drifts from a window, and I turn to see if she notices, and newly discover that she is not there: grief fills the cavern of my mouth with a taste like ancient metal, and loss like some sweeping hypothesis of ethereal physics floods the transparent volume between the grass and the clouds. Vast streets open up, stream outward, under the revelation, and the entire world, cities and trees, seems a negative imprint of her absence, a kind of tinted hollowness from which her presence might be rebuilt, as wooden artifacts, long rotted to nothing, can be re-created from the impress they have left in clay, a shadow of paint and grain more easily erased by a finger than the dusty pattern on a butterfly's wing.

Imagine a beach. At night. The usual immutable web of stars overhead. Boats anchored, lightly swapping slaps with the water, off the sand. Many people, a picnic; there is a large bonfire, lighting up faces. She is there. She, herself, is there, here. Cold with fear, under the mantle of darkness, I go up to her; restored beside my shoulder, her human smallness amazes and delights me. "How are you?"

"Fine, just fine."

"No. Really."

"Don't ask me. I'm all right. You're looking very well."

"Thank you."

The nervous glitter of her eyes, looking past my shoulder into the fire, translates into yet another dimension the fire my father had set to burning aeons ago. She looks at last at me. The fire goes out in her eyes. She asks, "Would you like some coffee?"

"I don't have a cup."

"I have a cup."

"Thank you. You're very kind." I add, touching the cup that she is touching (our fingertips don't touch), "Don't hate me."

"I don't hate you. I don't think I do."

The taste of metal follows the taste of coffee in my mouth. "I'm glad," I say. "For me, it's still bad."

"You like to think that. You enjoy suffering because you don't know what suffering is." And from the trapped quickness with which she moves her head from one side to the other, toward the fire and away, I realize that she is struggling not to cry; a towering exultation seizes me and for a moment I am again her master, riding the flood.

I protest, "I do know."

"No."

"I'm sorry you hate me," I say, to wrench a contradiction from her.

The contradiction does not come. "I don't think that's what it is," she says thoughtfully, and takes our cup from my hand, and sips as if to give her words precision. "I think it's just that I'm dead. I'm dead to you"—and with sweet firmness she pronounces my name. "Please try to understand. I expect nothing from you; it's a great relief. I'm very tired. All I want from you is to be left alone."

And I find myself saying, "Yes," as she walks away, her long hair bouncing on her back with the quick light step she has preserved, "yes," as if I am giving assent, aloof and scholarly, to the invincible facts around me: the rigid spatter of stars above, the sand that in passing accepts the print of my feet, the sea absent-mindedly tipping pale surf over the edge of darkness—ribbons of phosphorescent white that unravel again and again, always in the same direction, like a typewriter carriage.

Where am I? It has ceased to matter. I am infinitesimal, lost, invisible, nothing. I leave the fire, the company of the others, and wander beyond the farthest ring, the circumference where guitar music can still be heard. Something distant is attracting me. I look up, and the stars in their near clarity press upon my face, bear in upon my guilt and shame with the strange, liquidly strong certainty that, humanly considered, the universe is perfectly transparent:

we exist as flaws in ancient glass. And in apprehending this transparence my mind enters a sudden freedom, like insanity; the stars seem to me a roof, the roof of days from which we fall each night and survive, a miracle. I await resurrection. Archaeology is the science of the incredible. Troy and Harappa were fables until the shovel struck home.

On the beach at night, it is never totally dark or totally silent. The sea soliloquizes, the moon broods, its glitter pattering in hyphens on the water. And something else is happening, something like the aftermath of a plucked string. What? Having fallen through the void where the woman was, I still live; I move, and pause, and listen, and know. Standing on the slope of sand, I know what is happening across the meadow, on the far side of the line where water and air maintain their elemental truce. Harv is plowing now.

The Music School

My name is Alfred Schweigen and I exist in time. Last night I heard a young priest tell of a change in his Church's attitude toward the Eucharistic wafer. For generations nuns and priests, but especially (the young man said) nuns, have taught Catholic children that the wafer must be held in the mouth and allowed to melt; that to touch it with the teeth would be (and this was never doctrine, but merely a nuance of instruction) in some manner blasphemous. Now, amid the flowering of fresh and bold ideas with which the Church, like a tundra thawing, responded to that unexpected sun the late Pope John, there has sprung up the thought that Christ did not say *Take and melt this in your mouth* but *Take and eat*. The word is *eat,* and to dissolve the word is to dilute the transubstantiated metaphor of physical nourishment. This demiquaver of theology crystallizes with a beautiful simplicity in the material world; the bakeries supplying the Mass have been instructed to unlearn the science of a dough translucent to the tongue and to prepare a thicker, tougher wafer—a host, in fact, so substantial it *must* be chewed to be swallowed.

This morning I read in the newspaper that an acquaintance of mine had been murdered. The father of five children, he had been sitting at the dinner table with them, a week after Thanksgiving. A single bullet entered the window and pierced his temple; he fell to the floor and died there in minutes, at the feet of his children. My acquaintance with him was slight. He has become the only victim of murder I have known, and for such a role anyone seems drastically miscast, though in the end each life wears its events with a geological inevitability. It is impossible, today, to imagine him alive. He was a computer expert, a soft-voiced, broad-set man from Nebraska, whose intelligence,

138

concerned as it was with matters so arcane to me, had a generous quality of reserve, and gave him, in my apprehension of him, the dignity of an iceberg, which floats so serenely on its hidden mass. We met (I think only twice) in the home of a mutual friend, a professional colleague of his who is my neighbor. We spoke, as people do whose fields of knowledge are miles apart, of matters where all men are ignorant—of politics, children, and, perhaps, religion. I have the impression, at any rate, that he, as is often the case with scientists and Midwesterners, had no use for religion, and I saw in him a typical specimen of the new human species that thrives around scientific centers, in an environment of discussion groups, outdoor exercise, and cheerful husbandry. Like those vanished gentlemen whose sexual energy was exclusively spent in brothels, these men confine their cleverness to their work, which, being in one way or another for the government, is usually secret. With their sufficient incomes, large families, Volkswagen buses, hi-fi phonographs, half-remodelled Victorian homes, and harassed, ironical wives, they seem to have solved, or dismissed, the paradox of being a thinking animal and, devoid of guilt, apparently participate not in this century but in the next. If I remember him with individual clarity, it is because once I intended to write a novel about a computer programmer, and I asked him questions, which he answered agreeably. More agreeably still, he offered to show me around his laboratories any time I cared to make the hour's trip to where they were. I never wrote the novel—the moment in my life it was meant to crystallize dissolved too quickly—and I never took the trip. Indeed, I don't believe I thought of my friend once in the year between our last encounter and this morning, when my wife at breakfast put the paper before me and asked, "Don't we know him?" His pleasant face with its eyes set wide like the eyes of a bear gazed from the front page. I read that he had been murdered.

I do not understand the connection between last night and this morning, though there seems to be one. I am trying to locate it this afternoon, while sitting in a music school, waiting for my daughter to finish her piano lesson. I perceive in the two incidents a common element of nourishment, of eating transfigured by a strange irruption, and there is a parallel movement, a flight immaculately direct and elegant, from an immaterial phenomenon (an exegetical nicety, a maniac hatred) to a material one (a bulky wafer, a bullet in the temple). About the murder I feel certain, from my knowledge of the victim, that his offense was blameless, something for which he could not have felt guilt or shame. When I try to picture it, I see only numbers and Greek letters, and conclude that from my distance I have witnessed an almost unprecedented crime, a crime of unalloyed scientific passion. And there is this to add: the young priest plays a twelve-string guitar, smokes mentholated cigarettes, and seemed unembarrassed to find himself sitting socially in a circle of Protestants and nonbelievers—like my late computer friend, a man of the future.

But let me describe the music school. I love it here. It is the basement of a huge Baptist church. Golden collection plates rest on the table beside me. Girls in their first blush of adolescence, carrying fawn-colored flute cases and pallid folders of music, shuffle by me; their awkwardness is lovely, like the stance of a bather testing the sea. Boys and mothers arrive and leave. From all directions sounds—of pianos, oboes, clarinets—arrive like hints of another world, a world where angels fumble, pause, and begin again. Listening, I remember what learning music is like, how impossibly difficult and complex seem the first fingerings, the first decipherings of that unique language which freights each note with a double meaning of position and duration, a language as finicking as Latin, as laconic as Hebrew, as surprising to the eye as Persian or Chinese. How mysterious appears that calligraphy of parallel spaces, swirling clefs, superscribed ties, subscribed decrescendos, dots and sharps and flats! How great looms the gap between the first gropings of vision and the first stammerings of percussion! Vision, timidly, becomes percussion, percussion becomes music, music becomes emotion, emotion becomes—vision. Few of us have the heart to follow this circle to its end. I took lessons for years, and never learned, and last night, watching the priest's fingers confidently prance on the neck of his guitar, I was envious and incredulous. My daughter is just beginning the piano. These are her first lessons, she is eight, she is eager and hopeful. Silently she sits beside me as we drive the nine miles to the town where the lessons are given; silently she sits beside me, in the dark, as we drive home. Unlike her, she does not beg for a reward of candy or a Coke, as if the lesson itself has been a meal. She only remarks— speaking dully, in a reflex of greed she has outgrown—that the store windows are decorated for Christmas already. I love taking her, I love waiting for her, I love driving her home through the mystery of darkness toward the certainty of supper. I do this taking and driving because today my wife visits her psychiatrist. She visits a psychiatrist because I am unfaithful to her. I do not understand the connection, but there seems to be one.

In the novel I never wrote, I wanted the hero to be a computer programmer because it was the most poetic and romantic occupation I could think of, and my hero had to be extremely romantic and delicate, for he was to die of adultery. Die, I mean, of knowing it was possible; the possibility crushed him. I conceived of him, whose professional life was spent in the sanctum of the night (when, I was told, the computers, too valuable to be unemployed by industry during the day, are free, as it were, to frolic and to be loved), devising idioms whereby problems might be fed to the machines and emerge, under binomial percussion, as the music of truth—I conceived of him as being too fine, translucent, and scrupulous to live in our coarse age. He was to be, if the metaphor is biological, an evolutionary abortion, a mammalian mutation crushed underfoot by dinosaurs, and, if the metaphor is mathematical, a hypothetical ultimate, one digit beyond the last real number. The title of the book was to be "N + 1." Its first sentence went, *As Echo passed overhead, he stroked Maggy Johns' side through her big-flowered dress.* Echo is the artificial star, the first, a marvel; as the couples at a lawn party look upward at it, these two caress one another. She takes his free hand, lifts it to her lips, warmly breathes on, kisses, his knuckles. *His halted body seemed to catch up in itself the immense slow revolution of the earth, and the firm little white star, newly placed in space, calmly made its way through the older points of light, which looked shredded and faint in comparison.* From this hushed moment under the ominous sky of technological miracle, the plot was to develop more or less downhill, into a case of love, guilt, and nervous breakdown, with physiological complications (I had to do some research here) that would kill the hero as quietly as a mistake is erased from a blackboard. There was to be the hero, his wife, his love, and his doctor. In the end the wife married the doctor, and Maggy Johns would calmly continue her way through the comparatively faint . . . Stop me.

My psychiatrist wonders why I need to humiliate myself. It is the habit, I suppose, of confession. In my youth I attended a country church where, every two months, we would all confess; we kneeled on the uncarpeted floor and propped the books containing the service on the seats of the pews. It was a grave, long service, beginning, *Beloved in the Lord! Let us draw near with a true heart and confess our sins unto God, our Father.* . . . There was a kind of accompanying music in the noise of the awkward fat Germanic bodies fitting themselves, scraping and grunting, into the backwards-kneeling position. We read aloud, *But if we thus examine ourselves, we shall find nothing in us but sin and death, from which we can in no wise set ourselves free.* The confession complete, we would stand and be led, pew by pew, to the altar rail, where the young minister, a black-haired man with very small pale hands, would feed us, murmuring, *Take, eat; this is the true body of our Lord and Saviour Jesus Christ, given unto death for your sins.* The altar rail was of varnished wood, and ran around three sides, so that, standing (oddly, we did not kneel here), one could see, one could not help but see, the faces of one's fellow-communicants. We were a weathered, homely congregation, sheepish in our Sunday clothes, and the faces I saw while the wafer was held in my mouth were strained; above their closed lips their eyes held a watery look of pleading to be rescued from the depths of this mystery. And it distinctly seems, in the reaches of this memory so vivid it makes my saliva flow, that it was necessary, if not to chew, at least to touch, to embrace and tentatively shape, the wafer with the teeth.

We left refreshed. *We give thanks to thee, Almighty God, that Thou hast refreshed us through this salutary gift.* The church smelled like this school, glinting with strange whispers and varnished highlights. I am neither musical nor religious. Each moment I live, I must think where to place my fingers, and press them down with no confidence of hearing a chord. My friends are like me. We are all pilgrims, faltering toward divorce. Some get no further than mutual confession, which becomes an addiction, and exhausts them. Some move on, into violent quarrels and physical blows; and succumb to sexual excitement. A few make it to the psychiatrists. A very few get as far as the lawyers. Last evening, as the priest sat in the circle of my friends, a woman entered without knocking; she had come from the lawyers, and her eyes and hair were flung wide with suffering, as if she had come in out of a high wind. She saw our black-garbed guest, was amazed, ashamed perhaps, and took two backward steps. But then, in the hush, she regained her composure and sat down among us. And in this grace note, of the two backward steps and then again the forward movement, a coda seems to be urged.

The world is the host; it must be chewed. I am content here in this school. My daughter emerges from her lesson. Her face is fat and satisfied, refreshed, hopeful; her pleased smile, biting her lower lip, pierces my heart, and I die (I think I am dying) at her feet.

The Rescue

HELPLESSLY Caroline Harris, her husband and son having seized the first chair, found herself paired with Alice Smith. Together they were struck in the backs of their knees and hurled upward. When Caroline had been a child, her father, conceited in his strength, would toss her toward the ceiling with the same brutal, swooping lurch. Alice snapped the safety bar, and they were bracketed together. It was degrading for both of them. Up ahead, neither Norman nor Timmy deigned to glance back. From the rear, hooded and armed with spears, they were two of a kind, Timmy at twelve only slightly smaller than his father; and this, too, she felt as a desertion, a flight from her womb. While she was dragged through the air, rudely joggled at each pier, the whiteness of the snow pressed on the underside of her consciousness with the gathering insistence of a headache. Her ski boots weighted; her feet felt captive. Rigid with irritation and a desire not to sway, she smoked her next-to-last cigarette, which was cheated of taste by the cold, and tried to decide if the woman beside her were sleeping with Norman or not.

This morning, as they drove northward into New Hampshire, there had been in the automobile an excessive ease, as if the four of them knew each other better than Caroline remembered reason for. There had been, between Alice and Norman, a lack of flirtation a shade too resolute, while on sleepy, innocent Timmy the woman had inflicted a curiously fervent playfulness, as if warm messages for the father were being forwarded through the son, or as if Alice were seeking to establish herself as a sexual nonentity, a brotherly sister. Mrs. Harris felt an ominous tug in this trip. Had she merely imagined, during their fumbling breakfast at Howard Johnson's, a poignance in the pauses, and a stir of some-

144

thing, like toes touching, under the table? And was she para-
noid to have suspected a deliberate design in the pattern of
alternation that had her and her son floundering up the T-
bar together as the other two expertly skimmed down the
slope and waited, side by side, laughing vapor, at the end of
the long and devious line? Caroline was not reassured, when
they all rejoined at lunch, by Alice's smile, faintly flavored
with a sweetness unspecified in the recipe. Alice had been
her friend first. She had moved to their neighborhood a year
ago, a touching little divorcée with pre-school twins, utterly
lost. Her only interest seemed to be sports, and her marital
grief had given her an awkward hardness, as if from too
much exercise. Norman had called her pathetic and sexless.
Yet a winter later he rescued his skis from a decade in the
attic, enrolled Timmy in local lessons, and somehow guided
his wife in the same dangerous direction, as irresistibly as
this cable was pulling them skyward.

They were giddily lifted above the tops of the pines. Caroline, to brace her voice against her rising fear, spoke
aloud: "This is ridiculous. At my age women in Tahiti are
grandmothers."

Alice said seriously, "I think you do terribly well. You're
a natural dancer, and it shows."

Caroline could not hate her. She was as helpless as herself, and there was some timid loyalty, perhaps, in Norman's betraying her with a woman she had befriended. She
felt, indeed, less betrayed than diluted, and, turning with
her cigarette cupped against the wind, she squinted at the
girl as if into an unfair mirror. Alice was small-boned yet
coarse; muscularity, reaching upward through the prominent tendons of her throat, gave her face, even through the
flush of windburn, a taut, sallow tinge. Her hair, secured by
a scarlet ear warmer, was abundant but mousy, and her
eyes were close-set, hazel, and vaguely, stubbornly inward.
But between her insignificant nose and receding chin there
lay, as if in ambush, a large, complicated, and (Caroline supposed) passionate mouth. This, she realized, as the chair
swayed sickeningly, was exactly what Norman would want:
a mouse with a mouth.

Disgust, disgust and anger, swung through her. How
greedy men were! How conceited and heedless! The sky enlarged around her, as if to receive so immense a condemna-
tion. With deft haste Alice undid the safety bar; Caroline involuntarily transposed the action into an undoing of Nor-

man's clothes. Icy with contempt for her situation, she floated onto the unloading platform and discovered, slipping down the alarming little ramp, that her knees were trembling and had forgotten how to bend.

Of course, they were abandoned. The men had heedlessly gone ahead, and beckoned, tiny and black, from the end of a tunnel tigerishly striped with the shadows of birches. On whispering skis held effortlessly parallel, Alice led, while Caroline followed, struggling clumsily against the impulse to stem. They arrived where the men had been and found them gone again. In their place was a post with two signs. One pointed right to GREASED LIGHTNING (EXPERT). The other pointed left to THE LIGHTNING BUG (INTERMEDIATE-NOVICE).

"I see them," Alice said, and lightly poled off to the right.

"Wait," Caroline begged.

Alice christied to a stop. A long lavender shadow from a mass of pines covered her and for a painful instant, as her lithe body inquisitively straightened, she seemed beautiful.

"How expert is it?" The Harrises had never been to this mountain before; Alice had been several times. Caroline saw her surrounded by tan and goggled men, and perceived her own ineptitude at skiing to be a function of her failure to be divorced.

"There's one mogully piece you can sideslip," Alice said. "The Bug will take you around the other side of the mountain. You'll never catch the men."

"Why don't you follow them and I'll go down the novice trail? I don't trust this mountain yet." It was a strange mountain, one of the lesser Presidentials, rather recently developed, with an unvarnished cafeteria and very young boys patrolling the trails in rawly bright jackets chevron-striped in yellow and green. At lunch, Norman said he twice had seen members of the ski patrol take spills. His harsh laugh, remembered at this bare altitude, frightened her. The trembling in her knees would not subside, and her fingertips were stinging in their mittens.

Alice crisply sidestepped back up to her. "Let's both go down the Bug," she said. "You shouldn't ski alone."

"I don't want to be a sissy," Caroline said, and these careless words apparently triggered some inward chain of reflection in the other woman, for Alice's face clouded, and it was certain that she was sleeping with Norman. Everything, every tilt of circumstance, every smothered swell and deliberate contraindication, confirmed it, even the girl's very name, Smith—a nothing-name, a prostitute's alias. Her hazel eyes, careful in the glare of the snow, flickeringly searched Caroline's and her expressive mouth froze on the verge of a crucial question.

"Track!"

The voice was behind them, shrill and young. A teen-aged girl, wearing a polka-dot purple parka, and her mother, a woman almost elderly, who seemed to have rouged the tip of her nose, turned beside them and casually plunged over the lip of Greased Lightning.

Caroline, shamed, said, "The hell with it. The worst I can do is get killed." Murderously stabbing the snow next to Alice's noncommittal buckle-boots, she pushed off to the right, her weight flung wildly back, her uphill ski snagging, her whole body burning with the confirmation of her suspicions. She would leave Norman. Unsteady as a flame she flickered down the height, wavering in her own wind. Alice carefully passed her and, taking long traverses and diagrammatically slow turns, seemed to be inviting her not to destroy herself. Submitting to the sight, permitting her eyes to infect her body with Alice's rhythm, she found the snow yielding to her as if under the pressure of reason; and, swooping in complementary zigzags, the two women descended a long white waterfall linked as if by love.

Then there was a lazy flat run in the shadow of reddish rocks bearded with icicles, then another descent, through cataracts of moguls, into an immense elbow-shaped stage overlooking, from the height of a mile, a toy lodge, a tessellated parking lot, and, vast and dim as a foreign nation, a frozen lake mottled with cloud shadows and islands of evergreen. Tensely sideslipping, Caroline saw, on the edge of this stage, at one side of the track, some trouble, a heap of dark cloth. In her haste to be with the men, Alice would have swept by, but Caroline snowplowed to a halt. With a dancing waggle Alice swerved and pulled even. The heap of cloth was the woman with the red-tipped nose, who lay on her back, her head downhill. Her daughter knelt beside her. The woman's throat was curved as if she were gargling, and her hood was submerged in snow, so that her face showed like a face in a casket.

Efficiently, Alice bent, released her bindings, and walked to the accident. Each print of her boots in the snow was a

decisive, perfect intaglio. "Is she conscious?" she asked. "It's
the left," the casket-face said, not altering its rapt relation
with the sky. The dab of red was the only color not drained
from it. Tears trickled from the corner of one eye into a
fringe of sandy permed hair.

"Do you think it's broken?"

There was no answer, and the girl impatiently prompted,
"Mother, does it feel broken?"

"I can't feel a thing. Take off the boot."

"I don't think we should take off the boot," Alice said.
She surveyed the woman's legs with a physical forthright-
ness that struck Caroline as unpleasant. "We might disturb
the alignment. It might be a spiral. Did you feel anything
give?" The impact of the spill had popped both safety bindings, so the woman's skis were attached to her feet only by
the breakaway straps. Alice stopped and unclipped these,
and stood the skis upright in the snow, as a signal. She said,
"We should get help."

The daughter looked up hopefully. The face inside her
polka-dot parka was round and young, and a secondary
face, the angular face of a woman, had been stencilled over
its features. "If you're willing to stay," she said, "I'll go. I
know some of the boys in the patrol."

"We'll be happy to stay," Caroline said firmly. She was
conscious as she said this, of frustrating Alice and of declar-
ing, in the necessary war between them, her weapons to be
compassion and patience. She wished she could remove her
skis, for their presence on her feet held her a little aloof;
but she was not sure she could put them back on at this
slant, in the middle of nowhere. The snow here had the
eerie unvisited air of grass beside a highway. The young
daughter, without a backward glance, snapped herself into
her skis and whipped away, down the hill. Seeing how easy
it had been, Caroline dared unfasten hers and discovered
her own bootprints also to be sharp intaglios. Alice tugged
back her parka sleeve and frowned at her wristwatch. The
third woman moaned.

Caroline asked, "Are you warm enough? Would you like
to be wrapped in something?" The lack of a denial left
them no choice but to remove their parkas and wrap her in
them. Her body felt like an oversized doll sadly in need of
stuffing. Caroline, bending close, satisfied herself that what
looked like paint was a little pinnacle of sunburn.

The woman murmured her thanks. "My second day here, I've ruined it for everybody—my daughter, my son . . ."

Alice asked, "Where is your son?"

"Who knows? I bring him here and don't see him from morning to night. He says he is skiing, but I ski every trail and never see him."

"Where is your husband?" Caroline asked; her voice sounded lost in the acoustic depth of the freezing air.

The woman sighed, "Not here."

Silence followed, a silence in which wisps of wind began to decorate the snow-laden branches of pines with outflowing feathers of powder. The dense indigo shadow thrown by the woods grew heavy, and the cold pressed through the chinks of Caroline's sweater. Alice's thin neck strained as she gazed up at the vacant ridge for help. The woman in the snow began, tricklingly, to sob, and Caroline asked, "Would you like a cigarette?"

The response was prompt. "I'd adore a weed." The woman sat up, pulled off her mitten, and hungrily twiddled her fingers. Her nails were painted. She did not seem to notice, in taking the cigarette, that the pack became empty. Gesturing with stabbing exhalations of smoke, she waxed chatty. "I say to my son, 'What's the point of coming to these beautiful mountains if all you do is rush, rush, rush, up the tow and down, and never stop to enjoy the scenery?' I say to him, 'I'd rather be old-fashioned and come down the mountain in one piece than have my neck broken at the age of fourteen.' If he saw me now, he'd have a fit laughing. There's a patch of ice up there and my skis crossed. When I went over, I could feel my left side pull from my shoulders to my toes. It reminded me like having a baby."

"Where are you from?" Alice asked.

"Melrose." The name of her town seemed to make the woman morose. Her eyes focused on her inert boot.

To distract her, Caroline asked, "And your husband's working?"

"We're separated. I know if I could loosen the laces it would be a world of relief. My ankle wants to swell and it can't."

"I wouldn't trust it," Alice said.

"Let me at least undo the knot," Caroline offered, and dropped to her knees as if to weep. She did not as a rule like self-pitying women, but here in this one she seemed to confront a voluntary dramatization of her own inner sprain.

She freed the knots of both the outer and inner laces—the boot was a new Nordica, and stiff. "Does that feel better?"

"I honestly can't say. I have no feeling below my knees whatsoever."

"Shock," Alice said. "Nature's anesthetic."

"My husband will be furious. He'll have to hire a maid for me."

"You'll have your daughter," Caroline said.

"At her age, it's all boys, boys on the brain."

This seemed to sum up their universe of misfortune. Nothing was left to say. In silence, as dark as widows against the tilted acres of white, they waited for rescue. The trail here was so wide skiers could pass on the far side without spotting them. A few swooped close, then veered away, as if sensing a curse. One man, a merry ogre wearing steel-framed spectacles and a raccoon coat, smoking a cigar, and plowing down the fall line with a shameless sprawling stem, shouted to them in what seemed a foreign language. But the pattern of the afternoon—the sun had shifted away from the trail—yielded few skiers. Empty minutes slid by. The bitterly cold air had found every loose stitch in Caroline's sweater and now was concentrating on the metal bits of brassiere that touched her skin. She remembered how erotic her husband had pretended to find her when, dressing this morning, she had put on her Norwegian waffle-weave undershirt. "Could I bum another coffin nail?" the injured woman asked.

"I'm sorry, that was my last."

"Oh dear. Isn't that the limit?"

Alice, so sallow now she seemed Oriental, tucked her hands into her armpits and jiggled up and down. She asked, "Won't the men worry?"

Caroline took satisfaction in telling her, "I doubt it." Looking outward, she saw only white, a tilted rippled wealth of colorlessness, the forsaken penumbra of the world. Her private desolation she now felt in communion with the other two women; they were all three abandoned, cut off, wounded, unwarmed, too impotent even to whimper. A vein of haze in the sky passingly dimmed the sunlight. When it brightened again, a tiny upright figure, male, in green and yellow chevron-stripes, stood at the top of the cataracts of moguls.

"That took eighteen minutes," Alice said, consulting her wristwatch again. Caroline suddenly doubted that Norman, whose pajama bottoms rarely matched his tops, could love anyone so finicking.

The woman in the snow asked, "Does my hair look awful?"

Down, down the tiny figure came, enlarging, dipping from crest to crest, dragging a sled, a bit clumsily, between its legs. Then, hitting perhaps the same patch of ice, the figure tipped, tripped, and became a dark star, spread-eagled, a cloud of powder from which protruded, with electric rapidity, fragments of ski, sled, and arm. This explosive somersault continued to the base of the precipitous section, where the fragments reassembled and lay still. The women had watched with held breaths. The woman from Melrose moaned, "Oh dear, dear God." Caroline discovered herself yearning, yearning with her numb belly, for their rescuer to stand. He did. The boy (he was close enough to be a boy, with lanky legs in swankishly tight racing pants) scissored his skis above his head (miraculously, they had not popped off), hopped to his feet, jerkily sidestepped a few yards uphill to retrieve his hat (an Alpine of green felt, with ornamental breast feathers), and skated toward them, drenched with snow, dragging the sled and grinning.

"That was a real eggbeater," Alice told him, as one boy to another.

"Who's hurt?" he asked. His red ears protruded and his face swirled with freckles, he was so plainly delighted to be himself, so clearly somebody's son, that Caroline felt herself forced to share his absurd pride.

And as if with this clown there entered into vacuity a fertilizing principle, more members of the ski patrol sprang from the snow, bearing blankets and bandages and brandy, so that Caroline and Alice were pushed aside, as it were, from themselves. They retrieved their parkas, refastened their skis, and tamely completed their run to the foot of the mountain. There, Timmy and Norman, looking worried and guilty, were waiting beside the lift shed. Her momentum failing, Caroline Harris actually skated—what she had never managed to do before, lifted her skis in the smooth alternation of skating—in her haste to assure her husband of his innocence.

The Dark

THE DARK, he discovered, was mottled: was a luminous collage of patches of almost-color that became, as his open eyes grew at home, almost ectoplasmically bright. Objects became lunar panels let into the air that darkness had given flat substance to. Walls dull in day glowed. Yet he was not comforted by the general pallor of the dark, its unexpected transparence; rather, he lay there waiting, godlessly praying, for those vistations of positive light that was hurled, unannounced, through the windows by the headlights of automobiles pausing and passing outside. Some were slits, erect as sentinels standing guard before beginning to slide, helplessly, across a corner, diagonally warping, up onto the ceiling, accelerating, and away. Others were yellowish rectangles, scored with panes, windows themselves, but watery, streaked, the mullions dissolved, as if the apparition silently posed on a blank interior wall were being in some manner lashed from without by a golden hurricane.

He wondered if all these visitations were caused by automobiles; for some of them appeared and disappeared without any accompaniment of motor noises below, and others seemed projected from an angle much higher than that of the street. Perhaps the upstairs lamps in neighboring homes penetrated the atmosphere within his bedroom. But it was a quiet neighborhood, and he imagined himself to be, night after night, the last person awake. Yet it was a rare hour, even from two o'clock on, when the darkness in which he lay was untouched; sooner or later, with a stroking motion like a finger passing across velvet, there would occur one of those intrusions of light which his heart would greet with wild grateful beating, for he had come to see in them his only companions, guards, and redeemers.

Sounds served in a much paler way—the diminishing drone

of an unseen car vanishing at a point his mind's eye located beyond the Baptist church; the snatched breath and renewed surge of a truck shifting gears on the hill; the pained squeak, chuffing shuffle, and comic toot of a late commuting train clumsily threading the same old rusty needle; the high vibration of an airplane like a piece of fuzz caught in the sky's throat. These evidences of a universe of activity and life extending beyond him did not bring the same liberating assurance as those glowing rectangles delivered like letters through the slots in his room. The stir, whimper, or cough coming from the bedroom of one or another of his children had a contrary effect, of his consciousness touching a boundary, an abrasive rim. And in the breathing of his wife beside him a tight limit seemed reached. The blind, moist motor of her oblivious breathing seemed to follow the track of a circular running of which he was the vortex, sinking lower and lower in the wrinkled bed until he was lifted to another plane by the appearance, long delayed, on his walls of an angel, linear and serene, of light stolen from another world. While waiting, he discovered the dark to be green in color, a green so low-keyed that only eyes made supernaturally alert could have sensed it, a thoroughly dirtied green in which he managed to detect, under opaque integuments of ambiguity, a general pledge of hope. Specific hope he had long given up. It seemed a childhood ago when he had moved, a grown man, through a life of large rooms, with white-painted moldings and blowing curtains, whose walls each gave abundantly, in the form of open doorways and flung back French windows, into other rooms—a mansion without visible end. In one of the rooms he had been stricken with a pang of unease. Still king of space, he had moved to dismiss the unease and the door handle had rattled, stuck. The curtains had stopped blowing. Behind him, the sashes and archways sealed. Still, it was merely a question of holding one's breath and finding a key. If the door was accidentally locked—had locked itself—there was certainly a key. For a lock without a key is a monstrosity, and while he knew, in a remote way, that monstrosities exist, he also knew there were many more rooms; he had glimpsed them waiting with their white-painted and polished corners, their invisible breeze of light. Doctors airily agreed, but then their expressions fled one way—cherubic, smiling— while their words fled another, and became unutterable, leaving him facing the blankness where the division had occurred. He tapped his pockets. They were empty. He stooped to pick the lock with his fingernails, and it shrank from his touch, became a formless bump, a bubble, and sank into the wood. The door became a smooth and solid wall. There was nothing left for him but to hope that the impenetrability of walls was in some sense an illusion. His nightly vigil investigated this possibility. His discoveries, of the varied texture of the dark, its relenting phosphorescence, above all its hospitality to vivid and benign incursions of light, seemed at moments to confirm his hope. At other moments, by other lights, his vigil seemed an absurd toy supplied by cowardice to entertain his last months.

He had months and not years to live. This was the fact. By measuring with his mind (which seemed to hover in fear some distance from his brain) the intensity of certain sensations obliquely received, he could locate, by a kind of triangulation, his symptoms in space: a patch of strangeness beneath the left rib, an inflexible limitation in his lungs, a sickly-sweet languor in his ankles, which his mind's eye located just this side of the town wharf. But space interested him only as the silver on the back of the mirror of time. It was in time, that utterly polished surface, that he searched for his reflection, which was black as a Negro's, only thin-lipped and otherwise familiar. He wondered why the difference between months and years should be qualitative when mere quantities were concerned, and his struggle to make "month" a variant of "year" reminded him of, from his deepest past, his efforts to remove a shoehorn from between his heel and shoe, where with childish clumsiness he had wedged it. How impossibly tight the fit had seemed! How feeble and small he must have been!

He did not much revisit the past. His inner space, the space of his mind, seemed as irrelevant as the space of his body. His father's hands, his mother's tears, his sister's voice shrilling across an itchy lawn, the rolls of dust beneath his bed that might, just might, be poisonous caterpillars—these glints only frightened him with the depth of the darkness in which they were all but smothered. Everything in his life had been ordinary except its termination. His "life." Considered as a finite noun, his life seemed unequal to the infinitude of death. The inequality almost made a ledge where his hope could grip; but the leaden sighing of his wife's sagging mouth dragged it down. Faithlessly she lay beside him in the arms of her survival. Her unheeding sleep deserved only dull anger and was not dreadful like the sleep of his children, whose dream-sprung coughs and cries seemed to line the mouth of death with teeth. The sudden shortness of his life seemed to testify to the greed of those he had loved. He should have been shocked by his indifference to them; should have grubbed the root of this coldness from his brain, but introspection, like memory, sickened him with its steep perspectives, afflicted him with the nausea of futile concentration, as if he were picking a melting lock. He was not interested in his brain but in his soul, his soul, that outward simplicity embodied in the shards and diagonal panes of light that wheeled around his room when a car smoothly passed in the street below.

From three o'clock on, the traffic was thin. As if his isolation had turned him into God, he blessed, with stately wordlessness, whatever errant teen-ager or returning philanderer relieved the stillness of the town. Then, toward four, all such visits ceased. There was a quietness. Unwanted images began to impinge on the dark: a pulpy many-legged spider was offered wriggling to him on a fork. His teeth ached to think of biting, of chewing, eyes, fur . . .

It was time to imagine the hand.

He, who since infancy had slept best on his stomach, could now endure lying only on his back. He wished his lids, even if they were closed, to be pelted and bathed by whatever eddies of light animated the room. As these eddies died, and the erosion of sleeplessness began to carve his consciousness fantastically, he had taken to conceiving of himself as lying in a giant hand, his head on the fingertips and his legs in the crease of the palm, He did not picture the hand with total clarity, denied it nails and hair, and with idle rationality supposed it was an echo from Sunday school, some old-fashioned print; nevertheless, the hand was so real to him that he would stealthily double his pillow to lift his head higher and thereby fit himself better to the curve of the great fingers. The hand seemed to hold him at some height, but he had no fear of falling nor any sense of display, of being gazed at, as a mother gazes at the baby secure in her arms. Rather, this hand seemed something owed him, a basis upon which had been drawn the contract of his conception, and it had the same extensive, impersonal life as the pieces of light that had populated, before the town went utterly still, the walls of his room. Now the phosphor of these walls took on a blueness, as if the yellowness of the green tinge of the darkness were being distilled from it. Still safe in the hand, he dared turn, with cunning gradualness, and lie on his side and touch with his knees the underside of his wife's thighs, which her bunched nightie had bared. Her intermittently restless sleep usually resolved into a fetal position facing away from him; and in a parallel position—ready at any nauseous influx of terror to return to his back—he delicately settled himself, keeping the soft touch of her flesh at his knees as a mooring. His eyes had closed. Experimentally he opened them, and a kind of gnashing, a blatancy, at the leafy window, which he now faced, led him to close them again. A rusty brown creaking, comfortable and antique, passed along his body, merging with the bird song that had commenced beyond the window like the melodious friction of a machine of green and squeaking wood.

He smiled at himself, having for an instant imagined that he was adjusting his stiff arms around a massive thumb beside his face.

Comfort ebbed from the position; his wife irritably stirred and broke the mooring. Carefully, as gingerly as if his body were an assemblage of components any one of which might deflect his parabolic course, he moved to lie on his stomach, pressing himself on the darkness beneath him, as if in wrestling, upon some weary foe.

Panic jerked his dry lids open. He looked backward, past his shoulder, at the pattern of patches that had kept watch with him. A chair, with clothes tossed upon it, had begun to be a chair, distinctly forward from the wall. The air, he saw, was being visited by another invader, a creature unlike the others, entering not obliquely but frontally, upright, methodically, less by stealth than like someone hired, like a fine powder very slowly exploding, scouring the white walls of their moss of illusion, polishing objects into islands. He felt in this arrival relief from his vigil and knew, his chest loosening rapidly, that in a finite time he would trickle through the fingers of the hand; would slip, blissfully, into oblivion, as a fold is smoothed from a width of black silk.

The Bulgarian Poetess

"YOUR POEMS. Are they difficult?"

She smiled and, unaccustomed to speaking English, answered carefully, drawing a line in the air with two delicately pinched fingers holding an imaginary pen. "They are difficult—to write."

He laughed, startled and charmed. "But not to read?"

She seemed puzzled by his laugh, but did not withdraw her smile, though its corners deepened in a defensive, feminine way. "I think," she said, "not so very."

"Good." Brainlessly he repeated "Good," disarmed by her unexpected quality of truth. He was, himself, a writer, this fortyish young man, Henry Bech, with his thinning curly hair and melancholy Jewish nose, the author of one good book and three others, the good one having come first. By a kind of oversight, he had never married. His reputation had grown while his powers declined. As he felt himself sink, in his fiction, deeper and deeper into eclectic sexuality and bravura narcissism, as his search for plain truth carried him further and further into treacherous realms of fantasy and, lately, of silence, he was more and more thickly hounded by homage, by flat-footed exegetes, by arrogantly worshipful undergraduates who had hitchhiked a thousand miles to touch his hand, by querulous translators, by election to honorary societies, by invitations to lecture, to "speak," to "read," to participate in symposia trumped up by ambitious girlie magazines in shameless conjunction with venerable universities. His very government, in airily unstamped envelopes from Washington, invited him to travel, as an ambassador of the arts, to the other half of the world, the hostile, mysterious half. Rather automatically, but with some faint hope of shaking himself loose from the burden of himself, he consented, and found himself floating,

157

with a passport so stapled with visas it fluttered when pulled from his pocket, down into the dim airports of Communist cities.

He arrived in Sofia the day after a mixture of Bulgarian and African students had smashed the windows of the American legation and ignited an overturned Chevrolet. The cultural officer, pale from a sleepless night of guard duty, tamping his pipe with trembling fingers, advised Bech to stay out of crowds and escorted him to his hotel. The lobby was swarming with Negroes in black wool fezzes and pointed European shoes. Insecurely disguised, he felt, by an astrakhan hat purchased in Moscow, Bech passed through to the elevator, whose operator addressed him in German. "*Ja, vier,*" Bech answered, "*danke,*" and telephoned, in his bad French, for dinner to be brought up to his room. He remained there all night, behind a locked door, reading Hawthorne. He had lifted a paperback collection of short stories from a legation window sill littered with broken glass. A few curved bright crumbs fell from between the pages onto his blanket. The image of Roger Malvin lying alone, dying, in the forest—"Death would come like the slow apprach of a corpse, stealing gradually towards him through the forest, and showing its ghastly and motionless features from behind a nearer and yet a nearer tree"— frightened him. Bech fell asleep early and suffered from swollen, homesick dreams. It had been Thanksgiving Day.

In the morning, venturing downstairs for breakfast, he was surprised to find the restaurant open, the waiters affable, the eggs actual, the coffee hot, though syrupy. Outside, Sofia was sunny and (except for a few dark glances at his big American shoes) amenable to his passage along the streets. Lozenge-patterns of pansies, looking flat and brittle as pressed flowers, had been set in the public beds. Women with a touch of Western chic walked hatless in the park behind the mausoleum of Georgi Dimitrov. There was a mosque, and an assortment of trolley cars salvaged from the remotest corner of Bech's childhood, and a tree that talked— that is, it was so full of birds that it swayed under their weight and emitted volumes of chirping sound like a great leafy loudspeaker. It was the inverse of his hotel, whose silent walls presumably contained listening microphones. Electricity was somewhat enchanted in the Socialist world. Lights flickered off untouched and radios turned themselves on. Telephones rang in the dead of the night and breathed wordlessly in his ear. Six weeks ago, flying from New York City, Bech had expected Moscow to be a blazing counterpart and instead saw, through the plane window, a skein of hoarded lights no brighter, on that vast black plain, than a girl's body in a dark room.

Past the talking tree was the American legation. The sidewalk, heaped with broken glass, was roped off, so that pedestrians had to detour into the gutter. Bech detached himself from the stream, crossed the little barren of pavement, smiled at the Bulgarian militiamen who were sullenly guarding the jewel-bright heaps of shards, and pulled open the bronze door. The cultural officer was crisper after a normal night's sleep. He clenched his pipe in his teeth and handed Bech a small list. "You're to meet with the Writer's Union at eleven. These are writers you might ask to see. As far as we can tell, they're among the more progressive."

Words like "progressive" and "liberal" had a somewhat reversed sense in this world. At times, indeed, Bech felt he had passed through a mirror, a dingy flecked mirror that reflected feebly the capitalist world; in its dim depths everything was similar but left-handed. One of the names ended in "-ova." Bech said, "A woman."

"A poetess," the cultural officer said, sucking and tamping in a fury of bogus efficiency. "Very popular, apparently. Her books are impossible to buy."

"Have you read anything by these people?"

"I'll be frank with you. I can just about make my way through a newspaper."

"But you always know what a newspaper will say anyway."

"I'm sorry, I don't get your meaning."

"There isn't any." Bech didn't quite know why the Americans he met irritated him—whether because they garishly refused to blend into this shadow-world or because they were always so solemnly sending him on ridiculous errands.

At the Writer's Union, he handed the secretary the list as it had been handed to him, on U.S. legation stationery. The secretary, a large stooped man with the hands of a stonemason, grimaced and shook his head but obligingly reached for the telephone. Bech's meeting was already waiting in another room. It was the usual one, the one that, with small differences, he had already attended in Moscow and Kiev, Yerevan and Alma-Ata, Bucharest and Prague: the polished oval table, the bowl of fruit, the morning light, the gleaming glasses of brandy and mineral water, the lurking portrait of Lenin, the six or eight patiently sitting men who would leap to their feet with quick blank smiles. These men would include a few literary officials, termed "critics," high in the Party, loquacious and witty and destined to propose a toast to international understanding; a few selected novelists and poets, mustachioed, smoking, sulking at this invasion of their time; a university professor, the head of the Anglo-American Literature department, speaking in a beautiful withered English of Mark Twain and Sinclair Lewis; a young interpreter with a moist handshake; a shaggy old journalist obsequiously scribbling notes; and, on the rim of the group, in chairs placed to suggest that they had invited themselves, one or two gentlemen of ill-defined status, fidgety and tieless, maverick translators who would turn out to be the only ones present who had ever read a word by Henry Bech.

Here this type was represented by a stout man in a tweed coat leather-patched at the elbows in the British style. The whites of his eyes were distinctly red. He shook Bech's hand eagerly, made of it almost an embrace of reunion, bending his face so close that Bech could distinguish the smells of tobacco, garlic, cheese, and alcohol. Even as they were seating themselves around the table, and the Writer's Union chairman, a man elegantly bald, with very pale eyelashes, was touching his brandy glass as if to lift it, this anxious red-eyed interloper blurted at Bech, "Your *Travel Light* was so marvellous a book. The motels, the highways, the young girls with their lovers who were motorcyclists, so marvellous, so American, the youth, the adoration for space and speed, the barbarity of the advertisements in neon lighting, the very poetry. It takes us truly into another dimension."

Travel Light was the first novel, the famous one. Bech disliked discussing it. "At home," he said, "it was criticized as despairing."

The man's hands, stained orange with tobacco, lifted in amazement and plopped noisily to his knees. "No, no a thousand times. Truth, wonder, terror even, vulgarity, yes. But despair, no, not at all, not one iota. Your critics are dead wrong."

"Thank you."

The chairman softly cleared his throat and lifted his glass

an inch from the table, so that it formed with its reflection a kind of playing card.

Bech's admirer excitedly persisted. "You are not a *wet* writer, no. You are a dry writer, yes? You have the expressions, am I wrong in English, dry, hard?"

"More or less."

"I want to translate you!"

It was the agonized cry of a condemned man, for the chairman coldly lifted his glass to the height of his eyes, and like a firing squad the others followed suit. Blinking his white lashes, the chairman gazed mistily in the direction of the sudden silence, and spoke in Bulgarian.

The young interpreter murmured in Bech's ear. "I wish to propose now, ah, a very brief toast. I know it will seem doubly brief to our honored American guest, who has so recently enjoyed the, ah, hospitality of our Soviet comrades." There must have been a joke here, for the rest of the table laughed. "But in seriousness permit me to say that in our country we have seen in years past too few Americans, ah, of Mr. Bech's progressive and sympathetic stripe. We hope in the next hour to learn from him much that is interesting and, ah, socially useful about the literature of his large country, and perhaps we may in turn inform him of our own proud literature, of which perhaps he knows regrettably little. Ah, so let me finally, then, since there is a saying that too long a courtship spoils the marriage, offer to drink, in our native plum brandy *slivovica,* ah, firstly to the success of his visit and, in the second place, to the mutual increase of international understanding."

"Thank you" Bech said and, as a courtesy, drained his glass. It was wrong; the others, having merely sipped, stared. The purple burning revolved in Bech's stomach and a severe distaste for himself, for his role, for this entire artificial and futile process, focused into a small brown spot on a pear in the bowl so shiningly posed before his eyes.

The red-eyed fool smelling of cheese was ornamenting the toast. "It is a personal honor for me to meet the man who, in *Travel Light,* truly added a new dimension to American prose."

"The book was written," Bech said, "twelve years ago."

"And since?" A slumping, mustached man sat up and sprang into English. "Since, you have written what?"

Bech had been asked that question often in these weeks and his answer had grown curt. "A second novel called

Brother Pig, which is St. Bernard's expression for the body."

"Good. Yes, and?"

"A collection of essays and sketches called *When the Saints.*"

"I like the title less well."

"It's the beginning of a famous Negro song."

"We know the song," another man said, a smaller man, with the tense, dented mouth of a hare. He lightly sang, "Lordy, I just want to be in that number."

"And the last book," Bech said, "was a long novel called *The Chosen* that took six years to write and that nobody liked."

"I have read reviews," the red-eyed man said. "I have not read the book. Copies are difficult here."

"I'll give you one," Bech said.

The promise seemed, somehow, to make the recipient unfortunately conspicuous; wringing his stained hands, he appeared to swell in size, to intrude grotesquely upon the inner ring, so that the interpreter took it upon himself to whisper, with the haste of an apology, into Bech's ear, "This gentleman is well known as the translator into our language of *Erewhon.*"

"A marvellous book," the translator said, deflating in relief, pulling at his pockets for a cigarette. "It truly takes us into another dimension. Something that must be done. We live in a new cosmos."

The chairman spoke in Bulgarian, musically, at length. There was polite laughter. Nobody translated for Bech. The professorial type, his hair like a flaxen toupee, jerked forward. "Tell me, is it true, as I have read"—his phrases whistled slightly, like rusty machinery—"that the stock of Sinclair Lewis has plummeted under the Salinger wave?"

And so it went, here as in Kiev, Prague, and Alma-Ata, the same questions, more or less predictable, and his own answers, terribly familiar to him by now, mechanical, stale, irrelevant, untrue, claustrophobic. The door opened. In came, with the rosy air of a woman fresh from a bath, a little breathless, having hurried, hatless, a woman in a blond coat, her hair also blond. The secretary, entering behind her, seemed to make a cherishing space around her with his large curved hands. He introduced her to Bech as Vera Something-ova, the poetess he had asked to meet. None of the others on the list, he explained, answered their telephones.

"Aren't you kind to come?" As Bech asked it, it was a genuine question, to which he expected some sort of an answer.

She spoke to the interpreter in Bulgarian. "She says," the interpreter told Bech, "she is sorry she is so late."

"But she was just called!" In the warmth of his confusion and pleasure Bech turned to speak directly to her, forgetting he would not be understood. "I'm terribly sorry to have interrupted your morning."

"I am pleased," she said, "to meet you. I heard of you spoken in France."

"You speak English!"

"No. Very little amount."

"But you *do*."

A chair was brought for her from a corner of the room. She yielded her coat, revealing herself in a suit also blond, as if her clothes were an aspect of a total consistency. She sat down opposite Bech, crossing her legs. Her legs were very good; her face was perceptibly broad. Lowering her lids, she tugged her skirt to the curve of her knee. It was his sense of her having hurried, hurried to him, and of being, still, graciously flustered, that most touched him.

He spoke to her very clearly, across the fruit, fearful of abusing and breaking the fragile bridge of her English. "You are a poetess. When I was young, I also wrote poems."

She was silent so long he thought she would never answer; but then she smiled and pronounced, "You are not old now."

"Your poems. Are they difficult?"

"They are difficult—to write."

"But not to read?"

"I think—not so very."

"Good. Good."

Despite the decay of his career, Bech had retained an absolute faith in his instincts; he never doubted that somewhere an ideal course was open to him and that his intuitions were pre-dealt clues to his destiny. He had loved, briefly or long, with or without consummation, perhaps a dozen women; yet all of them, he now saw, shared the trait of approximation, of narrowly missing an undisclosed prototype. The surprise he felt did not have to do with the appearance, at least, of this central woman; he had always expected her to appear. What he had not expected was her appearance here, in this remote and abused nation, in this room of morning light, where he discovered a small knife in his fingers and on the table before him, golden and moist, a precisely divided pear.

Men travelling alone develop a romantic vertigo. Bech had already fallen in love with a freckled Embassy wife in Prague, a buck-toothed chanteuse in Rumania, a stolid Mongolian sculptress in Kazakhstan. In the Tretyakov Gallery he had fallen in love with a recumbent statue, and at the Moscow Ballet School with an entire roomful of girls. Entering the room, he had been struck by the aroma, tenderly acrid, of young female sweat. Sixteen and seventeen, wearing patchy practice suits, the girls were twirling so strenuously their slippers were unravelling. Demure student faces crowned the unconscious insolence of their bodies. The room was doubled in depth by a floor-to-ceiling mirror. Bech was seated on a bench at its base. Staring above his head, each girl watched herself with frowning eyes frozen, for an instant in the turn, by the imperious delay and snap of her head. Bech tried to remember the lines of Rilke that expressed it, this snap and delay: *did not the drawing remain/ that the dark stoke of your eyebrow/ swiftly wrote on the wall of its own turning?* At one point the teacher, a shapeless old Ukrainian lady with gold canines, a *prima* of the thirties, had arisen and cried something translated to Bech as, "No, no, the arms free, *free!*" And in demonstration she had executed a rapid series of pirouettes with such proud effortlessness that all the girls, standing this way and that like deer along the wall, had applauded. Bech had loved them for that. In all his loves, there was an urge to rescue—to rescue the girls from the slavery of their exertions, the statue from the cold grip of its own marble, the Embassy wife from her boring and unctuous husband, the chanteuse from her nightly humiliation (she could not sing), the Mongolian from her stolid race. But the Bulgarian poetess presented herself to him as needing nothing, as being complete, poised, satisfied, achieved. He was aroused and curious and, the next day, inquired about her of the man with the vaguely contemptuous mouth of a hare—a novelist turned playwright and scenarist, who accompanied him to the Rila Monastery. "She lives to write," the play-wright said. "I do not think it is healthy."

Bech said, "But she seems so healthy." They stood beside a small church with whitewashed walls. From the outside it looked like a hovel, a shelter for pigs or chickens. For five centuries the Turks had ruled Bulgaria, and the Christian churches, however richly adorned within, had humble exteriors. A peasant woman with wildly snarled hair unlocked the door for them. Though the church could hardly ever have held more than thirty worshippers, it was divided into three parts, and every inch of wall was covered with eighteenth-century frescoes. Those in the narthex depicted a Hell where the devils wielded scimitars. Passing through the tiny nave, Bech peeked through the iconostasis into the screened area that, in the symbolism of Orthodox architecture, represented the next, the hidden world—Paradise—and glimpsed a row of books, an easy chair, a pair of ancient oval spectacles. Outdoors again, he felt released from the unpleasantly tight atmosphere of a children's book. They were on the side of a hill. Above them was a stand of pines whose trunks glistened with ice. Below them sprawled the monastery, a citadel of Bulgarian national feeling during the years of the Turkish Yoke. The last monks had been moved out in 1961. An aimless soft rain was falling in these mountains, and there were not many German tourists today. Across the valley, whose little silver river still turned a water wheel, a motionless white horse stood silhouetted against a green meadow, pinnned there like a brooch.

"I am an old friend of hers," the playwright said. "I worry about her."

"Are the poems good?"

"It is difficult for me to judge. They are very feminine. Perhaps shallow."

"Shallowness can be a kind of honesty."

"Yes. She is very honest in her work."

"And in her life?"

"As well."

"What does her husband do?"

The other man looked at him with parted lips and touched his arm, a strange Slavic gesture, communicating an underlying racial urgency, that Bech no longer shied from. "But she has no husband. As I say, she is too much for poetry to have married."

"But her name ends in '-ova.' "

"I see. You are mistaken. It is not a matter of marriage; I am Petrov, my unmarried sister is Petrova. All females."

"How stupid of me. But I think it's such a pity, she's so charming."

"In America, only the uncharming fail to marry?"

"Yes, you must be very uncharming not to marry."

"It is not so here. The government indeed is alarmed; our birth rate is one of the lowest in Europe. It is a problem for economists."

Bech gestured at the monastery. "Too many monks?"

"Not enough, perhaps. With too few of monks, something of the monk enters everybody."

The peasant woman, who seemed old to Bech but who was probably younger than he, saw them to the edge of her domain. She huskily chattered in what Petrov said was very amusing rural slang. Behind her, now hiding in her skirts and now darting away, was her child, a boy not more than three. He was faithfully chased, back and forth, by a small white pig, who moved, as pigs do, on tiptoe, with remarkably abrupt changes of direction. Something in the scene, in the open glee of the woman's parting smile and the unselfconscious way her hair thrust out from her head, something in the mountain mist and spongy rutted turf into which frost had begun to break at night, evoked for Bech a nameless absence to which was attached, like a horse to a meadow, the image of the poetess, with her broad face, her good legs, her Parisian clothes, and her sleekly brushed hair. Petrov, in whom he was beginning to sense, through the wraps of foreignness, a clever and kindred mind, seemed to have overheard his thoughts, for he said. "If you would like, we could have dinner. It would be easy for me to arrange."

"With her?"

"Yes, she is my friend, she would be glad."

"But I have nothing to say to her. I'm just curious about such an intense conjunction of good looks and brains. I mean, what does a soul do with it all?"

"You may ask her. Tomorrow night?"

"I'm sorry, I can't. I'm scheduled to go to the ballet, and the next night the legation is giving a cocktail party for me, and then I fly home."

"Home? So soon?"

"It does not feel soon to me. I must try to work again."

"A drink, then. Tomorrow evening before the ballet? It is possible? It is not possible."

Petrov looked puzzled, and Bech realized it was his fault, for he was nodding to say Yes, but in Bulgaria nodding meant No, and a shake of the head meant Yes. "Yes," he said. "Gladly."

The ballet was entitled *Silver Slippers*. As Bech watched it, the word "ethnic" kept coming to his mind. He had grown accustomed, during his trip, to this sort of artistic evasion, the retreat from the difficult and disappointing present into folk dance, folk tale, folk song, with always the implication that, beneath the embroidered peasant costume, the folk was really one's heart's own darling, the proletariat.

"Do you like fairy tales?" It was the moist-palmed interpreter who accompanied him to the theatre.

"I *love* them," Bech said, with a fervor and gaiety lingering from the previous hour. The interpreter looked at him anxiously, as when Bech had swallowed the brandy in one swig, and throughout the ballet kept murmuring explanations of self-evident events on the stage. Each night, a princess would put on silver slippers and dance through her mirror to tryst with a wizard, who possessed a magic stick that she coveted, for with it the world could be ruled. The wizard, as a dancer, was inept, and once almost dropped her, so that anger flashed from her eyes. She was, the princess, a little redhead with a high round bottom and a frozen pout and beautiful free arm motions, and Bech found it oddly estatic when, preparatory to her leap, she would dance toward the mirror, an empty oval, and another girl, identically dressed in pink, would emerge from the wings and perform as her reflection. And when the princess, haughtily adjusting her cape of invisibility, leaped through the oval of gold wire, Bech's heart leaped backward into the enchanted hour he had spent with the poetess.

Though the appointment had been established, she came into the restaurant as if, again, she had been suddenly summoned and had hurried. She sat down between Bech and Petrov slightly breathless and fussed, but exuding again, that impalpable warmth of intelligence and virtue.

"Vera, Vera," Petrov said.

"You hurry too much," Bech told her.

"Not so very much," she said.

Petrov ordered her a cognac and continued with Bech

their discussion of the newer French novelists. "It is tricks," Petrov said. "Good tricks, but tricks. It does not have enough to do with life, it is too much verbal nervousness. Is that sense?"

"It's an epigram," Bech said.

"There are just two of their number with whom I do not feel this: Claude Simon and Samuel Beckett. You have no relation, Bech, Beckett?"

"None."

Vera said, "Nathalie Sarraute is a very modest woman. She felt motherly to me."

"You have met her?"

"In Paris I heard her speak. Afterward there was the coffee. I liked her theories, of the, oh, *what?* of the *little* movements within the heart." She delicately measured a pinch of space and smiled, through Bech, back at herself.

"Tricks," Petrov said. "I do not feel this with Beckett; there, in a low form, believe it or not, one has human content."

Bech felt duty-bound to pursue this, to ask about the theatre of the absurd in Bulgaria, about abstract painting (these were the touchstones of "progressiveness"; Russia had none, Rumania some, Czechoslovakia plenty), to subvert Petrov. Instead, he asked the poetess, "Motherly?"

Vera explained, her hands delicately modelling the air, rounding into nuance, as it were, the square corners of her words. "After her talk, we—talked."

"In French?"

"And in Russian."

"She knows Russian?"

"She was born Russian."

"How is her Russian?"

"Very pure but—old-fashioned. Like a book. As she talked, I felt in a book, safe."

"You do not always feel safe."

"Not always."

"Do you find it difficult to be a woman poet?"

"We have a tradition of woman poets. We have Elisaveta Bagriana, who is very great."

Petrov leaned toward Bech as if to nibble him. "Your own works? Are they influenced by the *nouvelle vague?* Do you consider yourself to write anti-*romans?*"

Bech kept himself turned toward the woman. "Do you want to hear about how I write? You don't, do you?"

"Very much yes," she said.

He told them, told them shamelessly, in a voice that surprised him with its steadiness, its limpid urgency, how once he had written, how in *Travel Light* he had sought to show people skimming the surface of things with their lives, taking tints from things the way that objects in a still life color one another, and how later he had attempted to place beneath the melody of plot a countermelody of imagery, interlocking images which had risen to the top and drowned his story, and how in *The Chosen* he had sought to make of this confusion the theme itself, an epic theme, by showing a population of characters whose actions were all determined, at the deepest level, by nostalgia, by a desire to get back, to dive, each, into the springs of their private imagery. The book probably failed; at least, it was badly received. Bech apologized for telling all this. His voice tasted flat in his mouth; he felt a secret intoxication and a secret guilt, for he had contrived to give a grand air, as of an impossibly noble and quixotically complex experiment, to his failure when at bottom, he suspected, a certain simple laziness was the cause.

Petrov said, "Fiction so formally sentimental could not be composed in Bulgaria. We do not have a happy history."

It was the first time Petrov had sounded like a Communist. If there was one thing that irked Bech about these people behind the mirror, it was their assumption that, however second-rate elsewhere, in suffering they were supreme. He said, "Believe it or not, neither do we."

Vera calmly intruded. "Your personae are not moved by love?"

"Yes, very much. But as a form of nostalgia. We fall in love, I tried to say in the book, with women who remind us of our first landscape. A silly idea. I used to be interested in love. I once wrote an essay on the orgasm—you know the word?—"

She shook her head. He remembered that it meant Yes.

"—on the orgasm as perfect memory. The one mystery is, what are we remembering?"

She shook her head again, and he noticed that her eyes were gray, and that in their depths his image (which he could not see) was searching for the thing remembered. She composed her fingertips around the brandy glass and said, "There is a French poet, a young one, who has written of this. He says that never else do we, do we so gather up, collect into ourselves, oh—" Vexed, she spoke to Petrov in rapid Bulgarian.

He shrugged and said, "Concentrate our attention."

"—concentrate our attention," she repeated to Bech, as if the words, to be believed, had to come from her. "I say it foolish—foolishly—but in French it is very well put and *correct*."

Petrov smiled neatly and said, "This is an enjoyable subject for discussion, love."

"It remains," Bech said, picking his words as if the language were not native even to him, "one of the few things that still deserve meditation."

"I think it is good," she said.

"Love?" he asked, startled.

She shook her head and tapped the stem of her glass with a fingernail, so that Bech had an inaudible sense of ringing, and she bent as if to study the liquor, so that her entire body borrowed a rosiness from the brandy and burned itself into Bech's memory—the silver gloss of her nail, the sheen of her hair, the symmetry of her arms relaxed on the white tablecloth, everything except the expression on her face

Petrov asked aloud Bech's opinion of Dürrenmatt.

Actuality is a running impoverishment of possibility. Though he had looked forward to seeing her again at the cocktail party and had made sure that she was invited, when it occurred, though she came, he could not get to her. He saw her enter, with Petrov, but he was fenced in by an attaché of the Yugoslav Embassy and his burnished Tunisian wife and, later, when he was worming his way toward her diagonally, a steely hand closed on his arm and a rasping American female told him that her fifteen-year-old nephew had decided to be a writer and desperately needed advice. Not the standard crap, but real brass-knuckles advice. Bech found himself balked. He was surrounded by America: the voices, the narrow suits, the watery drinks, the clatter, the glitter. The mirror had gone opaque and gave him back only himself. He managed, in the end, as the officials were thinning out, to break through and confront her in a corner. Her coat, blond, with a rabbit collar, was already on; from its side pocket she pulled a pale volume of poems in the Cyrillic alphabet. "Please," she said. On the flyleaf she had written, "to H. Beck, sincerelly, with bad spellings but much"—the last word looked like "leave" but must have been "love."

"Wait," he begged, and went back to where his ravaged pile of presentation books had been and, unable to find the one he wanted, stole the legation library's jacketless copy of *The Chosen*. Placing it in her expectant hands, he told her, "Don't look," for inside he had written, with a drunk's stylistic confidence,

Dear Vera Glavanokova—

It is a matter of earnest regret for me that you and I must live on opposite sides of the world.

The Family Meadow

THE FAMILY always reconvenes in the meadow. For generations it has been traditional, this particular New Jersey meadow, with its great walnut tree making shade for the tables and its slow little creek where the children can push themselves about in a rowboat and nibble watercress and pretend to fish. Early this morning, Uncle Jesse came down from the stone house that his father's father's brother had built and drove the stakes, with their carefully tied rag flags, that would tell the cars where to park. The air was still, inert with the postdawn laziness that foretells the effort of a hot day, and between blows of his hammer Jesse heard the breakfast dishes clinking beneath the kitchen window and the younger collie barking behind the house. A mild man, Jesse moved scrupulously, mildly through the wet grass that he had scythed yesterday. The legs of his gray workman's pants slowly grew soaked with dew and milkweed spittle. When the stakes were planted, he walked out the lane with the REUNION signs, past the houses. He avoided looking at the houses, as if glancing into their wide dead windows would wake them.

By nine o'clock Henry has come up from Camden with a carful—Eva, Mary, Fritz, Fred, the twins, and, incredibly, Aunt Eula. It is incredible she is still alive, after seven strokes. Her shrivelled head munches irritably and her arms twitch, trying to shake off assistance, as if she intends to dance. They settled her in an aluminum chair beneath the walnut tree. She faces the creek, and the helpless waggle of her old skull seems to establish itself in sympathy with the oscillating shimmer of the sunlight on the slow water. The men, working in silent pairs whose unison is as profound as blood, carry down the tables from the barn, where they are stacked from one year to the next. In truth, it has

172

been three summers since the last reunion, and it was feared that there might never be another. Aunt Jocelyn, her gray hair done up in braids, comes out of her kitchen to say hello on the dirt drive. Behind her lingers her granddaughter, Karen, in white Levis and bare feet, with something shadowy and doubtful about her dark eyes, as if she had been intensely watching television. The girl's father—not here; he is working in Philadelphia—is Italian, and as she matures an alien beauty estranges her, so that during her annual visits to her grandparents' place, which when she was a child had seemed to her a green island, it is now she herself, at thirteen, who seems the island. She feels surrounded by the past, cut off from the images—a luncheonette, a civic swimming pool, an auditorium festooned with crêpe paper—that represent life to her, the present, her youth. The air around her feels brown, as in old photographs. These men greeting her seem to have stepped from an album. The men, remembering their original prejudice against her mother's marrying a Catholic, are especially cordial to her, so jovially attentive that Jocelyn suddenly puts her arm around the girl, expressing a strange multitude of things; that she loves her, that she is one of them, that she needs to be shielded, suddenly, from the pronged kidding of men.

By ten-thirty Horace's crowd has come down from Trenton, and the Oranges clan is arriving, in several cars. The first car says it dropped Cousin Claude in downtown Burlington because he was sure that the second car, which had faded out of sight behind them, needed to be told the way. The second car, with a whoop of hilarity, says it took the bypass and never saw him. He arrives in a third car, driven by Jimmy and Ethel Thompson from Morristown, who say they saw this forlorn figure standing along Route 130 trying to thumb a ride and as they were passing him Ethel cried, "Why, I think that's Claude!" Zealous and reckless, a true believer in good deeds, Claude is always getting into scrapes like this, and enjoying it. He stands surrounded by laughing women, a typical man of this family, tall, with a tribal boyishness, a stubborn refusal to look his age, to lose his hair. Though his face is pitted and gouged by melancholy, Claude looks closer to forty than the sixty he is, and, though he works in Newark, he still speaks with the rural softness and slide of middle New Jersey. He has the gift—the privilege—of making these women laugh; the women uniformly run to fat and their laughter has a sameness, a

quality both naïve and merciless, as if laughter meant too
much to them. Jimmy and Ethel Thompson, whose name is
not the family name, stand off to one side, in the unscythed
grass, a fragile elderly couple whose links to the family
have all died away but who have come because they received a mimeographed postcard inviting them. They are
like those isolated corners of interjections and foreign syllables in a poorly planned crossword puzzle.

The twins bring down from the barn the horseshoes and
the quoits. Uncle Jesse drives the stakes and pegs in the
places that, after three summers, still show as spots of depressed sparseness in the grass. The sun, reaching toward
noon, domineers over the meadow; the shade of the walnut
tree grows smaller and more noticeably cool. By noon, all
have arrived, including the Dodge station wagon from
central Pennsylvania, the young pregnant Wilmington
cousin who married an airline pilot, and the White Plains
people, who climb from their car looking like clowns, wearing red-striped shorts and rhinestone studded sunglasses.
Handshakes are exchanged that feel to one man like a
knobbed wood carving and to the other like a cow's slippery, unresisting teat. Women kiss, kiss stickily, with little
overlapping patches of adhesive cheek and clicking conflicts
of spectacle rims, under the white unslanting sun. The very
insects shrink toward the shade. The eating begins. Clams
steam, corn steams, salad wilts, butter runs, hot dogs turn,
torn chicken shines in the savage light. Iced tea, brewed in
forty-quart milk cans, chuckles when sloshed. Paper plates
buckle on broad laps. Plastic butter knives, asked to cut
cold ham, refuse. Children underfoot in the pleased frenzy
eat only potato chips. Somehow, as the first wave of appetite subsides, the long tables turn musical, and a murmur
rises to the black sky, a cackle rendered harmonious by a
remote singleness of ancestor; a kind of fabric is woven and
hung, a tapestry of the family fortunes, the threads of
death by war, death by automobile, insanity—a strangely
prevalent thread, the thread of insanity. Never far from a
farm or the memory of a farm, the family has hovered in
honorable obscurity, between poverty and wealth, between
jail and high office. Real-estate dealers, schoolteachers, veter-
inarians are its noblemen; butchers, electricians, door-to-
door salesmen its yeomen. Protestant, teetotalling, and un-
daring, ironically virtuous and mildly proud, it has added to

America's statistics without altering their meaning. Whence, then, this strange joy?

Watermelons smelling of childhood cellars are produced and massively sliced. The sun passes noon and the shadows relax in the intimate grass of this antique meadow. To the music of reminiscence is added the rhythmic chunking of thrown quoits. They are held curiously, between a straight thumb and four fingers curled as a unit, close to the chest, and thrown with a soft constrained motion that implies realms of unused strength. The twins and the children, as if superstitiously, have yielded the game to the older men, Fritz and Ed, Fred and Jesse, who, in pairs, after due estimation and measurement of the fall, pick up their four quoits, clink them together to clean them, and alternately send them back through the air on a high arc, floating with a spin-held slant like that of gyroscopes. The other pair measures, decides, and stoops. When they tap their quoits together, decades fall away. Even their competitive crowing has something measured about it, something patient, like the studied way their shirtsleeves are rolled up above their elbows. The backs of their shirts are ageless. Generations have sweated in just this style, under the arms, across the shoulder blades, and wherever the suspenders rub. The younger men and the teen-age girls play a softball game along the base paths that Jesse has scythed. The children discover the rowboat and, using the oars as poles, bump from bank to bank. When they dip their hands into the calm brown water, where no fish lives, a mother watching from beneath the walnut tree shrieks, "Keep your hands inside the boat! Uncle Jesse says the creek's polluted!"

And there is a stagnant fragrance the lengthening afternoon strains from the happy meadow. Aunt Eula nods herself asleep, and her false teeth slip down, so her face seems mummified and the children giggle in terror. Flies, an exploding population, discover the remains of the picnic and skate giddily on its odors, the softball game grows boring, except to the airline pilot, a rather fancy gloveman excited by the admiration of Cousin Karen in her tight white Levis. The Pennsylvania and New York people begin to pack their cars. The time has come for the photograph. Their history is kept by these photographs of timeless people in changing costumes standing linked and flushed in a moment of midsummer heat. All line up, from resurrected Aunt Eula, twitching and snapping like a mud turtle, to the unborn baby in the belly of the Delaware cousin. To get them all in, Jesse has to squat, but in doing so he brings the houses into his viewfinder. He does not want them in the picture, he does not want them there at all. They surround his meadow on three sides, raw ranch shacks built from one bastard design but painted in a patchwork of pastel shades. Their back yards, each nurturing an aluminum clothes tree, come right to the far bank of the creek, polluting it, and though a tall link fence holds back the children who have gathered in these yards to watch the picnic as if it were a circus or a zoo, the stare of the houses—mismatched kitchen windows squinting above the gaping cement mouth of a garage—cannot be held back. Not only do they stare, they speak, so that Jesse can hear them even at night. *Sell*, they say. *Sell.*

The Hermit

HE HAD HAD BROTHERS—brothers older than he, and younger. He remembered his childhood as a tussle, a noisy competition for food, for clothes that fitted, for attention. Now, in the woods, there was no noise. There was sound, but not noise. In the beginning, during the first nights, the scrabbling and travelling of animals—the house apparently adjoined a confluence of paths—felt loud and harsh to him, a crackling and rustling that overflowed his consciousness, which was held cupped for sleep. Now he no longer heard these sounds, as a mechanic is deaf to a machine that is working smoothly. As he settled in, as March yielded to April and April to May, everything in his sudden environment sank into invisibility, into the utter transparency of perfect order.

And yet never in his life had he seen so well, seen so much. He had never excelled at school or in the competition within the family; something he could not quite believe was as simple as stupidity clouded his apprehension. Something numbed his grip at the moment of grasping, unfocused his wits at the demand for concentration, scattered his purpose when it needed to be single. It was as if his mind, or that set of switches and levers that translated his mind into the motions of the outer world, was too finely adjusted to bear the jostle of others, to function in the heavy damp climate human activity bred. The climate of humanity, he saw now, had never been native to him.

He had found the house while hunting, deep in the tract of second- or third-growth forest owned by a steel company. The steel company was at the other end of the state, in Pittsburgh. Fifteen years ago it had bought local land wholesale, on the speculation that it contained low-grade iron ore. The company had not yet mined it and perhaps

177

never would. In the meantime, these hundreds of acres grew
wild, submerging their interior demarcations—old boundary
stones and dissolving dry walls and rusting barbed-wire
fences like strands of a forgotten debate.

The house frightened him when he first saw it. A roofless
sandstone shell with some cedar shingles still clinging to a
lean-to, it had no business being there. Its ghostly presence
turned the wilderness menacing. How old was it? The trees
around it were tall but not thick, and a vestigial farmyard
remained, earth too packed to encourage roots. Perhaps the
land had been cleared a century ago, perhaps it had been
farmed as recently as before the war. He saw no sign of a
fire in the ruin. Not only the roof but the floor had been carried away by weather; the cellar hole, brimming with tumbled rocks and matted brambles, gaped between the floor
beams, which were still solid enough to support his weight.
Their spacing struck him as harplike, and when he looked
up, the blue sky showing between the naked rafters exhila-
rated him, as if, a little dizzily, he had taken flight in a
skeletal basket attached to a great blue balloon. With necessarily rhythmic motions he stepped from beam to beam, remembering an uncle of his who played the organ in the Lu-
theran church, and how precisely this uncle's feet would
dance on the pedal keyboard.

Part of the house was still sheltered. What must have
been the kitchen, the lean-to, still held its roof and its floor.
There was even part of an interior wall—papered pine
boarding rather than plaster-and-lath—and a doorframe
from which the door had long vanished. Another doorless
rectangle led outdoors across a sandstone threshold bearing
two damp depressions—puddles smaller than saucers—and
a patch of parallel grooves left by the mason's serrated
chisel. The stone was intact, and the timbering that boxed in
the shattered windows seemed, though pitted and warped,
sound enough. With doors, fresh sashes, some reboarding
and shingling, the room could be made weathertight. He
wondered why no one else had thought of it. The site
seemed ignored even by vandals. The initials gouged here
and there were as gray as the wood. The cola cans scattered
in the cellar hole were laden with rust, and the empty shotgun shells below one sill seemed older than last hunting season. Perhaps, he thought, groping, the steel company had
found a way to discourage trespassers and then itself lost in-
interest, in the lordly way of easy victors. Certainly the house

seemed to be waiting for no one but him, not even for lovers.

His younger brother, the schoolteacher, was the first to visit him. He had not been there a week and was still engaged in carpentry. A factory-puttied window sash, each pane labelled with the purple emblem of the glass company, was leaning against a birch, giving the bits of moss and grass around the roots the refracted, pampered look of greenhouse shoots. It was March, and the undergrowth was still simple and precious. Each bit of skunk cabbage nosing its way up through the leaf mold wore an air of surprise. A smothered spring made the ground on this side of the house very damp.

"It's not your land, Stanley," his brother told him. "It's not even government land."

"Well, they can kick me off, then. All I can lose is the lumber and nails."

"How much do you want to use it?"

"I don't know yet."

"Is there a woman you're going to bring up?" Morris's delicate skin registered a blush; Stanley had to laugh. Morris was the youngest of his brothers, younger even than his years. He was now in his late twenties, and had grown a mustache; it was as if a child had painted a male doll with the rosy pink of a girl and then, realizing its mistake, had solemnly dabbed beneath the nose.

Stanley said, "Couldn't I use my room for a woman?" It was an unkind joke, for Morris had complained about such use. Their rooms were side by side on the third floor of the parental house. There all of the brothers lived except Tom, who had moved to California. Their parents were dead. Bernard, the oldest brother, a contractor, with his wife and two sons occupied most of the house, though it was never quite clear if he had inherited it outright or they all owned it equally. Stanley's right to live there had never been questioned.

Morris winced, and spoke rapidly. "I guess," he said. "You have before. Anyway, none of your whores could hike this far." To emphasize his sharpness and coldness of voice he kicked a clump of skunk cabbage, smashing it, so that its scent of carrion flooded the air. "You'll make a fool of the family," he added, and Stanley was struck by how loud, for all of Morris's rosy delicacy, how loud his presence was, how he seemed to fill, with the speed of a spreading odor, so much of the bowl-shaped greening space around the house.

Stanley felt pressed, defensive. "Nobody need know."

"Will you work?"

Stanley could not quite grasp the essence of this question. He had two jobs; he was a custodian—a janitor—at the school where Morris taught, and in the summer he worked for Bernard, as a common laborer, digging trenches, mixing cement, knocking together forms, since he had some skill as a carpenter. Though he had always seemed to himself on the verge of a decisive inner graduation, Stanley had not finished the eleventh grade; there was a light above him he could not rise to out of the surrounding confusion.

"Well why not?" he answered, and Morris grunted, satisfied.

But it had been a good question, for in fact the trek through the two miles of woods to the town seemed to lengthen rather than, as is the way with most distances, shorten with use. Each piece of furniture fetched from his room to the old kitchen added weight to each departure. It was especially unnatural to set out at dawn, in the moist brown muddle before the slanting light had sorted out the tree trunks, when the twigs were heavy with clouded drops that seemed congelations of the transparent night; Stanley felt, pushing out from his clearing, as if he were tearing a skin, forcing a ripeness. His house had grown tight around him. He liked especially the contrast between the weathered lumber, seeming to seek through wind and rain its original knotted state, and his patches of fresh pine, trim and young-smelling and tight. Patchwork, with its sensations of redemption, had always pleased him. He had preferred, once past the stylishness of adolescence, to wear old clothes skillfully held back from the rag pile, in this way frustrating time—though the presence of these mended rents and barely visible patches had given him, for all their skill, a subtly forlorn and crazy aura. And this same instinctive hatred of waste, a conservative desire for postponement, led him to prolong the periods between haircuts and to shave only on alternate days, doubling the life of the blades. So that his passionate inward neatness was expressed in outward dishevelment—an inversion typical of his telescopic relations with society. He found himself increasingly unwilling to enter this society, even by way of the subterranean passages of the high-school basement. The students, he knew, mocked his stoop, his considerate slowness. Tentatively, expecting, as in his early experiments with sex, to be rebuked and instead emptying his sin into a strange indifference, he stayed away from work an odd day now and then, and then a week. He let himself grow a beard. To his surprise it came out red, though his hair was black. His older brother came to see him.

Bernard's presence, though less sharp than Morris's, was bigger; his voice, to ears accustomed to nothing more declamatory than bird song and the rustle of evening crawlers, seemed huge, a massive rupture in the web of life. Bernard was wearing a dark suit in the green glade; it was Sunday. He was sweating, angry. "I had hell's own time finding you."

"There's a stone wall you must keep on your left. I used to get lost myself." Stanley's voice sounded strange to him, a dry crackling; he had not used it for days except, in a vague way, to sing.

"Tell me one thing. Are you as crazy as you look?"

"I can shave when I go to town."

"I didn't mean just the beard—but speaking of that, do you know it's come out orange?"

"I know. I have a mirror."

"My boys ask, 'Where's Uncle Stan?' "

"Bring them out. They can spend the night if they'd like. But just them, not their friends. I couldn't put up too many."

"Then in your mind this is camping out?"

Stanley wanted to understand; so much importance seemed attached to his understanding. "Camping out?"

"You know what they're saying in town?"

"About me?"

"They say you've become a hermit."

An odd joy, the tepid blow of morning light, touched Stanley. Dignity and certainty were assigned to the vague thing he had been doing. He had been becoming a hermit. One brother was a contractor, another taught school, another lived in California, and he was a hermit. It was better than a diploma; but he hadn't earned it. He said cautiously, "I hadn't thought of it that way."

Bernard in turn seemed pleased. He shifted his feet as if he had at last found sockets solid enough for their intense black weight. "How had you thought of it exactly? Does this have to do with Loretta, or Leinbach, or who?"

Stanley remembered these names. Leinbach was the head custodian and Loretta was a woman who lived alone in a trailer. Leinbach was slender and fussy, with sunken temples and bright broken veins in his nose. Each day he wore a freshly laundered gray shirt to work, carrying his wife on his back in the sheen of her ironing. He demonstrated such jealous concern for the school's four great boilers that it seemed their heat kept his own blood warm. Loretta was pink and white and smooth, and loved her beer, and laughed when she thought of how life had unhitched her trailer and stranded her here, on the edge of a cornfield. Morning-glories twined up the cinderblock supports that had replaced the trailer's wheels. Stanley was always delighted by how the bathroom and kitchen fixtures, unfolding on nickel-coated hinges, were fitted into their envelopes of space. But at times Loretta was frantic and bitter; a coarse grief and sourceless storm of outrage would overwhelm her smoothness and shake the trailer's dainty compartments. He gathered that somehow even he, Stanley, was wronging her. Once, on the last day before Christmas vacation, he had accidentally smothered the fire in the third boiler with too great a draught of pea coal. Leinbach, his face gray, his veins livid, had rushed to revive the flames with such fierce haste and spat such vile German that Stanley wondered if it had been a quadrant of Leinbach's own heart he had mistakenly allowed to flicker and choke. This glimpse into a possible system cooled, strangely, his feelings for Loretta. There was a passion loose in the world that might burn him. He told Bernard, "No, it's nobody in particular."

"Then what? What's this about? You'll rot here."

"Have you seen Leinbach?"

"He told me to tell you to stay away. The school can't keep a queer on the staff, they must think of the kids."

This ugly word "queer" (he could see Leinbach's mouth twist, pronouncing it) made Stanley stubborn. "Because of where I live?"

"And he hasn't even seen the beard. When are you going to shave?"

"Not when Leinbach tells me."

Bernard laughed; the noise broke like a shot. "Stay, then. You can start work for me early. I've commenced a row of foundations out toward the cemetery hill."

"If you don't need me yet, I'd just as soon wait a while."

Bernard took off his coat and appeared to enter, combatively, into the spirit of the woods. "I don't need *you*," he said. "It's the other way around." When Stanley neither admitted this nor argued, Bernard said, louder, "Go crazy, then."

"It's the other way. I'm trying to clear my head."

"Sit and stink out here. Squat on your own shit. You'll be crawling down soon enough. Here. I'll leave you my cigarettes."

"Bernie, thanks, but I don't smoke that much now."

Stanley was left, after the thrashing footsteps receded from his ears, with the ringing sense—heartening, on the whole—of having struggled with his brother and having achieved the usual postponement of total defeat.

With tendrils of habit the hermit rooted himself in the woods. Solitude is a two-dimensional condition whose problems can be neatly plotted. Pure water ran in a nearby rivulet. Stanley cooked, on a double kerosene burner, canned foods bought once a week at the dying corner store on the near edge of town, a store grateful for his business. Though he had his gun, he shot nothing, for fear of poaching and offending the invisible authorities who left him undisturbed. The cooking conveniently partitioned the days, and, rewarming and combining leftovers, he was able to indulge his fondness for patchwork. The problem of elimination he solved with a succession of deeply dug and gradually refilled holes that he imagined would always exist, as wells of special fertility in the woods. For exercise, he cut fallen wood, and for warmth burned it in the ancient kitchen fireplace that he had cleared in the classic way, by pulling a small pine tree down the chimney. He read very little. Kerosene, lugged through the woods in a five-gallon can, was too precious to be used for light. On one of his scavenging trips to his old home he went into the dark attic and took two books at random from the dusty stacks his mother had accumulated. She had been a tireless reader—a hermit in her way. Downstairs he found in his hands a dun-colored novel of English society dated 1913 and the moss-green memoirs of an actress who had toured the American West after the Civil War. He read a few pages from one or the other each twilight, in the magical spirit in which people used to read the Bible, expecting not continuous sense but abrupt, fragmentary illumination. And indeed, he was rarely disappointed, for whether the scene was the ballroom of a Sussex manor house or an improvised arena in Dodge City, the events (the daughter of an impoverished nobleman declines to dance with the son of a powerful industrialist; a Mexican bandit is assassinated during the mad scene of *King Lear*) had the same brilliant surprisingness, quick high tints suggestive of a supernatural world.

> The gallant old Duchess, her hopes so insolently dashed, indicated with a discretionary murmur her desire to be carried from the room, toward a sanctum where their scintillating fragments could be considered with a loving eye, perhaps, to their reassembly.

It was a rare page that did not contain some sentence striking in its oblique pertinence, curving from the page upward into Stanley's eyes, his mind, his life.

> I felt the presence of Panic in the audience. I maintained my prattling song uninterruptedly but the menacing murmur swelled. Inspired by desperation, I stood, tore off my cap and bells, and allowed my long hair to cascade around my motley. Better than I had dared dream, the revelation that the Fool was a Woman shocked the crowd into silence and composure. The ovation which I received at the end of the act from these rough men left me weak and weeping.

In such passages Stanley seemed to encounter some angel within himself, a woman sexlessly garbed, demanding he continue his climb up the very thin steps of his days toward the plateau of final clarification.

Though the days submitted to symmetry, the nights proved slippery; an uncontrollable intruder appeared—insomnia—to ravage and mock the order of his existence. Several nights, sleep evaded him entirely; often he awoke under a cold moon and, hurrying with closed eyes back through the dark door that had blown ajar, found it locked until dawn, with a breath of light, blew it open again. It was as if in lightening himself of so much of the world he had made himself too buoyant to sink, as if in purging himself of so much evil he had violated an animal necessity that took its revenge on his stripped nerves, like teeth that hurt after a cleaning. To relax himself, he would remember women, but his emissions into these ghosts merely amplified his hollowness. Lying awake, he dreamed he was a stone drained of weight, a body without personality, and wondered if his personal existence had ever been actual or was merely an illusion that women had given him. First there had been his mother, shaping with her preoccupied eyes every inch of his growth, and then the kind succession ending with Loretta, who in intimacy had praised the masculine beauty of his chest, so that the memory of her, or even the vision of her two-toned trailer sitting with its hitch ensnarled in vines, physically broadened his chest, turned its skin taut, glossy, and tan. Why, indeed, did he keep a mirror but as a kind of woman, in whom he sought—cocking his head this way and that, smoothing his beard, smiling secretively—the angles previously made vivid by admiration? He was glad when Loretta came to see him. It happened late in April. His chest solidly flooded with relief as her incongruous body, in a blue dress and gray sweater, approached through the trees and waded across the treeless farmyard. The farmyard was now filled with ferns that swallowed her ankles. Her ankles were fine for so fat a woman.

"Well, Jesus," she said, halting. "Look at you,"

"Look at *you*," he said. "I didn't know you could walk so far."

Unlike the others, she had come toward evening. She asked, "Aren't you going to have me in?"

"Sure," he said. Her advance was smooth, unstoppable. "It's not as neat as your trailer." He felt fussed and pleased, invaded to his bones, as she stepped across the grooved and pitted threshold and examined the efficient interior he had formed, and found nothing to laugh at.

"You've done all right," she said seriously, awed. Then she laughed.

"What are you laughing at?"

"It reminded me of something, and now I know what. I once knew a Chinese bachelor who lived like this, in the middle of Philly. It smelled like this. Maybe it's the kerosene. Let me smell you." She unbuttoned the two top buttons of his shirt, tugged down the neck of his undershirt, put her stub nose against his skin, and sniffed. "You don't smell Chinese yet, you still smell like Stanley. Your heart's beating."

"It's been a time."

"I didn't think you wanted me to come."

"I don't think I did want you to come."

"But I'm here now, huh?"

"You're here."

"How cold does it get at night?"

"Not so bad now. We'll be O.K. Are you hungry?"

"Thirsty."

He looked down into her face to see in what sense she meant thirst, but the sun was low and his own body blocked her from the window light, so all he felt of her face was its shadowy warmth and a gingery perfume that perhaps dwelled in her hair. He gave her the cot and put a blanket on the floor beside it, so that each time he awoke that night he saw her above him, her bare bent arm luminous, her heavy body floating cloudlike on the spindly X-legs of the cot and bellying the underside of the canvas. As if it had become possible to tamper with the sky and move the moon, he reached and touched, and then became confused, for as her body encircled his and slipped across his finger-tips, she seemed now vast and now terribly thin, thin with a child's listening thinness as her frame yearned toward some sought position in relation to the fixed stars of his own system.

He slept late, awaking to the sound of her working on his stove. The metallic rummaging annoyed him; she seemed to be tinkering inside his head. From the back, in faded blue, she looked fat, having feasted on him. She cursed his kerosene burners, which were reluctant to light. He turned her from his stove and, naked, used his body as a wedge to separate her from the instruments, the stove and pans, of his private life. She yielded complacently at first, but by the time he was through her eyes were strained by anger. Dabs of sunlight shuffled on the coarse floor like coins perpetually being counted. He lay upon an adversary who in a single space of breathing might swell enough to overthrow him. They rose, and her storm came—the tears, the scorn, the stony-voiced repetitions, the pitiable reversals toward an abysmal tenderness. Looking past her head, his chin burning in the halo of her uncombed hair, he saw the window giving on the morning woods as an aquarium from whose magic jagged world of green leaves stricken with sunshine this weeping would keep him forever sealed. He gave her breakfast and walked her to the edge of the land, where the NO TRESPASSING signs were posted.

"I won't come again," she said.

"It's too hard for you," he told her.

"You know what you're doing?" she asked, and then answered, "You're pouring yourself down the drain."

"I'm just like you in the trailer," he said, smiling and watching her face for the reflection of his smile.

"No," she said, in the tone of dry calm that followed each of her storms, "It's been forced on me. But you're choosing."

How grateful he was, after all, to his visitors!—for each of them left him something to clarify his situation. He was choosing, yes, and, treading back through the woods, welcomed by the calls of unseen birds and the gestures of unnamed plants, he sought for some further choice, some additional dismissal with which he could atone for the night's parasitic ecstasy. He smashed the mirror. He held it squarely above the hearthstone, so the last thing it reflected was a slice of the blue zenith, and let it drop. The fragments he swept up and buried in a place far from the house, covering the earth with leaves so he could not find the spot again. But from that sector of woods, for a while, he felt watched, by buried eyes. The sensation passed in daylight but persisted at night, when it gave his sleep depth, as had the knowledge when he was a child that at an unknown hour his mother, though still downstairs, on her way to bed would come into his room and touch his forehead and tuck the kicked covers around him. Insomnia ceased to visit him. After Loretta's visit, he grew drowsy at twilight, was often unable to read a word, and rose with the sun.

He never saw so well, saw so much. Chill April yielded to frilly May. Buds of a hundred designs had broken unbidden. He became aware, intensely, of tiny distinctions—shades of brown and gray in the twigs, differences in the shapes of leaves, the styles of growing, a cadence expressed in the angle at which a hoofed branchlet thrust from the parent branch. That he could not articulate these distinctions, could hardly name a dozen trees and flowers, bathed the myriad populations of growth in a glistening transparency like that left by mist; as his mind slowly sorted the sea of green into types, he greeted each recognized specimen not with its name but with its very image, as one remembers a sister whose name, through marriage, has ceased to apply. His mind became a beautiful foreign book whose illustra-

tions were enhanced, in precision and wonder, by the unin-
telligibility of the text. First venturing onto the spaced
beams of the floorless house, he had thought of a harp, and
now these finely tuned strata of distinctions, fixed yet pliant,
seemed a greater harp, either waiting to be struck or else
played so continually that an instant of silence would have
boomed in his ears. The patient intricacy of moss and grass
fascinated him. There was no realm so small that it repelled
the rule of distinctions. Stanley felt the green and scurvy
mass around him as so infinitely divisible that the thickness
of a veil was coarse in comparison; Nature, that sturdy net
of interlocking rapacity, dissolved for him in its own unsay-
able exactness, and ceased to exist, or existed merely as the
description of something else.

Some boys came to see him: his two nephews and a
friend. The friend was thin, new in the town, with a close-
cropped skull and brown eyes so dark they seemed round.
Stanley felt, awkwardly entertaining his guests, that he was
addressing mostly this stranger, for the familiar leeringness
and the competitive jostling of his brother's boys were
things which he had determinedly ignored even when he
shared a house with their noise. His visitors seemed chastened by his strangeness. He could not think what to show
them; these boys had expected, perhaps, some piece of
work, some monument to testify to the accumulation of his
days. But there was nothing, nothing except the shelter on
which he had long ago ceased to make improvements—that,
and Stanley's delicately altered sense of actuality. He
walked them through the woods, showed them the faint rectangle of rubble where a barn must have stood, pointed out
the pleasant deposits of pellets with which the smaller mam-
mals of the woods declared their presence, bid them bend
with him to examine a bank where a combination of exposed roots, rocks, moss, and erosion had created a castle,
or chain of castles, inhabited by ants. The boys began to
crush the ants; Stanley shouted, and they backed from him,
and he glimpsed his gauntness, his bristling red beard, in
their eyes. They explored, taking him farther in the woods
than he had ever thought to go alone, to a point from which
the smoking chimney of a house and glinting strip of highway could be seen. On the way they made themselves clubs
and smashed them against dead branches and pitched their
entire weight against dead young trees whose skeletons had

hung vertical, undisturbed, for years, upheld by the arms of the trees that had stifled them. Wherever they circled, the boys flushed death, finding the cough balls of owls wadded with mouse bones, the bloated elongated corpse of a groundhog mangled by dogs, the mysteriously severed forefoot of a deer. The matrix of abundant green life held for them only these few jewels. Stanley gave them each an apple to provision their trek home, and sent them off with no invitation to return. In parting he sensed a susceptibility in the third boy, a curiosity in those round eyes not quite satisfied, a willingness to be taught that offered itself to Stanley, in the midst of his slow learning, as a new and subtler temptation. But the boy disappeared with the others.

Stanley, who when he had lived among men had rarely bathed, because the drawing and pollution of water seemed a waste, now bathed often, because in the nearby rivulet the water ran pure night and day and not to have used it would have been waste. The stream was only inches deep and a man's width wide; to wet himself Stanley had to lie on the bed of red sand and smoothed sandstones and make of himself a larger stone that the little stream, fumbling at first, icily consented to lave. To wet his back he would roll over and lie staring up at the explosive blue rents in the canopy of leaves, like a drowning man frozen during his final glimpse of sky. Then he would rise, dripping, a silver man, and walk naked back, slightly uphill, through the warm ragged mulch of last autumn's leaves. He had thought of building a dam, but the thought offended him. Still water would attract mosquitoes. More obscurely, the gap of water while the stream pooled would carry through the woods toward the sea as a kind of outcry betraying his existence here. Yet, though there was no natural pool where he could so much as squat, it was important in this bathing that every inch of him, even his eyelids, know the water. Otherwise he could not walk through the woods unashamed, a thoroughly silver man.

One day, thus returning, he was conscious of being watched, but blamed the buried mirror until he saw, standing startled in the lake of ferns in front of the house, the third boy, alone. The boy was the first to speak. "I'm sorry," he said, and turned to run, and Stanley, seized by an abrupt fear of loss, of being misunderstood, ran after him —a terrifying figure, probably, gaunt and wet and wordlessly openmouthed among the serene verticals of the trees, his

penis a-bobble. The boy ran faster, and Stanley soon
stopped. His pounding heart seemed to run a few paces farther and then return to the protection of his shaking rib
cage. He was amazed at himself, ashamed. His spurt of pur-
suit had reversed months of patient waiting, waiting—he
saw now—for himself to be overtaken. He saw how narrowly he had escaped a ruinous distraction, a disciple who
would have diluted his vulnerable solitude and siphoned
goodness from him faster than it could be secreted.

Now, each morning, he awoke with a sense of having
been called. At first, it was the slightest of sensations, im-
parting a shadowy, guilty restlessness to his first waking motions. Gradually, as the sensation was repeated on the following three mornings, the unheard voice gathered to itself
clear impressions of masculinity, of infinite gentleness and
urgency. It was distinct from any dream; he knew what
dreams were, and this call clove through them. The call
took place, as near as he could judge, in the instant between
his dreams' stopping and his eyelids' opening. But also it
seemed to underlie the dreams, as a telephone ringing in the
rooms below underlies an act of love, so that the phantoms
transposed from his memories of humanity were mocked
and made doubly phantasmal, performing in patterns constantly twisted and interrupted by an unsympathetic pressure. In his desire to hear the voice, as it were, face to face,
to grasp its masculinity and taste its sweet urgency direct,
Stanley fell asleep as if diving toward a rendezvous. For
two nights, in reprimand, the voice was silent. A humble
learner, he concluded that the voice had been unreal, that
he was drawing close, as Bernard had predicted, to going
crazy. The next morning, the seventh since the sensation
had first touched him, it touched him most strongly, just as
the dark was softening. He sat up as if in answer to a command spoken in the room and perceived that the call was a
condensation, like the dawn dew, of a reality that existed
continually, that persisted through daylight. He felt it, saw
it, as an overwhelming fineness in things; the minute truth
of bark textures, the many-layered translucence of leaves,
the stately gliding intervals between tree trunks all bespoke
something that wanted to be answered, a silence unsure of
itself. But it was so shy, so tactful, that to hear it distinctly
would be like—as Stanley had once read of counterfeiters

doing—dividing a dollar bill edgewise with a razor blade.

Though he turned aside to cook, to eat, to swing his axe into a fallen birch, the sensation remained, singing in the spaces between axe strokes, permeating the day. It was within reach, the graduation he sought, the final clarity, a tissue width removed from apprehension; it was waiting for him to be totally still. Then, he knew, this vaporous presence would condense into words and pour itself lavishly into his mind. He bathed, dried himself, dressed in fresh clothes he had himself washed in the brook and to whose clean faded fibres adhered a few reddish granules like sacred salt. He composed himself on the broad flat threshold, and listened. A single twig lay half in, half out of an oval of moisture the shape of the stone had collected. A breeze transparently touched the treetops, and in a flickering of green the high leaves sharpened themselves against the whetstone of light. A silence embraced all phenomena; the sound beneath the silence approached. Stanley leaned his back against the wood, wondered vaguely which was which, and relaxed into a joy indistinguishable from fear.

The forest shattered; Morris broke from the trees and ran panting toward him, shook him, cursed him. "You've ruined us. You've made us all fools."

Stanley could not speak, he was so deeply locked in the fibrous grasp of what had almost overtaken him. He looked up at his brother and saw a walking fever, a flushed pink skin that seared his green mind painfully.

"What got into you? The kid was so scared he went for days without telling. Bernie's been fighting to keep you out of jail. They're right behind me. I ran ahead to get you to put your clothes on."

But he had them on. Though tempted to protest, and aware that Morris wanted a response, Stanley chose not to desecrate his portion of the silence. He turned his head and saw the erect shadows that had appeared on the far edge of the field of ferns. Bernard, his two boys eager like hounds, the third boy, quailing, transfixed in the cataract of misunderstanding. There were two other men. One wore wine-colored slacks, a zebra shirt, and sunglasses, which he removed. It was Tom, come from California, clothed more strangely than a hermit. And a man in a gray business suit: with his new clarity of vision Stanley saw that he was a medical officer, or an agent of the steel company. He saw them all as standing upon a sea of more than crystalline fragility, achieved cell by cell in silence. Then they came rapidly toward him, and there was a thumping, a bumbling, a clumsy crushing clamor.